SPECIAL PURPOSES

FIRST STRIKE WEAPON

An Abaddon Books™ Publication
www.abaddonbooks.com
abaddon@rebellion.co.uk

First published in 2017 by Abaddon Books™, Rebellion Intellectual
Property Limited, Riverside House, Osney Mead, Oxford, OX2 0ES, UK.

10 9 8 7 6 5 4 3 2 1

Editor-in-Chief: Jonathan Oliver
Commissioning Editor: David Moore
Cover: Clint Langley
Design: Maz Smith
Marketing and PR: Rob Power
Head of Comics and Book Publishing: Ben Smith
Creative Director and CEO: Jason Kingsley
Chief Technical Officer: Chris Kingsley

Tomes of The Dead™, Special Purposes, Abaddon Books and Abaddon
Books logo are trademarks owned or used exclusively by Rebellion
Intellectual Property Limited. The trademarks have been registered or
protection sought in all member states of the European Union and other
countries around the world. All right reserved.

ISBN: 978-1-78108-521-9

Printed in Denmark

SPECIAL PURPOSES

FIRST STRIKE WEAPON

GAVIN G. SMITH

ABADDON
BOOKS

To Kiera & Bill, who are
also fans of splattery messes.

CHAPTER ONE

1604 Eastern Standard Time (EST), 16th November 1987
Grand Central Station, New York City

THE SCREAMING WAS more distant now, and the gunfire had stopped.

Captain Vadim Scorlenski had blood on his face and meat in his mouth. He spat out the gobbets of raw flesh and tried not to look at them.

He held his Stechkin pistol loosely in his right hand and looked across the Park Avenue Viaduct over 42nd Street, towards the dark mouth of the Park Avenue Tunnel. At his back was the colonnaded frontage of the huge, square, neoclassical building that was Grand Central Station. Ancient Roman imperialism, complete with statues of Hercules, Minerva and Mercury, reimagined in the early 20th century and transplanted to America. It was dark now, or as dark as it seemed to get in this city. The tall buildings running down either side of the viaduct were well-lit. Focusing on them, it was easy to believe that nothing was happening. They provided a counterpoint to the wreckage spread out in front of him: the bullet-riddled police cars and yellow cabs, the Emergency Services Unit SWAT van on its roof, cars crushed underneath it where the RPG hit had flipped it into the air, and the burning wreckage of an NYPD helicopter. Everywhere, a carpet of empty shell casings, and so much blood on the ground; but so few bodies.

Other than the distant screaming echoing through the concrete and glass canyons, the only other sounds were the steady drip of blood and tinny music coming from someone's transistor radio. The insipid American teen, singing about how they were alone now, contrasted obscenely with what he'd done, they'd done. The crime he'd helped commit. Vadim had thought himself a monster. He believed that he had come to terms with it. Now he realised he had never really known what a monster was. It had been a long time since Vadim had felt capable of weeping, and now the tears could not come. He was not as he had been. Instead he started to laugh, until the laughter became a dry, painful sob. Or it *would* have been painful, if pain were something he still felt.

He had no idea how he'd ended up out front of the grand train station. He was missing time, and his face was covered in someone else's blood. The last thing he remembered was being in the lower levels, amongst the platforms, looking for a way out for his squad. He had turned to find a terrified New York City Transit Police officer raising his revolver. He had been little more than a boy. Vadim hadn't been able to bring up his AK-74 quickly enough. The police officer had just been doing his job, protecting the passengers on the platform. For some reason, Vadim found this comforting. He hoped the boy and the passengers had lived, though he knew it was unlikely.

He saw the bright light first. He closed his eyes and it shone through his eyelids, but not bright enough to damage his retinas permanently, assuming that was still an issue. They hadn't targeted New York itself; the detonation had been to the west somewhere. Another bright light followed moments later; the oil refineries in New Jersey, maybe. The high-rise canyons of New York protected Vadim from the worst of the skin-burning flash.

The white light turned the city into a photographic negative for a moment. Then another flash from the south and he knew that Philadelphia had gone. The ground and the mighty buildings shook, the road over the viaduct cracked. The firestorm had blown itself out by the time it had reached Manhattan Island, leaving only hot, radioactive winds to howl through the artificial canyons.

"Fools," he tried to say to himself. His voice sounded dry, like the crack of wood snapping in a fire. It didn't sound like him anymore. He wondered, if he stood up and looked to the west, would he see mushroom clouds?

Lights in the surrounding buildings winked out, but he could still hear the tinny American pop music; the electromagnetic pulse had apparently not reached

Manhattan. Presumably, it had taken out a facility that supplied power to the city. Lights flickered on in some of the surrounding buildings as emergency power kicked in. Some of the light was red, which seemed appropriate to Vadim for a number of reasons. He almost started laughing again, but he knew that if he did, he wouldn't stop, until he put the Stechkin to his head and blew his brains out. Even then, he wasn't sure that would stop him now.

He felt cold. No, that wasn't true. He didn't really feel *anything*. He *knew* he was cold, though. He couldn't feel his heart beating, his chest rising and falling, he couldn't even feel his wounds. The only thing he felt was the hunger; the need to hunt, to feed. It was all-encompassing. It took everything he had to remain sitting there, not to answer the hunger's call, not to let go of himself. He wondered if he'd still be there, locked in behind his eyes, witness to atrocities at a new level. He suspected, however, that it would be a sweet release from the war inside himself. He had to do the right thing.

Just for once, he thought. He tasted the Stetchkin's barrel, felt it grind against his teeth as he angled it up. He started to squeeze the trigger, watched the hammer click back.

Then he saw her. The Fräulein, his massively built East German second-in-command. Sergeant Liesl Sauer of the East German Army had been transferred to the Spetsnaz company he now commanded. After Skull, the Fräulein had been with him the longest. She was moving between the bullet-riddled police cars amongst the flames, covered in blood. Some of it was undoubtedly hers, but the blood on her face probably wasn't.

Vadim had no idea why he was still in control of his body, still sentient, but he owed it to the Fräulein to put her out of her misery before seeing to himself. He stood up and made his way across the viaduct towards her. The Fräulein's head twitched around to look at him as soon as he moved. Vadim raised the pistol as he approached. She was staring at him.

He needed to get close. He had no idea where his rifle was, and he had to shoot her in the head, at least twice. To make sure that she was at peace before he followed.

She waited for him, her flat, brutish face lit by the orange flickering flame of the burning helicopter. Then he saw it in her eyes: recognition, intelligence. Liesl was still in there somewhere.

"Vadim?" a Ukrainian-accented voice asked from behind him.

CHAPTER TWO

0452 Afghanistan Time (AFT), 6th November 1987
North-Eastern Badakshan Province, Afghanistan

THE VILLAGE WAS burning, and the Spaniard was dead. The Hind D attack helicopter had dropped incendiaries to soften up the mujahideen before landing Vadim and his people. The helicopter had then circled the area, staying low and using the surrounding mountainous terrain as cover, whilst providing the squad with air support, should they need it. The nap-of-the-earth flying was prudent; after all they were here hunting American Stingers, man-portable surface-to-air missiles. The missiles were the mujahideen's most effective weapon against the *Shaitan-Arba*, or 'Satan's Chariot', as they called the fearsome Hind gunships. Vadim and his squad were acting on intelligence provided by the KGB. An American mercenary in the pay of their CIA was rumoured to be bringing the Stingers in from nearby northern Pakistan.

Vadim shifted slightly, his boots crunching the snow underfoot. He was watching a burning tree, foolishly destroying his night vision. Beyond the tree were the snow-covered peaks of the Hindu Kush. The mountains were truly what people meant when they used the word 'majestic'; ancient and enduring, they couldn't care less about the petty squabbles of humans that set villages alight and bloodied the crisp new snow.

Nothing was how it was supposed to be. He was supposed to be second-in-command of the company, but the major had been killed more than three months ago. So he had ended up in command, except their operational tempo had been such that he had less than a squad left. Thanks to bullshit like this morning's mission. They hadn't been allowed to plan the operation themselves. One squad in one gunship for an entire village of Tajiks. It was a platoon-strength job, for at least two gunships. Vadim hadn't wanted to drop incendiaries on the village. His company had a rule: don't kill them unless they're armed. It had nothing to do with sentiment. They just didn't feel like providing the various Afghan peoples with any further reason to hate them. That said, he had a moral responsibility to get as many of his people home as possible, and if that meant burning a village, then so be it.

The surviving villagers were mainly frightened children and weeping women, and a few very old, but still steely-eyed men staring at the Spetsnaz commandos with undisguised hatred. All of them were kneeling on the open ground where the village met the high plateau. Against Vadim's better judgement, Gulag – Private Nikodim Timoshenko – was watching over the prisoners. Like the rest of them, the Muscovite wore a white snow smock over his uniform, but the hood was down and Vadim could see the prison tattoos creeping up over his neckline. The tattoos marked him as one of the *Bratva*, the 'Brotherhood,' Mother Russia's unacknowledged organised crime network. His gloved hands hid the two fingers he'd lost to frostbite in the Siberian forced labour camp. His face was lean and hungry, and there was something animalistic just under the surface. Calculating eyes always looking for a weakness. Open contempt on his face as he looked down at the villagers.

The sun was little more than a distant glow behind the mountains in the east; most of the illumination came from the fires still burning in the village. He could make out the Fräulein standing a little way from him, watching his back. She was holding Princess's AKS-74, her own RPKS-74 light machine gun slung across her back. The snipers, Princess and Skull, were above the village in the mountains, hunting for the Spaniard's killer. The Hind gunship was playing bait for the snipers; recklessly, to Vadim's mind. He checked his watch; Princess and Skull were due back soon and he hadn't heard any gunfire. Not that he necessarily would.

He glanced at the Spaniard's body. Not even he knew where Sergeant Pavel Orlinsky had gotten the nickname, and out of everyone in the squad he had known him the longest. They had met in Angola, and spent time in Cuba, and South and Central America together.

They had been debussing from the helicopter; Vadim had been last out. The squad had taken up positions surrounding the Hind, checking all around them, and Pavel had stood up to move. One second he was there, the next he was on the ground, six feet back from where he'd been standing, his rib cage hollowed out and his head blown clean off. They'd scattered for cover as another round hit the Hind, sparking off the flying tank's armour as it took off and peeled away from the village. A third round had blown a hole the size of a car wheel in the mud-brick wall of one of the houses. The shots were still echoing over the plateau when Skull and Princess had shouted out that they were dropping their carbines and heading into the mountains. Vadim had told them to be back before 5am. Skull, the Chechen sniper, would want to be back for morning prayer anyway. The two snipers had pulled the hoods of their concealment suits over their heads and run into the rocks above the village. Another shot had echoed out, powdering a boulder behind Princess's heels. Vadim still had no idea where the sniper was, but judging by the delay between the report and the hit, it was quite some distance. He'd heard the *whoosh* of rockets being fired from the pods under the Hind's stubby wings; he guessed the crew of the gunship had seen something. A line of fireballs rolled across a steep, shale-covered slope in the distance. The gunship closed and strafed the impact area with rounds from the 12.7mm four-barrel Yak-B machine gun under its nose. Vadim had no idea if the rockets had hit anything, but no more shots were forthcoming. It was still a while before they emerged from cover.

"Boss," the Fräulein said quietly. On day one of the brutal Spetsnaz training, every recruit was given a nickname, hence 'the Fräulein.' Some stuck, others didn't. Vadim had never liked his nickname, but Spetsnaz units tended to be informal, so he answered to either Boss or Vadim.

"I can hear it," he told his newly promoted second-in-command. A lone helicopter – a Mi-8 transport helicopter, at a guess – making its way through the twilight gloom, threading in and out of the high mountain passes at close to its operational ceiling.

"We expecting anyone?" she asked.

Vadim just shook his head.

"This can't be good."

Vadim and the Fräulein moved towards where Gulag was standing over the prisoners as the ungainly-looking Mi-8 clattered in to land. A platoon of VDV airborne troops piled out of the transport. Vadim vaguely recognised the lieutenant in charge of them. He didn't know the man with him, but he wore the rank and uniform of a lieutenant in the KGB border guards. The Fräulein glanced at Vadim as the two officers approached. The KGB officer's uniform looked crisp and clean. They came to a halt and the KGB officer saluted, earning a withering look from the VDV officer.

"Put your damn hand down," Vadim snapped. The KGB officer looked as though he'd been slapped.

"Comrade captain, I am Lieutenant Ivack. And I may well just be a lieutenant, but I am a lieutenant in the KGB. My position holds more authority than my rank. I was merely showing courtesy." Young and keen and rake thin, he would have been handsome but for the familiar fanatic's gleam in his eyes. Children like this made Vadim feel every one of his fifty-three years. That and the all the pains in his joints, how much he now felt the cold, and how easily he got out of breath these days.

"Your courtesy could get him killed," the VDV officer muttered.

"We don't salute out here, lieutenant. It tells any watching snipers who's in charge," Vadim explained before turning to the VDV officer. "Lieutenant, I have a squad covering a lot of ground. Could we rotate your men onto security and guarding the villagers while I bring my people in?"

The VDV officer nodded. He looked haggard, like every other soldier serving in this war.

"Thank you, please coordinate with Sergeant Sauer." Vadim gestured to his second-in-command. The VDV officer nodded curtly and strode over to the Fräulein and began conversing. He didn't even introduced himself; probably too tired.

Vadim turned back to Ivack, trying not to sigh. "Frankly, lieutenant, I could have done with the extra manpower and another helicopter three hours ago."

"Did you find the Stingers?" the lieutenant all but demanded. Vadim narrowed his grey eyes. It was clear what Ivack had done: let Vadim and his squad do the dirty work so he could fly in at the last moment, with a platoon of VDV no less, and claim the find as his own.

"I'm afraid not," Vadim said, through clenched teeth.

"What is the reason for your failure?" Ivack demanded.

"Mostly the absence of any Stingers."

"The intelligence was good!" Ivack insisted.

"And yet..."

"Did you find any trace of them? Did you take any of the mujahideen prisoner?"

"Anyone fit enough to hold a gun is in the mountains," Vadim told him. *We burned this village for nothing*, he decided not to add.

"So you found nothing, but still managed to get one of your men killed. What extraordinary incompetence," Ivack said, smiling coldly. Vadim knew he was trying to goad him, and frankly, he was doing a good job. Under normal circumstances he would have ignored the young fool, but he'd had little sleep in the last ten days.

"We think we encountered your American, though," Vadim said. He saw the rest of the squad approaching out of the corner of his eye. They weren't bunching together, they were sticking close to cover and keeping up their situational awareness. They were, however, close enough to hear Ivack, which probably wasn't ideal for morale. Vadim nodded towards the Spaniard's body. They'd laid him on his poncho, used two fence poles to turn it into a stretcher. The Mongol, the squad's hulking medic, had lodged their dead comrade's severed head in his ruined chest cavity to stop it from rolling around; he was their friend, but they were all practical people. Ivack blanched when he saw the mess the corpse was in. "Looks like he's been hit by a *Dashka*, doesn't he?" The *Dashka* was the DShK 12.7mm heavy machine gun. "Except it was fired from a sniper rifle. That's a big round for a sniper rifle. Is there anything the KGB wants to share?" Vadim stretched his aching back and shifted his slung AK-74 into a slightly more comfortable position.

"Do you have the sniper?" Ivack managed. He looked as though he was about to throw up.

"I have my own snipers hunting him."

"Then let us hope they can salvage something from your failure," Ivack snarled, lips pulled back from his teeth. He was trying to brazen his way through his obvious horror at the Spaniard's ruined body. It was clear Ivack had not been in Afghanistan very long; this sort of thing was positively commonplace. Vadim hadn't stopped maintaining situational awareness either – it was a good reason not to have to look at Ivack. He was aware, and less than pleased, that Gulag had moved in closer, presumably to better hear what Ivack had to say.

Farm Boy had moved in as well. Skull's AKS-74 looked like a toy in the big Georgian's hands. At close to six and a half feet tall, blond, blue-eyed, Private First Class Genadi Nikoladze looked like some kind of Aryan ideal. He was by far the fittest member of the squad.

Birdcall. Vadim looked over at the Fräulein. She'd heard it and was speaking urgently to the VDV officer, who ordered his men not to shoot as Skull and Princess grew out of the snow-covered landscape. They pushed the hoods back on their concealment suits as they made their way into the village. Princess made for Farm Boy, pulling the concealment suit off, and Skull headed towards Vadim and the KGB lieutenant.

Princess, at four months, was the newest member of their squad. Private Tasiya Yubenkova was athletic, slender, with crystalline blue eyes, platinum silver hair and the cheekbones of a Romanov. She was quite striking, a trait that tended to cause her nothing but trouble. Vadim tried not to grind his teeth as Ivack leered at her. His weren't the only eyes following her, however, as she slid her Dragunov sniper rifle into a hard leather back sheath and crouched down to fold the concealment suit back into her pack.

"Report!" Ivack demanded as Skull approached. The Chechen sniper ignored him. After the Spaniard, Skull had been with Vadim the longest. He had been part of the 'Moslem Battalion' that had spearheaded the Soviet invasion of Afghanistan and assassinated Prime Minister Hafizullah Amin. Junior Sergeant Elimkhan Kulikova's nickname was well-earned: dark-haired, olive-skinned, and always trying to grow a beard in the field, he had a gaunt face, and the skin on his head looked oddly taut, as if stretched across bone. Some of the more superstitious soldiers in the Soviet 40th Army, those who were frightened of Asians, considered him a spectre of death, a reputation only enhanced by his aptitude as a sniper.

"How'd she do?" Vadim asked. He couldn't help himself. He knew that Princess was more than capable: she was a world-class shot and had been attached to an anti-assassination squad within the Russian Olympic team, until the war had become such a drain on personnel that she had been transferred to a combat unit. For some reason, however, he couldn't force himself to stop feeling protective of her, something she knew and resented.

Skull hesitated for a moment as he unscrewed the homemade suppressor from the barrel of his .303 Lee Enfield rifle. He'd taken the old bolt-action rifle from a mujahideen sniper he'd had a two-day-long duel with. It was more accurate than the Dragunov SVD rifle that most Soviet snipers carried. The previous owner had carved designs into the wooden furniture of the rifle, but they were obscured by the white pieces of fabric that Skull had tied to the weapon to camouflage it. The slight smile on the sniper's thin lips was almost a grimace. It made him look more like a death's head than ever.

"She did fine," Skull told him.

"Soldier, I gave you an order!" Ivack shouted. Eyes turned their way, and Vadim saw the squad tense. Princess had shouldered her pack and taken her AKS-74 back from Farm Boy. Her eyes were boring into the back of Ivack's head like a pair of blue lasers. The two snipers were very close, understandably. Skull ignored the KGB lieutenant.

"Find anything?" Vadim asked.

"He shot from about half a mile out, moved position each time. Whatever he used was big and heavy, much more than even big bore hunting rifles." Skull removed a magazine of sub-sonic rounds from the .303 and replaced it with a magazine of normal rounds. The brigade armourer had to custom manufacture ammunition for Skull's rifle, though the sniper took a lot from dead mujahideen as well.

"Soldier, that weapon is clearly not regulation!" Ivack had drool running down his chin now.

"Local footwear," Skull continued, still ignoring the KGB officer. "But judging by the tracks, length and depth of stride: tall, heavy..."

"Well fed," Vadim finished. Skull nodded. Their American mercenary.

"Why did you return before you had completed the task set to you!" Ivack was all but screaming now. Vadim felt like backing away from the lieutenant and into the lee of the transport helicopter; he was sure the American sniper would be able to hear the KGB officer no matter where he was.

"Because I told him to," Vadim snapped, with command in his voice. Ivack's mouth snapped shut, though he glared at the captain. "Anything else?"

"Present for you," Skull said and produced a shell casing from one of the pouches on his webbing and handed it to Vadim. "He was careless." Vadim examined the shell casing. He checked the figures stamped into the metal on the bottom of it. Ivack held out his hand.

"Give me that bullet, captain," he said.

"It's not a bullet, lieutenant," Vadim said mildly, still studying it. "It's a shell casing. The bullet probably blew a hole in that wall over there, or bounced off the gunship's armour." He looked up at Ivack. "Or blew my friend's head off." He held up the casing. "This is a fifty-calibre round. NATO use these in their heavy machine guns. Why is it being fired from a sniper rifle?" Ivack still had his hand out.

"I said –" Ivack started.

"Captain, may I?" Skull asked, glancing at his watch.

"Of course," Vadim told the sniper. "Tell the lieutenant – the other lieutenant – that I said the prisoners can as well." Vadim watched as Skull walked over to where the Fräulein was looking after his gear. He grabbed a rolled-up mat from his pack and crossed over to the airborne lieutenant and spoke with him. The VDV officer glanced Vadim's way, but nodded to the sniper.

"What's he doing?" Ivack demanded. Skull was talking to one of the elderly men with the prisoners. Vadim knew the sniper had only a few words in Dari, which the Tajiks spoke, but the sniper spoke Pashto quite well. It looked as though the sniper was managing to make himself understood, though distrust visibly radiated from the villagers. Skull unrolled his prayer mat and knelt down as the villagers turned to face Mecca and began to pray.

"It's called the *Fajr* prayer. *Fajr* means 'dawn' in Arabic," Vadim told Ivack.

"That man's a disgrace, and presumably you know the State's position on Islam! I'll have you both on a charge. Now give me the shell casing, captain!"

Vadim was worried that if Ivack didn't stop shouting at him, one of the squad was going to kill him. Vadim tucked the shell casing into a pouch on his webbing and turned to face Ivack. The captain had starved during the siege of Stalingrad as a child, and since then had never managed to put on any weight. His physical fitness belied his gauntness, of course, though age was catching up with him quickly. He was tall, though, much taller than Ivack, who was the sort of person that it was easy to look down on.

"Lieutenant, I think my men are here as bait." He leaned in close to Ivack, who took a step back. "I think there is a CIA-backed mercenary sniper in these mountains with a new weapon, a heavy sniper rifle, and I think it would be something of a coup for you to capture it."

The truth of it was written all over the ambitious young fool's face. Ivack swallowed and then glanced at Skull, praying with the prisoners.

"There's no man of fighting age here," Ivack snapped. "This is clearly a mujahideen stronghold. I want these prisoners executed!" And Ivack was probably right. The men would be up in the mountains, waiting until they had gone.

"And what purpose would that serve?" Vadim asked.

"It would teach them the futility of opposing the will of the Union of Soviet Socialist Republics and the Red Army!"

Somehow Vadim was still surprised at the nonsense he had just heard. Ivack turned to glare at Gulag, who was openly laughing at the KGB lieutenant.

"No, it wouldn't. It would just make them angry, more committed to the fight."

Now Ivack leaned in closer to Vadim, though he had to look up.

"Captain, it is clear that this squad is a hotbed of sedition, possibly treason. Now either follow my orders or I will have no choice but to put you under arrest."

Vadim gave this some thought.

"Very well," he said. "But we'll do it at the very last moment before we take off, as the menfolk are probably watching us right now. The VDV will have to leave first so we can get the Hind down."

"Do you think I'm a fool, captain?" Ivack asked, and it took everything Vadim had not to answer. "You would watch me leave and then disobey my order. I will stay and see that the executions are carried out."

Are you sure you have the stomach for it, little man? Vadim wondered.

"Lieutenant, the Hind is only capable of carrying eight men. I'm afraid there is no room for you," Vadim pointed out.

Ivack pointed at the Spaniard's body. "You forget, there's only seven of you now."

"Comrade lieutenant, you make an excellent point." Vadim turned away from Ivack and beckoned to the VDV officer.

THE SUN WAS up and *Fajr* prayer, which Vadim had always found quite beautiful, was over by the time the Mi-8 clawed itself up into the cold, thin mountain air and clattered off between the snow-covered peaks. Vadim was still more than a little surprised that Ivack had decided to remain.

He'd had Farm Boy radio the Hind and tell the crew to get ready to pick them up. The gunship crew had done an exemplary job in supporting the squad, particularly given the potential threat from SAMs.

"Well?" Ivack demanded, nodding towards the prisoners.

"Oh, yes," Vadim said. "Gulag?" Gulag wandered insouciantly over to both the officers. He pulled a claw hammer from his webbing and a bag of nails from a pouch.

"Gulag used to have another nickname," Vadim told Ivack. "He was called the Carpenter. Do you know why?"

"Just get on with it, captain!" Ivack demanded. A number of the squad bristled, but Gulag just smiled his predatory smile.

"Do you know how Spetsnaz execute prisoners, comrade lieutenant?" Gulag asked. He held up a nail and the hammer. "Tap, tap, crunch. In the back of the head. Saves bullets. Run out of nails, you can use shell casings." Gulag dropped the bag of nails and the hammer at Ivack's feet.

"What do you think you're doing?" the KGB lieutenant demanded. "Just get on with it!" He hadn't noticed Skull and the Fräulein moving closer to him.

"You want them dead, then you do it," Vadim told him. Ivack stared at him, fear and anger warring on his face. Vadim was almost impressed that anger won out.

"I'll see you all in a gulag. No! I'll have you all *shot!* This is *treason!*"

Vadim spent a moment looking at the prisoners, and then the village. The low buildings were mostly smouldering now. He wondered how many charred bodies were amongst the wreckage. He looked down at the snow at his feet. Even churned up by their boot prints, it was still pristine, white. It looked so pure.

"You're right, it is," Vadim said and then looked up at the lieutenant. "But only a small one, and out here, who'll notice?"

Ivack was staring at him, perhaps only now realising the mistake he'd made. Vadim nodded to Farm Boy, who started calling the gunship in.

The butt of Skull's .303 caught Ivack in the face, spreading the KGB lieutenant's nose across it, putting him on his back in the snow. Then the Fräulein was on him, kneeling on his throat as he clawed at her massively muscled leg. She removed his knife and pistol, handing them off to Skull. Then, with a roar, she grabbed him by the neck and lifted him into the air. She had been a power lifter on the East German team during the 1980 Olympics in Moscow; when she'd joined the army, she'd had to wean herself off steroids and reduce her bulk, but she was still powerfully built and heavily muscled. She rammed Ivack into a mud brick wall.

"You never speak to one of us that way, you do not eye-fuck Princess, and you certainly never raise your voice to the captain, do you understand me, you little KGB shit?" she screamed. The Fräulein was properly angry, it seemed. Ivack didn't answer, because breathing was a significant problem for him. The Fräulein may have quit steroids, but sometimes Vadim wondered if the rage had ever left her. She turned to look at him. Vadim knew he was being asked if he wanted the KGB officer killed.

Gulag was watching, smiling. Skull was wiping blood off the carved butt of his rifle with snow. Farm Boy was watching what was happening as he talked to the approaching gunship over the squad's radio. He didn't look happy, he'd never liked this sort of thing. Only the Mongol, the hulking, bullet-headed medic, was keeping an eye on their surroundings. This was sloppy, but they were all so tired.

Private First Class Nergui Tsogt was the only other member of the team comparable in body mass to the Fräulein, though he had more fat on him. The Mongol had grown up hunting in his native Mongolia. Vadim wasn't sure how he'd ended up in the Spetsnaz, though the USSR had close links with Mongolia, but the cheerful medic had been a very useful addition to the squad.

"Put him down," Vadim told his second-in-command. Reluctantly the Fräulein let Ivack go and he slid, gasping, down to the snow. "Leave the hammer and the nails!" Vadim shouted over the noise of the Hind-D as it came in to land, whipping the snow up all around them.

THEY LEFT THE hatch to the passenger compartment open, letting in the frigid alpine wind as the gunship banked over the village. Vadim watched as the villagers gathered around Ivack. He was sure he saw one of the children pick something up from the snow.

Vadim laid his hand on his friend's body. He'd *told* Ivack there wasn't room; after all, the Spaniard had been one of them.

CHAPTER THREE

0540 AFT, 8th November 1987
Fayzabad Airport, Badakhshan Province, Afghanistan

VADIM COULDN'T JUST stare at the poncho-wrapped corpse of his old friend. He had to look away, watch the rock walls of the twisting valleys following the course of the frozen Kokcha River below them. Normally they would be trying to suppress the anxiety of a possible missile attack, that feeling of helplessness that came with being a passenger in a flying target. Vadim had been in his fair share of helicopter crashes, as had most of the squad.

The passenger compartment was cramped, and the dripping body wasn't helping. They'd left the hatch open to deal with the inevitable smell of evacuated bowels. It was an undignified way to die, but they all were.

"You shouldn't have hit him with the three-oh-three," Princess admonished Skull. Skull was trying to adjust the scope on his rifle. The impact with Ivack's face had knocked it out of alignment.

"Watch yourself," Gulag snapped. The rifle was ungainly in the cramped passenger compartment of the gunship. Vadim understood wanting to keep busy, he understood that Skull wanted everything working optimally before they returned to Fayzabad. Their camp was little guarantee of safety; they had been hit by any number of mortar attacks, and at least one frontal assault.

"Take it easy," Farm Boy told Gulag. The big gentle Georgian and the stolid medic were two of the very few people the gangster actually listened to.

Skull stopped fussing with his scope and pointed the weapon up, out of everyone's way. Farm Boy went back to staring out the hatch. Clearly the Georgian didn't want to look at the body either, although it was stretched across his lap. The captain had thought Farm Boy was simpleminded the first time he met him. As time passed, Vadim had realised the Georgian was a quiet, thoughtful man, whose experiences in Afghanistan troubled him deeply. Softly spoken, Farm Boy was too gentle for the Spetsnaz, or for this war. Vadim had no idea how the boy had made it through the meat labyrinth, the maze of viscera-filled channels designed to inure recruits to the gory horrors of the battlefield, in basic training.

Mongol's lips were moving, presumably praying to whatever it was he believed in. The captain had decided a long time ago never to interfere with their beliefs. Only Skull really made his beliefs obvious; some form of rebellion, Vadim guessed. It did sometimes cause problems. This hadn't been the first member of the KGB they'd 'misplaced.'

"Boss?" It took Vadim a moment to realise Farm Boy was talking to him. He moved slightly, making the body shift. They were flying over a gorge that emptied out into a broad, snow-covered plain. Fayzabad, a small city of some fifty thousand people, lined the right-hand bank of the river, a sprawling collection of low timber, clay and mud brick buildings, contrasting with the brutal poured concrete of Soviet state architecture. "Do you know why he was called the Spaniard?" His nickname held nearly as much mystery as Vadim's own.

"It's because Vadim and the Spaniard both fought with the International Brigades during the Spanish Civil War," Gulag said and laughed at his own joke. Pavel had been popular with everyone, except Gulag. Gulag didn't give a shit.

"Shut up, Gulag," the Fräulein told him. He blew her a kiss and she narrowed her eyes.

"How old do you think I am?" Vadim asked. There were a few dry chuckles. The helicopter was descending towards Fayzabad Airport.

"I think you stood at Lenin's side," Mongol suggested. A few more laughs, though Gulag's face looked sour for some reason.

"Maybe the colonel," the Fräulein suggested. Now there was more laughter, and even Vadim chuckled. Colonel Dmytro 'The Red Cossack' Krychenko, the de facto commander of the 15th Spetsnaz Brigade, was something of a legend, but not quite old enough to have fought in the October Revolution.

"Boss?" Farm Boy asked, prompting him. They were coming in to land. It was little more than an administration building and their *zastava*, their fortified camp, what the Americans called a Forward Operating Base. The Hindu Kush mountains towered above it. Vadim turned to look down at his friend's body and shook his head.

"I don't know, he never told me."

He saw the Fräulein start as she stepped out of the helicopter, and Farm Boy and Mongol, who were carrying the body, looked in the same direction as they emerged. Vadim stepped out onto the perforated steel planking of the runway behind them, to see an unexpected Antonov AN-72 transport plane. There were two men standing in front of it.

The younger of the two figures was wearing the heavy winter version of the VDV's khaki drab. There was no insignia on his uniform, which marked him as a member of the Spetsnaz. He had chiselled features and a square jaw, like a Western comic character, or a figure in a propaganda poster; but his expression was grim.

As Vadim approached, he recognised the young man as Private Orlov Razin. He had been a *razvedchiki*, a scout for the VDV airborne forces, when Vadim had noticed him and sent the boy back to Kiev for training.

More meat for the grinder, he thought grimly.

"Comrade captain..." Razin started as Vadim reached the two men.

"Vadim, or 'boss,' not 'captain'; do you understand me?" Vadim demanded. "Where are you from?"

"Ukraine, si –" Years of indoctrinated military discipline warred within Razin as he tried to bring himself to say Vadim's first name.

"Are you a Cossack, like this old fool?" Vadim asked, nodding towards the colonel. Razin actually blanched.

"Er... I mean... I'm..."

"Eloquent? It was a simple question, what are you ashamed of?"

Razin bristled, which pleased Vadim.

"Yes, I am a Cossack, Vadim." He pronounced the captain's name with just a little venom.

He has a backbone, Vadim thought.

"You see the big East German woman?" he asked.

"Yes si –" Razin looked down, shaking his head.

"You report to her."

Vadim watched as Razin, obviously uncomfortable, grabbed his pack and weapon and made his way toward the *zastava.*

"Bit hard on him, weren't you?" Colonel Krychenko asked, and Vadim turned to face his commanding officer. Tall and thin, the colonel had a narrow face that looked as though it had been formed by wind shear. Dark eyes and a goatee, he wore his salt and pepper hair almost down to his shoulders, because nobody could tell him otherwise. He wore a heavy grey greatcoat and a *ushanka* 'ear hat' made of real mink fur, as opposed to the synthetic fur hats that the rest of them wore, for much the same reason. He had an old, holstered Nagant M1895 revolver on one hip and a real Cossack sabre on the other. The colonel was in his mid-sixties, but Vadim couldn't help but think, as he pulled his winter smock tighter against the cold wind blowing in from the mountains, that his old friend looked in better shape than he did. Of course, the colonel wasn't jumping out of helicopters and shooting people on a daily basis anymore.

"We lost the Spaniard today," Vadim told him.

The colonel nodded. "I see, I'm sorry. He was the last of the old guard, wasn't he?"

Vadim didn't answer. The colonel reached into his greatcoat and pulled out a long hip flask and offered it. Vadim took a long pull from the flask, feeling the rough vodka hit the back of his throat and start to burn.

He was nine years old. Back in Stalingrad, standing over the body of a German soldier, his hands red and dripping. That was how a young Dmytro had found him. He had told Vadim that his first kill had earned him his first drink. Even then, Vadim had known that Dmytro had just been trying to help, but had no idea what to do with the boy. The 'vodka' – apparently made from potatoes and white spirit – had blinded him for the better part of an hour.

Vadim handed the flask back.

"Death to Hitler," the colonel said, and took a long swallow from the flask himself. "I'm sorry for your friend." He handed the flask back to Vadim. "He seems like an earnest young man." He nodded in the direction Razin had gone. Vadim was aware of raised voices. The rest of the squad had presumably started to give the new recruit a hard time.

The colonel wasn't praising the boy. The Spetsnaz didn't need earnest young men and women, it needed ruthless ones.

"He's good," Vadim said and then after a few more moments: "Perhaps I'm trying to make up for past mistakes."

"Timoshenko?" the colonel asked, meaning Gulag. Vadim nodded and took another drink before handing the flask back to the colonel. "Being a killer doesn't make you a good soldier."

"He likes it too much."

Gulag had been transferred from his Siberian work camp to a Motor Rifle Penal Battalion. His company had been caught in an ambush, and Vadim and his squad had been first on the scene. The penal company had given a good account of itself, but they had all been killed, bar Gulag. They found him amongst a pile of mujahideen bodies.

"Perhaps he's perfectly suited for this war," the colonel suggested. Vadim had thought the same thing. "You'll look after my fellow Cossack, though?"

"This place gets us all in the end," Vadim said quietly.

"You know I can have you court-martialled for calling me an old fool?" the colonel asked. Vadim smiled.

"I think you'll be at the end of a long queue."

"Yes, I noticed the good Lieutenant Ivack didn't make it back with you." The colonel's expression remained carefully neutral.

"He chose to stay," Vadim said, and the colonel nodded. "Why'd we get sent there?"

"Ivack went over my head. I'm sorry."

Vadim took a deep breath and looked away from his friend. The sun was up now, the mountains casting long shadows over the plain. The thin air was so fresh it hurt to breathe up here. There was just the slightest taint of oil and aviation fuel in the air.

"Why is a lieutenant in the KGB giving a colonel in the GRU orders? And why didn't the border guards do it, or Osnaz A?"

"Because they knew... *we* knew somebody would get killed."

Vadim almost wished he could feel betrayed, but he knew the colonel would have had no choice.

"Gorbachev has been arrested," the colonel told him, his voice even. You had to know him as well as Vadim did to see the emotion the old colonel was holding back. Mikhail Gorbachev, with his *perestroika* and *glasnost*, had seemed the best chance they had of an end to this grinding war. "He has been charged with treason against the State. For all I know they've already taken him into the yard at Dzerzhinsky Square and shot him."

Vadim had lived through Stalin's purges as young man. He didn't expect to feel such disappointment anymore. It was like a cold knife between the ribs. He was surprised to find he was frightened. He hadn't realised that he'd had enough hope left to invest any in Gorbachev.

"I should go in there," Vadim said, nodding towards the *zastava*, "and put a bullet in each of their heads. It would be quicker." He felt the colonel's hand on his shoulder.

"I do not think that it is what men like us do," he said. Vadim broke free of his grip and looked up at the mountains.

"Who's in charge now, in the Kremlin?"

"Varishnikov." Varishnikov was the hardest of the hard-liners and the head of the KGB. That explained the KGB pushing the GRU – Army intelligence, the parent organisation of Spetsnaz – around. "It was relatively bloodless, at least."

"They're going to kill us," Vadim said.

"Yes, both of us. A sad way for two Heroes of the Soviet Union to die, don't you think?" There was no humour in Vadim's answering laugh. "We have value to them only as good soldiers; the moment we stop..."

"We're bad soldiers, but excellent hunters," Vadim said. The colonel frowned, but held his peace. There hadn't been much light at the end of the tunnel, just a glimmer, and now it seemed like that had been snuffed out. Vadim didn't feel much like going on, but the colonel was right. They'd both lived through Stalingrad. They weren't the kind of men to put guns in their mouths. When they came for him, they would have a fight on their hands. He looked up at the Antonov.

"That's a big plane for just two people, even an officer of your stature," Vadim pointed out. The colonel, smiled but the smile didn't quite reach his eyes. Vadim wondered if this was it. A flight back to Bagram, and then two in the back of his head in the KGB compound in Kabul.

"We're going back west," the colonel said. "The whole brigade."

"Kiev?" Vadim asked, cursing the hope in his voice. He rarely went back to Stalingrad. The beautiful Ukrainian city where he'd done his officer training was the closest he had to a home.

"I don't know," the colonel said. He sounded uneasy.

"Is the war over? Are they pulling us out?" That didn't make sense; one of the main issues the hardliners had with Gorbachev was his intention to pull Soviet forces out of Afghanistan.

"Just the 15th Spetsnaz, and we're being replaced. The 40th Army is being reinforced. At least two more Armies."

Vadim suddenly felt cold.

"Two?"

"At least."

Vadim knew that this could only mean one thing.

"Pakistan or Iran?" he asked. It made perfect sense, of course. They couldn't control Afghanistan, so why not invade another country.

"I don't know. I suspect Iran, and then try for the rest of the Gulf. They need the oil."

Vadim stared at the colonel. He had wondered if it was going to happen in '79 when he'd flown into Kabul with the 'Moslem Battalion'.

"The Americans have to respond to this."

The colonel just nodded. It made sense that the 15th Spetsnaz Brigade were being pulled out; they were effective, but they had a reputation for being insubordinate – bordering, at times, on the seditious. The colonel liked to joke that this was down to his leadership. They also did not have a good relationship with the KGB. "They want to fight a war they can't win."

"Just like this one, my friend."

"But *nobody* can win this one," Vadim said very quietly. The colonel didn't say anything. Suddenly Vadim remembered how the gaunt, near-starving German soldiers thrown into the ruins of Stalingrad had looked like demons to him. Not for the first time, he wondered who the demons were now.

"Well, at least we'll get to put our training to use," he managed. Much of Spetsnaz training focused on cross-border, deep-penetration raids to destroy strategic resources, particularly nuclear weapons. He nodded towards the *zastava* where he could still hear the squad's voices. "What do I tell them?"

"What do you think?" the colonel asked.

THE COLONEL HAD returned to the Antonov; there were more members of the 15th to pick up from various airstrips in the north. Then they would return to

Bagram before joining the rest of the brigade to fly west en masse. The colonel felt that it should be Vadim himself who told his men.

He could hear them arguing, good-naturedly. The Fräulein was divvying out the Spaniard's belongings to the rest of the squad. They would have given Razin any gear that he needed, and the rest would be shared out according to sentimentality and requirement. The Spaniard didn't have much family. Given his off-duty habits, he almost certainly had bastard children everywhere he'd served, but they'd been unknown to him. Farm Boy had his parents and siblings back in Georgia, Mongol had a large extended family back in Mongolia, and, oddly, Gulag spoke of his father with near holy reverence, but none of them had immediate family. Their life wasn't really conducive to partners and children.

As he approached he could hear them calling Razin 'New Boy'. That's what he'd be called now until he earned back the nickname he'd been given in basic training, or a new one. He was new in from Kiev, so the rest of the squad would be going through his gear, looking for anything that was difficult to get hold of in Afghanistan – which was just about everything, but particularly sweets, alcohol, pornography and cigarettes. How New Boy took this blatant theft would play a large part in how he was accepted by the squad. You had to strike a balance between generosity and assertiveness. Even so, the rest of the squad would keep their distance until he had proven he wasn't a fool.

Their tent was pitched in a hole and surrounded by sand bags; you had to walk through a warren of trenches to reach it. It tended to turn into a boggy swamp when it rained, but in the snow, it was just cold. Gulag was lying across the top of the sandbags, smoking what Vadim assumed was one of New Boy's cigarettes.

"He didn't have any porn. I can only assume he's a monk. Didn't Marx have some quite strong things to say about religion?" Gulag took another drag of the cigarette. Vadim wasn't really in the mood for Gulag's brand of humour tonight. He started down the crumbling earthen steps into the tent. "Cosy little chat with the colonel: you both being heroes and everything?"

The Spetsnaz may have been more relaxed than the regular army, but even so, this crossed the line.

"You weren't beaten enough during basic training, were you?" Vadim asked. He was wondering if at his age he still had it in him to deliver a beating to a savage like Gulag. He wasn't sure he would like the answer.

"Oh, I was beaten," Gulag told him.

"I get that, just not *enough*."

"I was beaten growing up, I was beaten in the gulag, and I was beaten in basic training." He took another drag of his cigarette. He wasn't wearing his gloves now, despite the cold. Vadim could see the stumps of the two fingers on his left hand. "Made me the man I am today." Gulag sat up on the sandbags and grinned down at Vadim. "They don't beat me anymore, though. Now they just try and kill me. Tell me, captain, how many men under your command have made it back to Russia, or whatever disgusting shithole they come from?"

Vadim stared up at Gulag.

The criminal smiled back at him. "You're going to try and kill us all, aren't you?"

Not me, he wanted to tell Gulag, except it was his command, they were his people.

Gulag pushed himself off the sandbags, landing right in front of Vadim. He leaned in close, smelling of sweat, cigarettes and bad breath.

"Well you're not going to kill me, do you understand?"

Then he turned and stalked into the tent.

CHAPTER FOUR

1117 EST, 14th November 1987
The *Volga*, Lenok (India) Class Submarine, Laurentian Fan, Atlantic Ocean,
off the East Coast of Canada

THE SQUAD JOINED Colonel Krychenko in the Antonov, and the short-take-off-and-landing transport aircraft hopped from one airfield to the next, collecting the scattered 15th Spetsnaz Brigade. Vadim assumed that he would know most of the men and women that had joined them on the plane, but the rate of attrition had been such that a lot of the faces where new to him.

They landed at Bagram Airbase just outside Kabul, the main headquarters of the Soviet military effort in Afghanistan. The 15th Brigade had just about enough personnel left to warrant a heavy-lift Antonov AN-124 Ruslan aircraft. Even with them all in there, the huge cargo aircraft's interior seemed cavernous. The other men and women all looked like Vadim felt, tired and without hope. There was much speculation, but nobody was telling them anything. He'd used the time to catch up with those members of the brigade that he still knew. They shared the same stories: soldiers' lives wasted, the villainy of the KGB.

The plane landed a number of times to refuel and to drop people off. Initially Vadim wasn't sure where their final destination was, though he suspected East Germany. It was warmer here than it had been in Afghanistan, despite its being

November. They were loaded into trucks, and eventually debussed at the Baltic port of Rostock.

They were led into covered submarine pens to see two docked Lenok Class boats. They looked like most submarines Vadim had seen or operated from, except these had raised structures on their backs, carrying submersibles of a type Vadim didn't recognise. He could feel the questioning eyes of the rest of the squad, but this wasn't a good time to discuss anything.

There had been enough Spetsnaz in Rostock to form a patchwork company, which was split between the two subs and then broken down into squads. They were then ordered to give up their equipment, causing some heated discussion. No sailor had been permitted to carry a weapon in the Soviet fleet since the Kronstadt Mutiny, but Vadim and a number of other officers, backed by some increasingly angry soldiers, had pointed out that they weren't sailors. The naval officers had replied that a pressurised environment 700 feet beneath the surface is not a good place for high-velocity weapons and grenades. In all honesty, Vadim could see their point.

It was cramped on the sub, which smelled of diesel, sweat, military cooking and shit. The sub seemed to be running on a reduced crew to make room for the Spetsnaz commandos. The squads had been separated and isolated. This was standard operating procedure, helping compartmentalise what little information they knew. They had been at sea for more than seven days now. At least they had all managed to catch up on some much-needed sleep.

Vadim made his way through the narrow corridor from the commander's state room back towards the cramped bunk area his squad had been assigned. He had no idea how Farm Boy, Mongol and the Fräulein were managing to get around.

They were all sitting around a wooden crate, except for Gulag who was in his bunk, furtively masturbating.

"Fuck's sake, Gulag," Vadim muttered.

"I can't help it, boss, I can see Fräulein."

"I will tear it off and choke you with it, little man," the Fräulein threatened.

"Promises, promises…"

"Speaking as your medic, you're supposed to leave it alone when it starts to bleed," Mongol pointed out. There was some laughter. Gulag's mercifully dry hand emerged from beneath the sheets and he tried to wipe it on a protesting Farm Boy.

"Enough!" Vadim snapped. After the meeting he'd just had with the sub-commander and the political officer, he really wasn't in the mood. Even Gulag was paying attention now. The criminal sorted himself out and shifted to sit on the side of the bunk. Vadim nodded to Skull, who moved to stand by the curtain between the corridor and their bunkroom.

"Well?" Vadim asked Farm Boy. The big Georgian held up a half-full glass of water with a number of listening devices in it. Then he shook his head; he couldn't be sure that he'd found everything.

"Anything, boss?" Princess asked.

"The commander would like you to not break any more of his sailor's arms," he told the sniper.

"He grabbed my ass."

"I explained we have standing rules of engagement. If you're attacked, take whatever action you deem appropriate. Probably try not to kill anyone, though." There were a few smiles around the bunkroom and Princess nodded. It was the sub commander's job to control his men, not Princess's job to restrain herself.

"You can see why a man would, though," Gulag said. Vadim tried not to sigh.

"How will you masturbate when I break both your arms?" Princess asked.

"You are completely safe, my dear. I have eyes only for Fräulein." This wasn't true; Vadim had seen Gulag watching Princess. The gangster wasn't the only one in the squad, but his eyes were by far the most predatory.

"Well then, you're in luck, once Tas had broken both your arms I will snap your spine, which should enable your mouth to reach a cock even as small as yours," the Fräulein said. Even Vadim had to smile as laughter rolled around the room. "Now shut the fuck up and let Vadim speak."

"So... nothing," Vadim said. "The commander insists he's just a taxi driver, which I can believe. The political officer, who I'm pretty sure is actually calling the shots, says that we will be given our orders when we reach our destination. It's all compartmentalised, which makes a degree of sense if the different squads have different missions."

"Is the political officer KGB?" Farm Boy asked.

"Of course he is," Gulag told his friend.

"Without a doubt," Vadim affirmed. He left out that there were undoubtedly KGB-loyal crew on board, probably with access to small arms.

"Are we going to Am –" New Boy started.

"Shut up, you get to talk when you've been shot at." It seemed that Gulag still hadn't forgiven their new recruit for not having any pornography.

"I served in Afghanistan bef –"

"I said shut up," Gulag repeated. New Boy looked angry, but wisely decided not to push the matter. Farm Boy put his hand on Gulag's shoulder.

"Are we going to America?" Mongol asked. He was trying hard to keep the worry out of his voice, but not completely succeeding. He would be thinking about his family. Everybody was watching Vadim intently now.

"I don't know," Vadim said honestly. "They've done a good job in hiding the charts from me, but leaving from Rostock, this long at sea, it seems likely." There was some muttering and cursing from the squad. "Remember, this was what we were trained for." It was as much for anyone listening as to motivate the squad.

"Good thing I learned to speak Pashto," Skull said, smiling his death's head smile.

"How are we getting – ?" New Boy started.

Gulag swung round to face him. "What did I tell you?" he demanded.

Vadim was getting a little tired of this. Gulag always took this bullshit too far. He considered saying something, but it was better for the squad to sort it out themselves.

"Gulag," Mongol started, "let him talk."

Gulag opened his mouth to say something.

"You're either contributing or you're quiet, you understand me?" the Fräulein told him.

Gulag narrowed his eyes but managed to keep quiet.

"I don't know how we're getting back," Vadim said quietly. "The political officer told me I would be given all the details when we reached our destination."

The muttering was more subdued this time. Gulag laughed and lay back down on his bunk.

"You know what this sounds like, don't you, Vadim?" he asked. There was no need for the captain to answer. It sounded like a suicide mission, a one-way trip. Vadim found the Fräulein staring at him, a question in her eyes. *Should we take the sub?* He shook his head. For what it was worth, he was still a soldier of the USSR. Besides, if the sub was taking them to America, it would be easier to defect there, if that was what they decided. If the rumours he'd heard from the submariners were true – that the entire Soviet submarine fleet was preparing to put to sea to hunt NATO and SEATO ballistic missile boats in wolfpacks – it would be academic. What he didn't understand was why they were preparing to fight a war nobody could win.

Vadim climbed onto his bunk and lay down, picking up his novel. Whatever lay ahead, and despite being trapped in a pressurised tin can underwater with a lot of unhappy commandos, he was still enjoying the down time.

"Boss," New Boy began. Going by his tone, Vadim wasn't going to like the next question. "Why does Colonel Krychenko call you 'Infant'?" There was an almost perceptible intake of breath from the rest of the squad, except for Gulag, who was chuckling.

"Because he think's we're infantry," Gulag announced.

Vadim closed his eyes. He'd always hated the name.

0206 EST, 16th November 1987
The *Volga*, Lenok (India) Class Submarine, Napeague Bay, off the Coast of Long Island, New York State

THEY HAD BEEN given Western clothing and dry suits to put over the top of them, but no rebreathers, which meant a surface swim. They still had nothing but supposition about where they were. There was almost a revolt when they were told that their gear had already been loaded into the submersibles piggybacking the *Volga*. They wanted – needed – to check their equipment before they went ashore.

The next surprise had come when they'd climbed into the submersibles and realised they had caterpillar tracks. They had split into two fire teams of four: Vadim had New Boy, Gulag and Farm Boy in his sub. The submersible disconnected from the *Volga*, impellers lifting it out of its cradle, dimmed running lights playing across its mother-ship and sister submersible. The water through the viewport was in total darkness, specks of dust and scraps of seaweed floating into view in the craft's lights. He felt sure the sea wasn't deep here, but the impact with the bottom still came as something of a shock. The submersible's caterpillar tracks bit into the sea floor and started crawling, raising billowing clouds of silt. Vadim moved forward towards the submersible pilot and looked out the viewport. He could make out the other submersible just to the right and behind them. The clouds of silt reminded him of stagecoaches racing across dusty deserts in the Imperialist 'Westerns' he'd seen in Cuba.

The submersibles lurched to a halt. Looking up through the porthole, Vadim could just about make out where the top of the submersible had breached the surface. Gulag unscrewed the top hatch, and water spilled into the submersible as he pushed it up. The sea smell and fresh air was a blessed relief after eight days stuck in the stinking tin can of the *Volga*. Gulag was first out, followed by New Boy.

"This bullshit's for naval Spetsnaz," Farm Boy muttered as he tried to squeeze his bulk through the hatch. Vadim passed up the waterproof flotation sacks their gear had been packed into. They felt light. Then he followed.

He found himself less than sixty feet off a sandy beach edged by wooded hills. The beach and the surrounding area appeared deserted. To his right he could see the lights of houses, the Western equivalent of dachas, he guessed; even from here they looked large and comfortable, decadent. To his back were two islands, and further away, a headland with a few scattered lights on it. Beyond it were the lights of what looked like a reasonable sized town. At a guess, the few vessels he could see were small pleasure craft. They were unlikely to be crewed at this time of year.

Vadim glanced over at the other submersible, which was just breaking the surface now. Princess, Skull and Mongol were all in the water, holding onto their flotation sacks; Princess had a hold of two. The Fräulein was struggling to pull herself through the hatch. Vadim pulled on his fins and slid into the water, barely feeling the cold. He took his sack from New Boy, checked the Fräulein had managed to make it into the water, and started to swim toward the shore. He heard the hatches on the submersibles close; when he glanced behind him, they'd gone.

"Vadim," the Fräulein said. They were just inside the tree line now, looking out over the beach and into the bay. They'd opened up the flotation sacks to find Western luggage that contained their gear. They'd used their *saperkas*, the sharpened entrenching tools they all carried, to dig a pit for the sacks and dry suits, but they hadn't buried them yet. Vadim, Skull, Princess and New Boy had stood guard armed with suppressed Stechkin pistols, whilst the Fräulein had gone through the gear. "I don't like it." She had moved up to where Vadim was standing in the shadow of a tree.

"What?" Vadim asked. They were still speaking Russian; without further information it was a little hard to decide what else to do.

"We've got our weapons, plus webbing to carry it all. That's about it."

"The RPGs?"

"RPGs, grenades for the launchers, hand grenades, even Skull's old three-oh-three, all of it."

"Radio?" Not that he was sure what he would do with one.

The Fräulein shook her head. "No radio, no night vision and no body armour." That got his attention. "But all the ammunition in the world. There's one other thing." She pulled at her jumper and her jeans. "Western clothes, but no Western weapons. Easier to fit in, easier to find parts and ammunition for." In the East German Army, the Fräulein had been part of a special divisionary battalion, training on US equipment captured by the NVA in Vietnam. In the event of a conflict with the Western powers, their job would have been to drive over the border into West Germany, infiltrate NATO lines and wreak havoc. "It looks like we've been equipped for a fast, dirty op, not a long-term infiltration."

He nodded. Even in the darkness he could see the concern on her face. It felt like the jaws of a bear trap closing around them.

"Okay, keep the gear stowed, we carry concealed weapons only: knives, sidearms. Make sure everyone has their suppressors on." The Fräulein nodded.

Birdsong. People froze, or moved into cover. Suddenly everyone had a Stechkin in their hand. There was no sign of Skull.

"Hello, is there anyone the – !" The sentence was cut off by a frightened squeal, and Vadim heard something hit the ground. He hoped Skull hadn't killed the speaker. There was a reason why Gulag hadn't been on guard. Vadim signalled for New Boy to follow him and for the rest of them to remain on watch around the gear. At least they knew for sure where they were. The speaker had called out in English, with a pronounced American accent.

Vadim and New Boy, pistols at the ready, advanced through the trees towards where the voice had come from. They found Skull lying on a path leading into the woods, both legs and one arm wrapped around a stranger and a NRS-2 survival knife held to the man's throat. New Boy kept watch as Vadim knelt down next to Skull and his captive, his suppressed Stechkin levelled at the man's face. He nodded to Skull, who loosened his grip enough for his captive to speak.

"You guys are Spetsnaz, right?" He had floppy blond hair and a build that looked like he spent some time in a gym. Even in the darkness, Vadim could make out the tan, which seemed out of place at this time of year, on what he assumed was America's East Coast. He wore a thick coat over a ridiculously coloured suit that looked too large for him, and a grotesquely colourful shirt open at the neck. "My name's Eugene. I'm your contact. I've never been asked to do anything like this before, it's very cool."

He was clearly an idiot. Skull looked at him questioningly. Vadim was going to let the sniper kill him if he didn't use the contact phrase in the very near future. "Oh, shit, yeah! 'Alexander'."

"Nevsky," Vadim answered and didn't shoot Eugene in the face.

0438 EST, 16th November 1987
New York City, New York State

AFTER THE CONTACT phrase, they had thoroughly checked 'Eugene's' identity: his birth mark, fillings, questions about his cover. Vadim had the feeling Eugene wasn't an American who had been turned; he seemed to be trying too hard to be American, particularly with his ridiculous, over-sized clothes. He was pretty sure the man was a KGB infiltrator, probably trained at their mocked-up American town just outside Vinnytsia in the Ukraine.

A dirt path through the woods took them to a muddy track with a minibus parked on it. Eugene had got out of breath walking over the hills and Vadim had to stop him from smoking or using a torch. They put the luggage containing their gear onto the minibus's roof rack, which wasn't ideal. They had buried the drysuits, their fins and the flotation sacks back on the beach. With Eugene driving and all eight of them in the minibus, Vadim felt very conspicuous travelling the deserted roads at this time of the morning. Surely they would be screamingly obvious to any militia, or any members of America's state security apparatus.

They drove past dachas that Vadim assumed could only belong to the most powerful people in America. Then into suburbs where the houses still looked huge and luxurious compared to Soviet state housing. He could feel the squad struggling to maintain their situational awareness as they stared around themselves. The streets steadily became more and more built-up: leafy suburbs gave way to town houses, and in the distance he could see well-lit skyscrapers rise up into the sky. The city seemed to glow. Despite himself, Vadim was transfixed; and he didn't think he was the only one. Even Eugene, who had kept up a steady stream of nonsense in English since they had climbed into the minibus, had gone quiet.

"New York fucking City, baby," he told Vadim. Vadim continued ignoring the annoying man.

They crossed a river, glittering lights reflected in the water. Then they were into the city proper. Vadim wasn't quite sure what to think. Maybe he had spent too much time in the field in places like Afghanistan, Nicaragua, Angola and Vietnam, but even Moscow didn't compare to New York. The skyscrapers were causing a weird sort of vertigo. He understood that America was a new country, but even so, New York appeared to be from the future, something from one of Stanislaw Lem's fantasies. He caught glimpses of entire streets that seemed made of light, like some commercialised tawdry heaven. The skyscrapers were tall towers, fortress-like, the home to dark characters from a fairy tale; but at street level the cracks in the capitalist system were apparent. Rubbish-strewn roads, graffiti-covered concrete, broken glass refracting blinking streetlights, the poor made to sleep in the streets, wild dogs and rats picking at the garbage. There were pornographic cinemas and sex shops, prostitutes and drug dealers operating openly from the alleys and the kerbs. So much flesh on show, despite the rain and the cold, but there was little that was 'sexy' about the prostitutes. They looked cold and miserable, used and exploited by their petty bourgeois masters.

Vadim craned his neck, trying to look up at the towers on either side of the wet street as the minibus splashed through garbage-clogged puddles. There were clearly two very different worlds in this bizarre and alien city. He wondered what it took to get up into the towers. What kinds of crimes did one have to commit? Wonder and disgust warred within him as he tried to work out how he felt about this bizarre place.

It doesn't matter what you think of the place, you have a job to do, a decision to make, he thought.

"Why doesn't the government do anything about this?" Farm Boy asked, appalled.

"Free enterprise, dude," Eugene answered in English. "And you should probably try and get used to speaking English."

"We don't all *speak* English," Vadim told the infiltrator. Eugene stared at him before turning back to the road, shaking his head, as the minibus drove into a cloud of steam venting from a manhole cover.

"'Do something'?" Gulag asked. "This place looks like paradise."

"This is hell," Mongol muttered, his voice full of superstitious dread. Vadim glanced over at Skull and the Fräulein. He looked impassive, she looked tense.

The minibus came to a halt at a red light. Eugene was glancing around. A blue car, emblazoned with the letters *NYPD* and topped with a light, pulled up next to them. Suddenly Vadim's feeling of conspicuousness came flooding back as one of the uniformed police officers in the car looked up them. Eugene smiled back at them. Vadim could see suspicion written all over the jowly police officer's face. Gulag and New Boy, on the opposite side of the bus from the police car, had inched their Stechkins out of their holsters and were screwing suppressors into the barrels. Skull had his knife in his hand.

"Take it easy, everyone," Eugene managed through his fixed smile. "You, the pretty chick," he said to Princess, and then when she didn't answer: "Does she speak English?" he asked Vadim.

"Very well," Princess answered.

"Give them a smile," Eugene suggested.

"Why don't you go and fuck yourself?" Princess counter-suggested, practising her English.

"Woah! Hostile!" Eugene muttered, still grinning at the police officer. The choked-off caterwaul of the car's siren almost made Vadim jump. The minibus was bathed in a hellish red light as the police car pulled away from them.

"The light is green," Vadim pointed out.

Two walls of the apartment were floor-to-ceiling windows looking out over the city's lights. The apartment was huge, split level, open plan, with little more in it than a long, L-shaped sofa and some sort of entertainment centre that flashed and glittered like the cockpit of a fighter plane. A solitary picture hung on the whitewashed wall, two fields of subdued colour bisecting the canvas.

"How many people live here?" Vadim asked, crossing to the window and looking out. They were high above the street now, in a different world.

"Just me," Eugene said, sounding confused. Vadim had expected the answer, but it still managed to surprise him.

"And the State pays for all this?" Farm Boy asked, awe and disgust warring in his voice. Vadim could understand how the big Georgian felt: awe and disgust were pretty much all he'd felt since arriving in America.

"Where's all your furniture?" Gulag asked.

"It's called minimalism, man," Eugene told him and went to slap Gulag on the shoulder.

"Don't touch me," Gulag said and Eugene froze, arm still raised. "If this was my place, I would fill it with a *lot* of things."

"You've got to have style, you get me?" Eugene asked. Vadim was looking at a large, roughly square building, arched windows, a pillared frontage. It looked like a train station built by the decadent gods of Greek mythology. There was a broad skyscraper behind it, an ugly concrete block that ruined his appreciation of the station by reminding him of the brutal state architecture of the USSR.

He turned back to see the Fräulein organising the rest of the squad to thoroughly check through their gear. Mongol was kneeling over one of the bulky suitcases, shaking his head.

"No med kit," he said. Gulag glanced over at his friend, and then turned to look at Vadim. It was clear to the captain that if the squad decided they'd had enough, there wasn't a lot he could do about it over here. It would be very easy for them to defect right now.

"What's the mission?" Vadim asked Eugene. The spy looked around at the rest of the squad.

"Em… I think it's best that we speak alone." He'd actually lowered his voice to answer. Princess was closest to him.

"Princess," Vadim said quietly. Eugene screamed as she seized him, put him in a painful hold and showed him her knife. Most of the squad had stopped working, though New Boy had drawn his pistol and moved to the door. Vadim liked that.

"I have a number of misgivings, comrade Eugene," Vadim said as he started to pace. "The first is you don't seem very bright…" Eugene opened his mouth to protest. Princess hissed, almost sensuously, but the threat was apparent. He closed his mouth again. "For example, what possible reason could I have for hiding information from my people, and why would I risk losing something in translation? My second misgiving is that you seem to enjoy being American just a little too much…"

"I'm a loyal –" he started, giving a frightened yelp as Princess drew blood.

"…which makes me wonder if you've been compromised," Vadim continued. "And thirdly, you're annoying, and we're not renowned for our patience. So when any of us asks a question, I would like an answer. Do we have an understanding?"

Eugene opened his mouth to say something.

"Think about what you're going to say," the Fräulein warned him. In the end, he just nodded. He was pale and covered in sweat. Princess let him go.

"What is the mission?" Vadim asked again.

"I think you guys are here for the duration," Eugene said, shakily lighting a cigarette. Vadim wondered how this man had the nerve to be a spy. "I'm awaiting further orders, but initially it's very simple. They want you to pick up something from a locker in Grand Central Station."

Vadim pointed at the building far below.

"That station?" he asked. Eugene nodded, nervously sucking on the cigarette.

"Why can't *you* do it?" Gulag growled before standing up and taking Eugene's cigarette from him.

"That's what I asked," Eugene said fumbling for another cigarette. "Apparently there's a threat to the package, so they want you guys there and loaded for bear."

"Loaded for bear?" Farm Boy asked, frowning.

"Heavily armed," Vadim said. A building a little distance away had caught his attention: a silver, needle-like tower. It looked like something from a pre-war German Expressionist film he had seen at an illegal screening as a teenager. A city peopled by robots.

"Why weren't we given our body armour?" the Fräulein demanded.

"Or a medical kit?" Mongol added. Eugene stared at them.

"How would I possibly know that?"

"Why do they want us so heavily armed?" Skull asked quietly.

"I told you: a threat," Eugene protested. "Look, I think there will be more instructions with the package. You may be going straight on, catching a train to go and blow up Washington, or something. How would I know? This is what compartmentalisation is all about, *comprende*?"

Vadim stared at the spy, who look terrified. Gulag reached over, took Eugene's packet of cigarettes from his pocket and the second lit one from his unresisting hand. He offered it to Farm Boy, who shook his head. Gulag shrugged and started smoking both cigarettes.

Vadim didn't like any of this: the weapons, the missing equipment, the sparse brief, the trail of dead KGB they had left in Afghanistan. This stank of a setup.

"I'm sorry Eugene, but I don't believe you," Vadim said. "We're going to have to torture you until you tell us what the real plan is."

Mongol and Farm Boy shifted uncomfortably, but held their peace. New Boy didn't look terribly happy either. Skull and the Fräulein remained impassive, but Princess and Gulag smiled. Gulag wandered into the kitchen and started going through the drawers, pulling out knives and other utensils.

Eugene didn't try to run, and he certainly didn't go for a weapon. He was pale, shaking, tears rolling down his cheek, a growing wet patch on the front of his oversized trousers, piss running down his leg.

"Please..." he managed.

"You're fucking kidding me," Gulag muttered.

"Tell me the truth, Eugene," Vadim said quietly.

"I am!" he howled. "They don't tell me anything! I'm not good at this! I'm scared all the time! I don't know who's watching me! I live in fear constantly!" He sank to his knees in the puddle of his own piss. Princess looked disgusted, and Gulag shook his head. "I just want this to be over!" he sobbed. If it was an act, it was a damn good one; but it was the piss that convinced Vadim. He couldn't conceive of any man willingly pissing himself.

"Do you have equipment for detecting electronic surveillance?" Vadim asked, and Eugene nodded. Vadim pointed at Farm Boy. "You're going to show this man where it is and then you're going to show him where you believe all the listening devices are hidden." Eugene nodded again, utterly miserable.

THEY HAD EUGENE point out the listening devices and put the television on, before tying and gagging him and putting him in the bath. Then Farm Boy conducted another sweep with the bug detecting tools and found more listening devices.

"We have a decision to make," Vadim told them. They were all crouched, close together, speaking in a low voice in case Farm Boy had missed any of the bugs. "Do we do their bidding or not?"

The Fräulein frowned. Vadim suspected that she did not approve of the breakdown in military protocol.

"What are our alternatives?" New Boy asked carefully.

"We defect," Vadim said. They were all staring at him now, even Skull and Gulag.

"Even *I'm* not a *traitor*," Gulag spat.

"I believe we have been betrayed," Vadim said. "This feels like we're being set up, somehow."

"With all due respect," the Fräulein said, "are you sure you don't just have misgivings about the end result of the mission?"

Farm Boy was frowning. "What do you mean?" he asked.

"We have to be picking up an NBC weapon," Skull pointed out. Mongol drew back a little, and Gulag laughed humourlessly.

"He's right," Vadim said. "I suspect our job will be to pick such a weapon up, perhaps a suitcase bomb of some kind, and deliver it to a target. I think we're so heavily armed because we'll have to fight our way to the objective."

"Then why no body armour? No med kit?" Mongol asked.

It was a good question, and Vadim didn't have a good answer.

"Perhaps we'll be moving too fast for a med kit?" Farm Boy suggested, though he didn't sound like he really believed it.

"Too fast for body armour?" New Boy asked.

"It's the Red Army," Gulag said. "It's probably a logistics mistake." Except Vadim was pretty sure that the KGB had packed their gear. These weren't the kind of mistakes they made.

"So?" Vadim asked.

"What do you want to do, boss?" the Fräulein asked.

"I will act on whatever you decide."

"I have family back home," Mongol said. "I can't defect if there's even the slightest chance I can get home." Vadim could tell Mongol didn't like his chances of getting back.

"I owe the USSR nothing, I say we defect," Skull said. Suddenly everyone was staring at the sniper.

"I'm no traitor," New Boy managed. Princess glared at him.

"I say we do the job," she said. Then it went quiet.

"Fräulein?" Vadim asked.

"I am with you, whatever is chosen."

"This is your decision," Vadim told her.

"And I have made it," she told him evenly. Vadim turned to look at Farm Boy. The big Georgian was deep in thought. Gulag was watching his friend.

"I think..." Farm Boy finally said, "that it is not a good thing to turn your back on your loyalties" – he glanced over at Skull – "however they are imposed." Skull nodded. "I think we should follow our orders." All of them turned to look at Gulag, who in turn was staring at Vadim.

"You know we're all dead anyway, right? Smoking, radioactive corpses?"

he asked. Vadim nodded. Gulag glanced over at Farm Boy. "Fuck it, I'm in."

"You can go your own way," Vadim told Skull. The sniper just narrowed his eyes, offended at the suggestion he would leave the squad in the lurch.

CHAPTER FIVE

1500 Eastern Standard Time (EST), 16th November 1987
Grand Central Station, New York City

VADIM PUSHED HIS way through the door and into the cavernous edifice of Grand Central Station, New Boy beside him. Gulag and Farm Boy were a little way behind, far enough that the four didn't look as though they were together. At the other side of the concourse, the Fräulein and Princess, Mongol and Skull would be doing the same thing.

Looking around surreptitiously, he made his way down the grimy marble stairs into the main concourse, hefting his luggage, which carried much of his weaponry. There was no doubt it was a grand building, but it had seen better days; it reminded him a little of Leningrad in that respect. The domed ceiling high overhead was encrusted with soot. The dirty marble floor was covered in rubbish, which haggard-looking janitors pushed around with a brush. Ticket booths ran down one wall. A display board above them showed arrivals from places that Vadim had only heard of during intelligence briefings. A dirty, once-grand four-faced clock sat atop an information booth. Tawdry adverts covered the walls, offering a technicolor capitalist utopia for just the right amount of money. All of which seemed at odds with the hundreds of Americans crowding into the huge edifice, their heads down, moving with purpose as though performing some complex dance.

A raised walkway ran around the main concourse: Vadim caught a glimpse of the Fräulein pulling her wheeled suitcase around the long walkway, but he couldn't see the others. The idea was that the snipers and machine-gunners would act as fire support from an elevated position if things went wrong, while Vadim's team retrieved the package.

Vadim reached the bottom of the stairs, put his own wheeled suitcase down onto the grimy marble floor and looked around. New Boy joined him.

"Anything wrong?" New Boy asked quietly. Vadim was aware of Gulag and Farm Boy surreptitiously moving into covering positions on the stairs behind him. There wasn't anything wrong – not that Vadim could see – but something didn't seem right. He looked around at the commuters scurrying back and forth, on their way to and from work, going home, on their way to visit friends and relatives, families with children. It was hard to think of them as enemies, but he couldn't see the American authorities wanting to start a gunfight in the midst of them. Vadim shook his head and headed down the chandelier-lit slope between the stairs into the lower concourse.

WHERE THE MAIN concourse had been cavernous, the lower concourse seemed cave-like, perhaps thanks to the lack of natural light. Or perhaps he just felt trapped because this was a poor place for a fight. The sloping ceiling felt much lower than it actually was, and people buffeted him as they ran for the platforms on either side of the concourse; the air smelled of fried food, overflowing garbage bins and too many people, and it felt like every single transit cop was watching them as they passed.

The luggage storage area was in an alcove set back from the lower concourse. There were ten long rows of lockers. Vadim checked the key that Eugene had given him. They had discussed killing the spy, but decided to let him live in case he proved useful later on.

The locker they were looking for was in the fifth row. Gulag and Farm Boy took up position further back in the lower concourse, though still within view of the alcove. With a final look around them, Vadim and New Boy plunged into the luggage area.

They found the locker. Vadim took the key out, New Boy stood off a little. Vadim turned the key and opened the locker, revealing a brass cylinder filling the space inside. Vadim's heart sank. It was a biological or chemical weapon.

He had been hoping for something conventional; even a tactical nuclear suitcase bomb would have felt cleaner somehow. Then he heard a click. He looked on in horror as the top and bottom of the cylinder unscrewed itself. There was a distinct hissing noise. It made no sense to Vadim. Why send them all this way, just to kill them as part of a chemical weapons attack? He did something he hadn't even done as a child amongst the ruins of Stalingrad: he froze.

Then he heard movement coming from amongst the rows of lockers. The clink of weapons against webbing, the pad of booted feet trying to move stealthily. Instinct took over. The Stechkin APB was in one hand, a spare magazine in the other. Movement in his periphery. He turned to the left, made out the armoured, helmeted figure of a SWAT team member coming around the corner, triggered a three-round burst. The gun bucked in his hand, and the figure disappeared behind the lockers again. Vadim had no idea if he had hit him or not. New Boy was kneeling and opening the cases, rooting through their weapons. Vadim checked right and saw movement at the other end of the row. He fired a burst that way, then another. Then back to the left, firing again, alternating suppressing fire at each end of the row of lockers. It didn't matter who you were, you didn't walk into automatic weapons fire. He had no idea why they hadn't used a grenade yet, or used snipers on the way in. Perhaps it was some American sense of fair play. The twenty-round magazine in his pistol ran dry, and he ejected it, slid the fresh mag home and continued firing. The Stechkin was far from accurate on full automatic, but in an enclosed space like this it was good for making people keep their heads down.

"Grenade!" New Boy shouted in Russian and threw the grenade to Vadim's left into the next row of lockers. Another grenade was thrown to the right, also behind the lockers. Vadim was kneeling, head down, as he holstered his pistol and dropped the empty magazine down the front of his shirt. New Boy slid the captain's AK-74 along the floor, and Vadim grabbed the weapon; the safety was off. The first grenade exploded. Lockers toppled and bodies were flung into the air. There was another explosion, bright light and thunder. Presumably one of the SWAT members had been about to throw a stun grenade. New Boy's second grenade exploded. Over-pressure buffeted them, shrapnel tore at their clothes and Vadim only narrowly missed being decapitated by a spinning locker door. Blinking away spots of light, Vadim tried to shout at New Boy to clear right while he cleared left, but nothing came out. That was when he realised he'd gone deaf. He glanced behind him to see the younger man already stalking through the wreckage, rifle tucked into his shoulder. Vadim shouldered his AK-74 and did the same in the opposite direction.

There were two broken bodies at the end of the row, blackened from the explosion, red from shrapnel. One more was staggering around, probably as much from the effects of the stun grenade as anything else. It didn't look as though he could see. A fourth was curled up on the floor, hands over his ears, mouth open in a silent scream. The one on his feet was aware of Vadim somehow, he was grabbing for his sidearm. The captain squeezed the trigger, twice. The rifle kicked back into his shoulder and he leaned into it. The goggles the agent was wearing under his helmet filled with red and he collapsed to the ground. Vadim put two rounds into each of them. They couldn't leave anyone behind them.

Quickly Vadim checked the rest of the locker area. The SWAT team's members had the letters *FBI* painted on their body armour: American state security. They were not just police officers; they had been waiting for Vadim and his people.

The captain made his way back to where they had left their luggage. New Boy was already there. There were another four dead FBI agents amongst the wreckage at the other end of the row. New Boy had done his job. He was shaking his head as though trying to clear it; Vadim couldn't hear anything either, except a high-pitched whine. He signalled New Boy to cover him whilst he shrugged off his coat and grabbed his webbing from the suitcase, pulling it on and securing it tightly in place. He strapped on the back sheath holding his KS-23 shotgun, then straightened up and readied his rifle as New Boy put his webbing on. He was starting to hear muted sounds now: a voice shouting through a loudhailer in English and screaming, a lot of screaming and distant gunfire. The chatter of a light machine gun, Mongol's or the Fräulein's RPKS-74. Skull's .303 firing sounded like a cannon, and Vadim knew that up in the main concourse someone had just died.

Vadim and New Boy moved through what was left of the lockers into the mostly intact row closest to the lower concourse. They would provide only flimsy cover. Vadim ignored the demands to surrender from an authoritative voice, full of tension, shouting at them through a loudhailer. He signalled to New Boy to go left, and turned to check right.

At the end of the row he risked a glance into the main concourse. He had a moment to register the SWAT team officers in the open lower concourse before they opened up on him. He ducked back into the row, although all that really stood between him and the Americans' bullets were two flimsy pieces of sheet metal. If he was lucky the lockers had luggage in them. Fortunately the majority of the SWAT team were armed with submachine guns and shotguns, both fairly low-velocity weapons. Though he was still seeing holes appear in the lockers close to where his face had been.

As soon as the SWAT team had started firing, New Boy had moved around the opposite corner and returned fire. Their attackers switched target and New Boy ducked behind the lockers. Vadim swung round the corner. Three-round burst, the muzzle flash from the barrel, leaning into the hard kick of the recoil, shell casings flying into the air. Shift, aim, repeat. The SWAT team were probably highly trained, knew they had to cover both corners, but training is one thing, the adrenalin kicking in under live fire is another. They would not be used to facing trained special forces soldiers, armed with military weapons, with the sort of actual combat experience New Boy had gained with the VDV in Afghanistan. And Vadim had been fighting in wars since he was nine years old. He ducked back behind the lockers. He'd seen SWAT members go down under centre mass shots, but they were wearing body armour and he had no idea if they were dead or not.

Vadim heard the familiar pop of a grenade launcher. There was just a moment of panic, but the explosion was outside, in the lower concourse. The row of lockers buckled, threatening to topple over, as shrapnel from the 40mm fragmentation grenade tore through the flimsy metal. He didn't go deaf this time, though his ears were ringing. He heard the flat, hard staccato of AK-74s firing, burst after burst. Vadim and New Boy moved around the corners of the lockers. Broken bodies were scattered around on the ground. There were a few SWAT guys staggering around; fewer still had their weapons. Vadim and New Boy concentrated on those.

Gulag was stalking down the concourse past cowering commuters, firing at the remaining SWAT team members. Farm Boy was backing along behind him, firing in the other direction, exchanging shots with uniformed police officers. Between Gulag, New Boy and Vadim, the remaining members of the grenade-shocked FBI SWAT team were cut down in a vicious crossfire.

"Reloading!" Gulag shouted, pulling his magazine out and turning it over to insert the second magazine taped to it. A burly civilian launched himself off the ground and leapt on him. Gulag staggered, dropped the magazines, and almost went down. He awkwardly dragged his knife out of its scabbard with his left hand and stabbed the man repeatedly in the neck. The man staggered away from Gulag, clutching the wound. Gulag kicked him back, knocking him into the wall close to the entrance of one of the platforms, picked the magazine up, slid it home and shot his attacker twice in the face. Then it was quiet except for the cries of the injured and the whimpering of the terrified. Whoever had been shooting at Farm Boy had stopped. They took turns covering each other as they reloaded their weapons. Gulag reloaded the GP-25 Kostyor grenade launcher fixed to the barrel of his AK-74.

Vadim was looking around at the cowering commuters. The wrong place at the wrong time. Bullets, and shrapnel from the grenades, had hit a number of the civilians. Blood and shell casings covered the floor. Gunfire echoed down from the main concourse above them. He heard the LMGs, the sniper rifles, returning fire from SMGs, handguns and shotguns. He understood the civilians' response. There was nothing cowardly about it; simple self-preservation in the face of a threat they could do nothing about. Then he wondered about the chemical/biological agent they had triggered in the locker. He didn't feel any different, which suggested that it was biological rather than chemical. He had never liked fighting amongst civilians, but knew that sometimes it had to be done. Even so, the guilt of what he had done here gnawed at him. He glanced over at the corpse of the man that had attacked Gulag. Perhaps these Americans weren't the weak, decadent capitalists the Soviet Union wanted people to believe they were.

"Keep your heads down, stay out of our way and do not attempt to resist and we will not kill you!" Vadim shouted in English, making for the ramp that led to the main concourse. The other three followed in a diamond-shaped formation: Gulag and New Boy flanking him a little way back, Farm Boy directly behind him keeping an eye on their rear. People kept their heads down or scuttled into the platforms out of their way. They passed the uniformed transit police officer Farm Boy had killed.

VADIM AND GULAG were on one side of the sloping tunnel, New and Farm Boy on the other. Vadim watched as the blaze of tracers bounced off the marble floor. Either Mongol or the Fräulein was unwittingly firing at them. Their path passed under the double stairs leading to the raised walkway around the main concourse; it also led to one of the entrances. Vadim guessed the SWAT team had come in that way and got pinned down by the Fräulein's fireteam. Blood was dripping down into the mouth of the tunnel. Vadim communicated the plan to the others with hand signals. They nodded. They had to hope that when they moved, the Fräulein's fireteam didn't cut them down.

Vadim let his AK-74 drop on its sling and pulled a hand grenade from a pouch on his webbing. He removed the pin, let the spoon flip out and held the live grenade in his hand, cooking it, letting the fuse burn down. He stepped out of the tunnel mouth, the other three already moving behind him, and threw the grenade up over the railings onto the walkway. He heard cries of alarm, and followed Gulag out of cover. The grenade exploded almost immediately. Two bodies flew over the railings and landed on the edge of the ramp. Vadim and Gulag climbed the stairs, the criminal already firing. The SWAT team, already stunned and hurt, were dropping in front of them. Vadim heard the boom of Skull's .303 and the quieter crack of Princess's Dragunov sniper rifle.

Gulag reached the top of the stairs and moved sideways, still firing. Vadim reached the top of the stairs and did the same. Farm and New Boy remained on the stairs, catching the SWAT team in another crossfire. Sensing movement behind him, Vadim started to turn, seeing an agent levelling an SMG at his back. The top of the American's head came off as either Princess or Skull killed him.

A tracer round flew out of the barrel of Vadim's AK-74, telling him he only had three rounds left. One more burst and another SWAT team member was falling to the ground, but his comrade was still on his feet, frantically grabbing for his sidearm. Vadim let his AK-74 fall on its sling and grabbed the cut-down grip of the shotgun on his back, tearing it out of its sheath. He fired the 23mm buckshot round at nearly point blank range into the American's face. The face disappeared. It felt like the recoil had nearly torn his arm off, but the SWAT team were all on the ground. These ones had different uniforms. They were NYPD, the letters *ESU* on their body armour. Vadim had no idea what it stood for.

Something thumped into the meat of his upper right arm, spinning him around. It burned, feeling like something was burrowing through his flesh. Then he heard the gunshot and the smashing glass. He was facing the entrance now. It looked like everyone in New York had guns and was trying to get into Grand Central: uniformed police, plain-clothes officers, SWAT, all firing into the station. Vadim was backpedalling, working the slide on the pump-action and firing. The shotgun kicked back hard, and a police officer was taken off his feet.

He saw Farm Boy staggering back as a volley of bullets struck him, sending him tumbling down the stairs. Gulag was screaming. The police's relief force was in the station, on the walkway now. Tracer rounds started flying over the main concourse as the other fireteam rained fire on the police. Vadim fired the shotgun twice more, backing away, then switched the empty weapon into his left hand, drew the Stechkin and started burst-firing that. Gulag hadn't moved; he was screaming, firing his AK-74 in long, undisciplined bursts. A shotgun blast caught him in the chest, and he staggered back, but didn't go down. He tried to raise the AK-74 again, but several more rounds followed the first: undisciplined, inaccurate fire from frightened combatants, but it was enough. He hit the floor.

Vadim made it to the walled stairwell at the corner of the main concourse and took cover. He slid the shotgun back into its sheath, reloaded and holstered the Stechkin, and then reloaded the AK-74. He risked a glance through the doorway he'd just come through. The advancing police were being led by SWAT now. Bullets ricocheted off the stone, fragments cutting his face as the police closed in on his position. He removed the pin from another grenade, placed it at his feet and sprinted for the stairs, heading down. Above him, he heard the grenade exploding, followed by screams and cries of pain as he reached the doorway to the main concourse.

He edged out of the door, staying close to the wall. The police were on the walkway directly above him. On the other side of the main concourse, the other fireteam were conducting a fire-and–manoeuvre withdrawal, taking turns to lay down covering fire and move down the stairs. Vadim couldn't see Mongol. Terrified, cowering civilians lay on the floor of the concourse in the spreading pools of blood, interspersed with the dead.

Vadim edged along the wall, exposed. If he opened fire on the reaction force shooting at the other fireteam, it would warn the police directly above his head. He heard the shot, distinct from the SMGs, shotguns and pistols: a rifle, a marksman's weapon. He saw Skull's head snap back, and the sniper crumple on the stairs. Princess and the Fräulein glanced back, saw Skull was dead, then turned away and concentrated on the task at hand.

Vadim raised his AK-74 to his shoulder and fired on the police, across the main concourse, above the heads of civilians now too terrified to scream. One burst and then another, moving quickly, making for the ramp to the lower concourse. He swung around and looked up at the walkway just above him, seeing the police officers that had survived his grenade leaning over to locate him. He squeezed the trigger, shattering the stone balustrade, and the officers disappeared from view.

Vadim reached the ramp, where he was joined by New Boy. Princess and the Fräulein had already disappeared into the lower concourse on the other side of the station. New Boy covered him as he changed magazines. He was backing down the ramp when he noticed a SWAT shooter, who'd been lying in a puddle of blood in the middle of the main concourse, was standing up now. He must have been playing dead after being ambushed by the Fräulein's fireteam. Now he was standing up in the middle of a gunfight, just staring at Vadim. Vadim finished reloading his AK-74 and raised it to his shoulder, but didn't shoot. The man didn't have a weapon in his hand. He just stared until Vadim had backed out of sight. It was strange, but Vadim had been in enough battles to know that combat could do odd things to people's minds.

"Down! Down!" New Boy ordered in English. The civilians on the ground were trying to crawl out of the way of the two Spetsnaz commandos as they sprinted through the lower concourse. Vadim was looking for Princess and the Fräulein. If they could meet up with them, then they could escape along the tracks. He pushed away thoughts of how pointless escape was – presumably they'd be affected by whatever biological agent had been in the locker. All escape could provide was the opportunity to choose how to die. Somehow that seemed important.

Vadim glanced behind him and almost tripped over a commuter lying face-down on the floor, hands over his head. He couldn't see any police behind him. This would be a nightmare for them, hunting well-armed, well-trained, experienced soldiers in the tangled warren of tunnels beneath the main concourse. It reminded Vadim of hunting mujahideen in the *qanāt* irrigation tunnels, except now they were the guerrilla fighters.

Not guerrilla fighters: terrorists, he told himself. It wasn't evident yet what they had done, what he had done, but enemies or not, he was sure he had committed a monstrous war crime against these people.

Ahead of him he could see Princess and the Fräulein also sprinting through the lower concourse towards them. The surviving members of the other fireteam were almost level with the devastated baggage area when the fallen FBI SWAT team started standing back up. Vadim skidded to a halt and stared. It didn't make any sense. A couple of them might have survived, badly wounded, but not *all* of them; and all of them were standing up. New Boy stopped so quickly he slipped over, sliding into some of the cowering civilians. Vadim had thought he had seen every horror the human race could inflict on itself, but this was something else: the supernature that Communism denied, or else science gone mad. He couldn't quite process what he was seeing. Then the dead agents fell on the civilians. They didn't move like people, but like animals, pouncing on the screaming commuters. Vadim watched as teeth were sunk into flesh, blood gouting from fresh wounds. He watched as they started to feed. Starving people had been forced to eat the dead during the siege of Stalingrad, but that had been nothing like the feeding frenzy that was unfolding before their eyes.

We did this.

"Move! Run! That way! Now!" Vadim screamed, the muscles on his neck standing out. He pulled civilians to their feet, helping them back the way they came with the toe of his boot.

New Boy had moved against the wall by the entrance to one of the tunnels, and was trying to get a clear shot: Russian, American, it didn't matter. This was humans against something else.

"Run, you stupid bastards, run!" The panicking civilians knocked into Vadim as he tried to get a shot. He watched as one of the SWAT members pounced high into the air, bringing a screaming woman down. It reminded Vadim of lions hunting. *Not lions, baboon packs.* Another raised its head from its kill, tendrils of flesh dangling from a red mouth. A clear shot. The butt of the rifle hammering into his shoulder was almost comforting, the flickering muzzle flash turning the cave-like lower concourse into a picture of hell. The bloody-mouthed SWAT agent was knocked away from its prey by the three-round burst, but it was up again almost immediately. Vadim's eyes widened. For the first time in over forty years of conflict, he didn't know what to do. The thing charged him, dripping hands outstretched, reaching for him. Vadim fired again, convincing himself he had missed the first time, desperately searching for a rational explanation. Another hit. Three rounds, centre mass. The creature staggered slightly but continued charging.

Body armour, Vadim told himself. He was aware of New Boy firing as well, burning through ammunition. The charging, bloody creature was almost on him. Vadim flicked the AK-74's selector to single-shot, raised the weapon slightly, and fired. The once human creature's face caved in and it hit the ground, sliding towards him.

"Head shots!" Vadim shouted to New Boy. It was easier said than done. The SWAT team had been wearing Kevlar helmets. He could hear firing from the other side of the feeding pack: the Fräulein and Princess. Vadim realised that he had been so appalled by what he had seen he hadn't even considered that the other two remaining members of the squad would be in their field of fire.

"We have to get out of here!" New Boy shouted, shooting another charging corpse in the helmet, its jaw already hanging off. It barely seemed to register the impact. New Boy adjusted his aim and squeezed the trigger again, blowing the thing's brains out the back of its skull. He was right; they were about to be overrun. The Fräulein and Princess could look after themselves, and they had set up secondary and tertiary rendezvous points if things didn't go to plan.

"Platform!" Vadim shouted, and both of them ran.

THERE WAS A train at the platform. The closest thing Vadim had to a plan was to get in front of the train and make their way out of the station on the rails. He'd had better plans in his life.

He stopped and turned. Five of the things had chased New Boy and him onto the platform. Two of them leapt onto the train and more screams joined the cacophony. Vadim raised his AK-74 to his shoulder. His breath burned in his lungs. He was too old for this, and he knew it. He fired, missed. Tried to steady his aim and only then realised that, for the first time in decades, his hands were shaking. He tried to control his breathing, remember everything he knew about shooting. One of the creatures dropped, taken down by New Boy. The younger man was a better shot than he was. New Boy fired again, and another dropped.

Come on, old man. He squeezed the trigger. The third creature went down. There was shouting from behind him, and his busy mind tried to translate the panicked English as he turned. There was a young black man, little more than a boy, in a Transit Police officer's uniform. He held a revolver in two shaking hands, terrified civilians behind him. Everything seemed to slow down. He watched the hammer come down. The muzzle flash grew in slow motion from the barrel of the gun. The hammer blow to the chest. He was lying down, staring at the grimy ceiling.

I deserve this, worse than this. He had betrayed these people, these Americans, these humans. He was looking up at New Boy through a tunnel when one of the things jumped through the train's window, taking the younger soldier to the ground.

THEN EVERYTHING WENT red for a while.

CHAPTER SIX

1607 Eastern Standard Time (EST), 16th November 1987
Grand Central Station, New York City

"Vadim?" a Ukrainian-accented voice asked from behind him. Vadim didn't turn around immediately. He was still staring at the Fräulein.

She was red from head to toe. She'd taken multiple gunshot wounds, and in places was missing chunks of flesh. He could see human teeth marks in the wounds on her face, scraps of meat dangling from them. She was a mess. Her mouth opened and human flesh dribbled from it, an obscene red he'd seen in the aftermath of so many battles.

"Turn around slowly, hands raised. We have you covered."

The Fräulein's head twitched at the sound of the voice. He smelled it too, sensed it at some primal level: food, prey, or at least a respite for the hunger that suffused him. But he wasn't an animal, at least not at this moment, not as he had been. He turned around slowly, but he didn't raise his hands, nor did he drop his Stechkin.

New Boy and Princess stood in front of the blood-stained entrance to the terminal. Princess's sniper rifle was levelled at his face. The weapon's suppressor was screwed onto the barrel. She could not miss at this range. It would be easy, quick, an end to this non-life, an end to the hunger that gnawed at him like a beast imprisoned in his body. They were both pale and bloodstained. They looked strained and, unusually for Spetsnaz soldiers, visibly frightened. Both of them were also alive. Their blood sang to him. He could already taste their meat between his teeth. Red drool ran down his chin. He saw Princess's finger tighten around the trigger. She was wound tight.

The city was dark, stained red by the emergency lighting from the surrounding buildings. There was no starlight, no moonlight, all of it was obscured by the ash and dust thrown into the sky by the nuclear explosions.

It took him a moment to realise that the noise behind him was the sound of teeth clacking together, a dry, breathless larynx trying to form words in defiance of biology.

"Princess..." the Fräulein finally managed from behind him. A tear ran down Princess's cheek, but she didn't take her eye away from her scope, the Dragunov never wavered. New Boy swallowed hard, his own rifle levelled at the Fräulein.

"What *are* you?" New Boy managed. There was disgust in his voice. Vadim was sure the younger man knew the answer to his own question. They all did, if they were honest, but there was a gulf between knowing and accepting.

"I do not breathe. My heart does not beat," Vadim managed. It had taken him several attempts to make a noise that resembled speech. It felt unnatural, as though he no longer had the tools for the job. He wasn't sure whether he was imagining it or not, but New Boy and Princess's pulses were deafening, a beating drum between his ears. He found himself staring at Princess's pretty neck. Imagining tearing into it with his teeth. "I want... *need* to eat." He was trying to warn them. They tensed. He was surprised that neither of them fired.

"Please..." the Fräulein managed, staggering to his side. Vadim had no idea what she was asking for. Understanding? Mercy? A release? Food?

"Why can you talk?" New Boy demanded. "Why aren't you trying to feed?" Somehow the meat talking about feeding was too much. The hunger was the only real sensation he felt, the only thing that wasn't a muted, numbed echo of what his senses once were. The hunger was hot and red and washed over him... and he was gone.

HE HAD ONLY moved a few feet. New Boy was lying on the ground; he looked as though he'd stumbled backwards and tripped. His weapon was now pointed at Vadim, his face a mask of terror. Princess was the colour of snow under the blood spatter. He had no idea why he wasn't dead, why she hadn't pulled the trigger. Then he realised that someone was gripping his shoulder, tight. He looked over at the Fräulein. She was just shaking her head. He couldn't quite believe what he'd almost done. It started to rain. The rain was gritty and black. It had been the Fräulein's touch that had stopped him.

"Don't fucking do that!" New Boy barked as, still covering Vadim, he scrambled to his feet.

"I'm sorry," Vadim told him. He meant it, but it sounded so hollow, so utterly pointless given the situation. "You can't trust us."

They heard the scraping first. The sound of metal dragged across stone. Princess moved to the side, keeping her sniper rifle levelled at him but manoeuvring for a better shot at the Fräulein. New Boy spun around, covering the entrance, broken glass crunching underfoot. Vadim could see the large figure moving towards them, but he didn't get any sense of life. He glanced around, wondering where all the other bodies had run off to.

It was Mongol, dragging his RPKS-74 by the stock, the barrel scraping across the floor in a way that should have appalled Vadim, but such considerations were for the living. He looked good, as corpses go. He'd caught a shotgun blast to the chest, something that body armour might have saved him from. A bullet had torn open his cheek and smashed his teeth, revealing his jaw. The way he moved – stumbling, dragging his weapon behind him – it was easy to assume he was one of the mindless ones, but why wasn't he hunting?

"That's enough, Mongol," New Boy told him. Mongol kept on staggering towards him. "I mean it. I'll put a bullet in your head."

"Mongol!" the Fräulein snapped. Her voice still sounded wrong, hoarse and dry, but she was starting to sound more like herself. Mongol shuffled round to stare at the Fräulein. Dark eyes, as though from a haemorrhage. There was no spark there, no intelligence, no sign of recognition. Mongol opened his mouth, teeth bared obscenely through the torn skin. The noise he made sounded like a wounded animal. Vadim was pretty sure that it was only a matter of time before New Boy snapped and shot someone, then Princess would kill the rest.

"Your weapon!" the East German continued. Mongol looked down at the light machine gun for what seemed like a long time. Vadim waited to get a bullet in the face. Then Mongol lifted the weapon and put the sling over his head, letting it hang down, held at the ready but pointed well away from the anxious living. Vadim used the moment to holster his pistol. Mongol turned to stare at him.

"Wh…" he tried, the skin around his mouth flopping around. "Wh… What… have… we done?" he finally managed. There was something different about his eyes, now. Vadim shook his head slowly. He wasn't sure he had a good answer for the big medic.

"Did you know?" It was Princess who asked the question. Vadim shrugged.

"We all knew it was going to be bad, but this…" he managed. He wasn't sure if he'd even *thought* of such things before. It was far beyond even his experience.

"This isn't war," Mongol said. "This is black magic."

He was right. Vadim had been a good Communist; he hadn't been inside a church since before his parents were killed in the war. Their current situation belonged in the sphere of supernature. He had no frame of reference for any of this. He doubted anyone did.

"What happened?" he asked, nodding at the bloodied wreckage out the front of the train station. It was more for something to say than anything else. "I thought I saw one of them take you down."

"After you got shot," New Boy said, driving home to Vadim that he was dead, that he'd been killed in the tunnels below the station. "I managed to hold it off, stop it from biting me until I could stab it through the head. I heard the gunfire from Princess and Fräulein, and made my way across the tracks, through the trains, until I found them."

"There were too many of them down there," the Fräulein continued in her dry, rasping voice. "They were running through the carriages making more of themselves. We laid down a lot of fire, grenades, and managed to break contact, make it back up to the main concourse. But they were right behind us. Mongol…" She looked at the medic. "And Skull…"

"I saw Skull," Vadim said quietly. He wondered where the other sniper was. Was he wandering around here, or off hunting with the others?

Why are we different? he asked himself. It was only then he thought of Farm Boy and Gulag. They had both fallen, just the other side of those doors. It would be easy to look for their bodies, but Princess and New Boy both seemed a little too highly strung for him to show any initiative at the moment.

"We made it back up here and then ran into the police," New Boy told him, nodding towards the bullet-ridden wreckage of the police cars out front.

"The SWAT van? The helicopter?" Vadim asked.

"Fräulein," Princess said simply, though Vadim could hear the emotion in her voice. New Boy was looking at the big East German with something approaching awe in his eyes, and more than a little fear.

"The zombies were coming up behind us. We needed to break through. She – Fräulein hit the van with one of the RPGs," New Boy continued. "Then she laid down fire on the chopper. She... she got hit..."

"Over and over," Princess said evenly. "Even then, she kept firing. Told us to run. Then they fell on her from behind and fed." Somehow it was more uncomfortable having the Fräulein standing next to him listening to a description of her own death.

"How'd you get away?" he asked. It sounded somehow inane.

"We ran," Princess told him.

"Back down again. All the zombies were coming up anyway. We locked ourselves into a baggage car." New Boy's head dropped as though ashamed, but Vadim couldn't really see what else they could have done, other than die themselves. It sounded as though they were very lucky to be alive, although perhaps, given the situation, 'lucky' wasn't the right word.

"And then we were very, very quiet," Princess whispered. Vadim looked down at the ground, the big black drops of rain leaving greasy stains even over the blood. He wondered how much radiation they were taking from the fallout. Would it make a difference to the dead? Would it kill Princess and New Boy?

"Where did they all go?" the Fräulein asked.

"It was like an explosion," Princess told her. "It had an epicentre that spread out." *Or a virus*, Vadim thought. "They hunt the living, and then those they kill rise again. When they thought everyone here was dead, they moved on." She nodded out into the city. He imagined them streaming out of the station, running down pedestrians, dragging people from their cars, leaping through the windows of shops and restaurants. Running up through the high towers of these steel and glass canyons, killing and raising more and more of themselves, like a cancer consuming cells. In the moment of quiet, Vadim faintly wondered when the music had stopped. In the distance, he thought he heard gunfire.

All of them heard the sound of a horse's hooves echoing on the asphalt. The terrified animal galloped down 42nd Street in front of them. Princess lowered her weapon.

"What do we do now?" she asked. Vadim did not have an answer.

* * *

HAVING LOST HIS rifle, Vadim carried his now-reloaded shotgun as they re-entered the station, trying to move as quietly as they could through the carpet of empty shell casings. There was blood everywhere. The Fräulein found her RPKS-74, close to where she had fallen, and the three dead went first, New Boy and Princess following at a safe distance.

They were going through the motions. Vadim had no idea what to do now. His head was a whirl of thoughts and blunted emotions. He didn't think he was in charge anymore; that would be insane. Princess and New Boy couldn't trust any of them. He had to concentrate on other things just so he wouldn't leap at their throats.

Vadim checked the area where Gulag and Farm Boy had fallen. Their bodies were gone, although tellingly, neither of their weapons remained. Just for a moment, he wondered if the KGB had slipped them some kind of partial vaccine, perhaps in their food on the submarine. Something that allowed them to hold onto to just enough of their selves to function. Were they supposed to be the second stage of this horrifying new weapon, he wondered?

"Boss," said Mongol, and Vadim looked up. They'd found Skull, dead. A bloodstain on his sweater where his heart should be. A good shot. Killed by a fellow sniper. He was seated on a neatly stacked pile of bodies, bullet holes in their heads, as though enthroned. He was holding his .303 up in one hand, the butt on his leg, barrel pointing at the domed roof. They approached him carefully, fanning out, and he just watched, smiling. In the emergency lighting, Skull's eyes glittered. He was clearly sentient. Despite the smile, Vadim had known the sniper long enough to know he was angry, very angry.

"What did they do?" Skull asked. *They,* Vadim thought. It seemed Skull had decided to direct his anger.

"You killed all these things?" Mongol asked, nodding at the sniper's corpse throne. Skull turned to look at the medic, but said nothing.

"Skull?" the Fräulein asked. He ignored her and looked up at Princess. Vadim followed his gaze. She nodded at the other sniper but looked ready to kill him if she had to. Skull turned back to Vadim.

"Permission to fall in, captain?" he asked. He'd used Vadim's rank, and it wasn't a question you heard often in the Spetsnaz. Vadim just nodded, half-wondering why anybody was listening to him. Even through the whirl of his own thoughts he was aware that something seemed very wrong with Skull, beyond what was obviously very wrong with all of them.

* * *

THEY DID A sweep of the station – no sign of Gulag or Farm Boy – and set out for the secondary rendezvous point, in the underground car park beneath Eugene's building. Walking corpse or not, Vadim still found the deserted streets and blackened sky eerie.

Princess and New Boy were still, understandably, keeping their distance, as much covering their dead comrades as they were looking for the more mindless zombies.

They found Farm Boy first, in a pool of light created by the flickering emergency illumination in the underground car park. His arms were bound to his side, legs as well. He was thrashing against his bonds, drooling. His eyes were bloodshot, wide, no longer the eyes of a human being. He went wild when he sensed Princess and New Boy.

Vadim knew he wasn't thinking straight, but this was clearly bait. He started to turn to look around, Skull and the Fräulein doing the same. Gulag stepped out from behind a pillar, his rifle aimed at Vadim. Skull had his AKS-74 shouldered, levelled at Gulag, and Princess followed suit. The rest of them were checking the surrounding area.

"See, I knew you were trying to kill me." He was in shadow, the flickering light giving the occasional glimpse of his ruined form. Like the Fräulein, he'd taken a lot of damage, and at some point been chewed on.

"What are you doing, Gulag?" the Fräulein demanded.

"You're still playing soldier, comrade Fräulein?" Gulag said. Vadim found himself transfixed by the barrel of Gulag's rifle. It looked like a way out.

"Lower your weapon," the Fräulein told him.

"Or what?" the Muscovite demanded. "Administrative punishment, court-martial, firing squad, send me back to the gulag? All seems redundant now. We've blown up the world, but the funny part is: we can't die."

"You can still die," Princess promised him.

Gulag raised his ruined nose slightly and sniffed the air. "I smell life. My food is talking to me."

Princess tensed.

"What do you want?" Vadim asked, looking back down at Farm Boy, or what had once been him. He was trying to thrash his way across the floor towards New Boy, making the scout step backwards. New Boy lowered his rifle to cover the now mindless corpse of his squadmate.

"Don't you point your fucking gun at him!" Gulag screamed. Even Vadim flinched. New Boy looked unsure for a moment, but he didn't shift his aim. "I mean it. I'll do you next!"

"I asked you a question, Nikodim," Vadim said quietly. Then he looked away from the barrel and searched for Gulag's eyes in the flickering light.

"What did you do to me?" the gangster asked.

"You know I didn't do this. We could have walked away." *For all the good it would have done.* "I am as you are. So are Fräulein, Skull and Mongol. You know this. If it makes you feel better, then pull the trigger."

"You're one of us," the Fräulein said. "What are you doing?"

"Lower the gun, brother," Mongol told him, letting his own weapon dip. "There's just us here."

Skull and Princess still had Gulag covered. He glanced over at them.

"Is it your time now?" Skull asked him. "Do you want to leave?" It didn't sound like a threat. It sounded like sympathy, understanding.

"Farm Boy...?" Gulag asked. Even dead, his voice was wracked with anguish. Vadim looked down at the big Georgian. It didn't make sense; why had they retained their sentience, but not him? They had eaten the same food on the submarine.

"I don't know," Vadim said, shaking his head. Farm Boy had settled down a little, though he was emitting an odd keening noise, not unlike a beaten dog. Princess cursed and raised her weapon as the Fräulein walked in front of her, blocking Gulag's line of fire to Vadim. Skull raised his AKS-74 as well, shifted position so he could get a clearer shot, but didn't re-aim his weapon.

The Fräulein pushed Gulag's rifle down. Vadim could see the Muscovite's frame shaking, as he made a strange, dry hiccoughing noise. It took Vadim a few moments to realise that the hardened criminal, a man who had spent many of his formative years in a Siberian prison camp, was sobbing. The Fräulein just lay her hand on his shoulder.

Skull looked down at Farm Boy, and then Vadim. "Do you want me to do it?" he asked, and Vadim shook his head.

"It's my responsibility," said the captain, and in saying those words started to feel the enormity of what had happened; just how badly he had failed his people. He walked over to Farm Boy and put the barrel of his sawn-off KS-23 shotgun to the side of his head. The Georgian looked up at him. Vadim hoped for something, some spark of recognition, of intelligence, but there was nothing. He – it – didn't even understand that there was a weapon pressed against his head.

"I'm sorry," Vadim said, but he couldn't shake the feeling that this was better. He started to squeeze the trigger.

"Wait!" Gulag came out of the intermittent darkness to stand over his friend. "I'll do it." He handed Vadim his AK-74 and grabbed a second rifle he'd slung across his back, Farm Boy's own. He sighted down it.

"The noi –" New Boy started. The crack of the rifle echoed through the parking structure, the muzzle flash throwing them into harsh relief for a moment. "Never mind."

Farm Boy was still.

Vadim was grabbed and slammed against a concrete pillar, and Gulag's ruined face was suddenly nose-to-nose with his. He could still just about make out the Muscovite's tattoos under the scabbed, bloody grime. The Fräulein lumbered towards Gulag to drag him off, but Vadim saw something like a tear, thick and glutinous, run down the Muscovite's cheek. The captain held up his hand and the Fräulein stopped.

"If I ever find out that you had something to do with this," he said quietly, his voice full of menace, "I will hammer a shell casing into your skull, do you understand me?" Vadim could smell the meat on the other man's breath, see the dried blood on his teeth. Vadim leaned towards Gulag.

"What do you want, Nikodim?" he whispered. In part, because he had no idea what to do next, or where to go from here. Spetsnaz officers were supposed to have initiative, but nothing even remotely similar had been discussed during officer training in Kiev.

"I want to know *who did this*," Gulag hissed.

CHAPTER SEVEN

1905 EST, 16th November 1987
Eugene's Apartment, New York City

"HE'LL BE LONG gone," Mongol muttered as they trudged up the stairs. Vadim didn't feel a thing. There was no breath to feel out of, no aching muscles. He was aware of his body, but it felt muted somehow.

"Where's he going to *go?*" Gulag asked as they passed a long, smeared, bloody hand mark on the wall. Vadim caught shards of glistening skull on the rail. They had found a body at the base of the stairwell, far below. Vadim knew they were clutching at straws, trying to find a reason to continue existing. He had always prided himself on being clearheaded, regardless of the situation, but now it was a real struggle just to think straight. He at least should have told Princess and New Boy to make their own way; although perhaps their best chance at survival was with the dead members of the squad protecting them.

Skull was on point, Vadim following him. He had Gulag's rifle now; Gulag had kept Farm Boy's. The Muscovite had carved various obscenities into the wooden stock of his AK-74. They had split Farm Boy's grenades and ammunition between them. The Fräulein had taken the big Georgian's disposable RPG-18 to replace the one she'd used on the SWAT van.

Princess and New Boy were still some way behind them. He couldn't blame them. He wouldn't have wanted to be trapped in enclosed quarters with his dead squadmates either.

Skull reached Eugene's floor and opened the door a crack, bringing the sound of moaning and the scrape of fingers against wood. Skull glanced out into the corridor and signalled that the source of the noise was round the corner. Vadim indicated for everyone to switch to suppressed weapons. Princess unsheathed her Dragunov, attached the suppressor and swapped out the magazine for subsonic bullets. The rest of them slung their weapons and drew their Stechkins, screwing suppressors into the barrels. All except Gulag, but Vadim didn't have the capacity to deal with the criminal's bullshit today.

Vadim followed Skull through the door, Gulag right behind them. There was red on the walls, on the light, meat on the floor. They passed broken doors to bloodstained apartments and rounded the corner. There were six zombies: four of them pawing at Eugene's door with bloodied hands, and another two trying to get into the next apartment. A partially-eaten corpse lay on the floor.

Skull's Stechkin coughed and there was a small explosion of bone, dry flesh and brain. Vadim fired and his target hissed as the bullet caught it in the shoulder. *This should be easier, you're not even breathing*, he thought. He adjusted aim and fired again, and the zombie slid to the ground.

The others had noticed, faces raised like wild animals scenting prey. As Vadim passed Eugene's neighbour's door he heard sobbing from inside. Skull fired again, and another zombie dropped. They were on their feet now, charging. Vadim took his time, squeezed the trigger, and another one tumbled to the floor. A hole appeared in the head of the second-to-last zombie, and then Gulag pushed past them, sending Vadim's shot wide. He caught a glimpse of Skull's angry face as Gulag sidestepped the charging corpse and suddenly yanked the thing backwards off its feet. Vadim only realised what Gulag had done when the Muscovite started to saw at the zombie's neck with his garrotte. Three piano strings with diamonds intertwined in them, to saw through the victim's fingers if they managed to get them under the garrotte, as the zombie had.

"Shh!" Gulag soothed as he sawed through fingers and into the neck. Gulag had won the garrotte in a card game, from a member of the Bulgarian Committee for State Security's Service 7. Vadim had always been surprised that Gulag hadn't just fenced the diamonds. Instead, he'd used the garrotte to saw the heads off mujahideen sentries and then balance them back on their necks for their comrades to find. Vadim heard the spinal cord crack, the sound of the wire saw grating through bone. Blood seeped from the wound but didn't spurt. Gulag cried out, exultant, as the head came off.

"Don't do that again," Skull whispered, still covering up the hall. Vadim heard two shots from Princess's Dragunov round the corner and the thump of two bodies hitting the ground.

"Or what?" Gulag asked, making a smile out of his facial wounds. Vadim felt eyes on him, and glanced back to see the Fräulein staring at him.

"Hello?" A woman's voice, American, from the apartment next to Eugene's: the source of the sobbing. Like Eugene's apartment, the door was apparently strong enough to withstand the dead tearing through the building. Gulag strode over to the door and banged on it.

"Kill yourself! There's no hope out here!" he shouted. There was a startled cry, followed by more sobbing.

"It's unlikely she speaks Russian," Mongol pointed out.

"Someone's in there," Skull said, nodding towards Eugene's door. He fired another shot into the partially-eaten corpse on the floor, to be sure.

Vadim moved to the door and knocked on it.

"Eugene," he called. "It's us, let us in." He just heard laughing. "Eugene, open the door now."

Gulag shoved him aside and hammered on the door. Vadim felt his rage rising; he found himself staring at New Boy, down by the corner of the corridor, as he sought to control himself.

"Open the door, you fucking KGB cunt! Or we'll blast it open and cut off your feet, let you bleed!"

Vadim managed to control himself, and once more found the Fräulein watching him. The door opened a fraction and Gulag pushed hard against it. A chain snapped, and the door knocked into someone on the other side. Vadim followed Gulag in. Eugene was lying on the floor, scrabbling for a snub-nosed .38 revolver. Gulag put the boot in hard as Vadim reached down and picked up the .38, noticing with distaste that it was nickel-plated, with mother-of-pearl grips. He opened the cylinder and emptied out the bullets.

"Do you think we can make any *more* noise?" the Fräulein asked as she and Skull pushed past, weapons at the ready, to check the rest of the apartment.

"That's enough," Vadim told the Muscovite, who was trying to stamp on Eugene, now curled up in a ball. Gulag ignored him.

"Gulag!" Vadim very rarely raised his voice. It was still enough to get the other man's attention. Mongol was now in the doorway.

"Fuck's sake!" Eugene muttered from the ground. "Fuckin' kicking me, man!" He sounded angry, but not, Vadim noted, all that afraid.

"What, you think you're still a captain?" Gulag demanded, turning on Vadim. "You think *any* of that matters, now?"

Eugene sat up, laughing at them; he didn't seem to be the pants-pissing wreck they'd left a few hours before. Then Gulag turned to deliver another kick, and Eugene got his first good look at the walking corpse standing over him. He started scrabbling backwards across the floor, Gulag stalking after him.

"What the fuck! You're dead, why are you talking, you're just fucking zombies now! *Holy shit, you're going to eat me!*" *Now* he was frightened. Gulag yanked him to his feet. The spy was white.

"I'm going to hurt you *so much*. I'm going to take my time. Make you a woman, keep you alive as I slice bits off and eat them in front of your face. Fucking *understand me?*"

The shot narrowly missed Gulag's head; a small hole appeared in the window beyond him.

In the stunned silence that followed, Vadim lowered the rifle and met Gulag's eyes.

"The next bullet I will put in your head," he told him. "Let him go. Now."

Gulag kept hold of Eugene. "You know I have guns as well, right?" he asked.

"Try and use them," the Fräulein told him. She didn't exactly have her light machine gun pointed at the Muscovite, but she was making her point.

"We're all angry, we all want answers," Vadim told him. "We can't get them if you beat him to death."

"You need to calm down, Gulag," Mongol said over his shoulder from the doorway.

"Yeah, man, you need to chill, listen to your –" Eugene started.

"Shut up." Vadim's voice was like ice. The spy knew enough to be quiet. Gulag threw Eugene down on the sofa, and Vadim spotted a large, mostly-empty bottle of Jack Daniels and a huge pile of cocaine on the table. It might account for some of Eugene's newfound bravery; but Vadim was pretty sure the KGB agent had played them. He was only now starting to work out what must be going on.

"Mongol, see if Princess and New Boy are prepared to join us."

GULAG WAS GLARING at Vadim as Eugene did another line of coke. At this juncture, Vadim didn't see what difference it would make, beyond making the spy more talkative. It was clear that Eugene understood how narrow and unpleasant his future options were and was pretty much past caring. Princess and New Boy remained by the door to the apartment.

"What was the plan? Drink and snort yourself into oblivion and then put a bullet in your head?" Vadim asked.

"Pretty much," Eugene said, taking a belt of Jack Daniels.

"I don't think much matters anymore. Do I need to threaten you, or are you happy to speak to us?" Vadim asked. Eugene was sat on the sofa now, the dead commandos standing around him.

"No," Eugene nodded towards Gulag. "I think your road-kill friend here has made his position quite clear." Gulag actually growled at him. "You all look like shit, by the way; I mean really disgusting." Gulag took a step towards him, but the Fräulein put a restraining hand on his chest.

"You're a superb actor," Vadim said.

"It's the pissing myself. To guys like you, shitting yourself is a fight-or-flight response, maybe I can't help it; but pissing yourself? That's cowardly, beneath you." He looked at the Fräulein. "Unmanly."

Dead eyes stared back at him.

"You set us up," Mongol growled.

Eugene turned to look at him. "Grow up," he told him, and Mongol tensed. "You were sacrificed for the good of the Union of Soviet Socialist Republics." Then he laughed, as though he didn't believe it himself.

"You can't win a nuclear war," the Fräulein said quietly.

"You can if there's nobody around to retaliate," he told her. Then he did another line. His eyelids flickered, and for a moment Vadim thought he was going to pass out.

"The virus was a first strike weapon," Vadim said. He'd worked that much out. "America would be too busy dealing with the dead in their streets."

"They'd still press the button when they realised who'd done this, when the nukes started falling," Mongol pointed out. The big medic was clearly thinking about his extended family back home in Mongolia. Not for the first time, Vadim felt it would have been better if the Spetsnaz only recruited orphans like him. Of course, the KGB generally got to the orphanages and asylums first.

"Not if there's no-one around to press the button," Vadim said.

Eugene lit a cigarette and nodded, pointing at him.

"It was a decapitation strike wasn't it?" Vadim continued. "I'm guessing you made sure the infection reached NORAD and the White House?"

"And any silo we could manage, and some other strategic targets: the Pentagon, Fort Meade, military bases..."

"And of course civilian population centres, like..."

"New York." Eugene was grinning at Vadim. Vadim's expression didn't change, but he could have killed Eugene there and then.

"Limited nuclear strikes to cripple the country's infrastructure, make any response to the virus that much more difficult," Vadim said quietly. "And then we roll into Europe and the Middle East. NATO's crippled, and US soldiers in Europe will be more concerned with what's happening at home."

"The British, the French, they have missiles," the Fräulein added. "Bombers, submarines."

"The British and the French bases would have been attacked by your brethren," Eugene countered. "Bombers can be intercepted. And –"

"And the sub fleet went to sea in wolfpacks hunting NATO and SEATO subs," Vadim said, remembering the rumours at Rostock. "But that's not foolproof."

"No," Eugene admitted. "Russia will have been hit. There are still tactical devices in play. It will get messy."

"The virus will spread," Mongol put in. Vadim glanced at Gulag. The Muscovite was staring at Eugene; not at his face, at his neck.

"It was only used on America," Eugene told him.

"I don't think you understand how viruses work," the medic said.

"You've murdered an entire continent. Not just the imperialists; we have allies in South and Central America," the Fräulein pointed out. Eugene sagged on the sofa. He grabbed at the Jack Daniels and emptied the rest of it before turning to face the Fräulein.

"First of all, *I* haven't done shit," he told her. The phrase was presumably an Americanism, it sounded odd in Russian. "I'm just a tiny cog and a lot of what I'm telling you is supposition, because guess what? I wasn't told much either. But I mean really, how fucking naive are you? Did you not know you were here to spread chaos and terror? You think there's a difference between this and nerve gas, a nuke?"

"Yes," the Fräulein told him. "I do think there's a difference between dying in a flash of nuclear fire and being eaten to death by a loved one, only to be cursed to rise again."

"Listen to yourself," Eugene scoffed. "Sentimental hypocrites, you're just pissed off *you* got infected." Vadim was keeping an eye on Gulag, making sure he didn't kill Eugene before they found out what they needed to know.

"That was the point, wasn't it?" They all turned to look at New Boy, standing by the door. Vadim almost wished the younger man hadn't drawn attention to himself and Princess, and the smell of fresh meat he associated with them. "That's why we had all the ammunition and grenades in the world but no body armour, no other equipment. You wanted us to make bodies for the virus."

"Because you placed the canister in the locker and then reported us to the police," Vadim added. Eugene didn't say anything.

"Son of a whore," Gulag said quietly. It wasn't an insult he used often; Gulag's own mother had been a prostitute. The gangster drew his knife and took a step toward Eugene, who edged away from him.

"Wait," Vadim said. Gulag hesitated, but the captain could see he wasn't going to listen for very much longer. "Why do *we* retain our intelligence, our personalities? Why aren't we mindless, like the others?" Eugene was glancing warily between Gulag and Vadim. He kept an eye on the Muscovite as he leaned down to the glass table and snorted another line of cocaine.

"Sorry. You guys have been very patient with me, but I can tell you're getting close to the end of that patience. Probably best I'm as numb as possible when it happens, eh?"

"I asked you a question," Vadim said. It was suddenly very quiet and still in the apartment.

"How the fuck would I know? What, do I look like some kind of biochemist to you?"

"Motherfucker!" Gulag spat and reached for him.

"Wait, wait, wait!" Eugene cried. Vadim raised his hand and was surprised when Gulag hesitated.

"Wait for what?" Vadim enquired. He pointed round at the dead members of the squad. "Why was this done? Why didn't the last member of my squad stay sentient?"

"This wasn't done!" Eugene protested. "You weren't *supposed* to be fucking smart! I mean, why would they want smart, pissed off, trained Spetsnaz zombies? That'd be insane!"

"There was nothing in our food? We weren't given any kind of vaccine?" Vadim asked. Eugene just shook his head.

"My friend?" Gulag spat.

"Wasn't strong enough." They all turned to look at the Fräulein. Gulag's eyes were wide, clearly furious. "We have held onto ourselves through sheer force of will. Think of who we are, our training, what we have done. We are strong, that is why we can still think."

"Genadi was strong," Gulag insisted, but Vadim could hear the doubt in his voice.

"Genadi was a good man," the Fräulein said quietly. "The best, because he had a soft heart; and you know he did. How many times did you have to do something horrific because he didn't have the stomach to do it?"

"Shut up!" Gulag screamed at her. "Shut your fat fucking Nazi mouth!" Vadim watched the Fräulein tense. It was about the worst thing that Gulag could have said to her.

"You're not listening, Nikodim," Skull said, surprising the captain. "Genadi is not here with us now, living this hell, because he was a better person than us." Gulag stared at the sniper and then turned back to Eugene. Someone had to pay for the way the Muscovite felt right now. "Gulag, I pray, just a moment longer." The sniper looked to Eugene. "Who did this to us? Who gave you the orders?"

Eugene was already shaking his head.

"Look, this is mostly guesswork. You guys probably know as much as I do, but I don't do that. I'm not going to betray..."

"*What?*" Gulag screamed, spitting in Eugene's face. "It doesn't fucking *matter* anymore!"

"What do you think? The Supreme fucking Soviet! The head of the KGB! How the *fuck* should I know?" *Now* he sounded scared. *Now* he sounded desperate.

"The virus was a secret program, it had to be," Vadim said. Though Eugene was right: the rulers, the strategic planners, they would have had to know about it, to factor it in to their plans. *One step at a time*, Vadim thought. "I want to know who you answered to, so you need to decide how much Gulag needs to torture you before you tell us."

"His name is Yurinov, Major Yurinov, that's all I fucking know, okay?" Eugene told them.

"Where is he!" Gulag screamed in the spy's face.

"How the fuck would I know! Russia! He's probably a pile of radioactive ash by now!"

Gulag looked up at Vadim. Vadim nodded. Teeth sank into flesh. The smell of blood filled the air. Vadim didn't even hear the screaming. He had gone by then.

VADIM HAD NO idea how or why he recovered. His face and hands were deep in Eugene's chest cavity, and he had a mouthful of viscera. With difficulty, he managed to push himself back, leaving bloody handprints on the white carpet. His revulsion at himself warred with the red hunger. He dry heaved, spitting out the foulness in his mouth.

New Boy, Princess were nowhere to be seen. The door to the apartment was wide open. Mongol, the Fräulein, Gulag, Skull, they weren't soldiers anymore, his comrades, they were carrion eaters now, a pack of wild animals like the hyenas he'd seen in Africa. His AK-74 was still hanging off his front. Blood-slippery hands grasped the soiled weapon. He would kill the others and then himself. He should have stuck to his original plan. He raised the weapon to his shoulder. The Fräulein's head rose, face covered in blood, looking like a wolf. She drew back from Eugene's corpse and held up a dripping hand.

"Wait," she managed and then she half-belched, half-retched, blowing a blood bubble.

"Why?" Vadim demanded. "We're monsters."

The Fräulein slumped against the no-longer white sofa. "We always were," she told him. "You... you have to lead... We have unfinished business."

It wasn't much. In fact, it was more of the same. More wading neck-deep into violence. And it would be pointless. It was all far too late. But Vadim had just been going through the motions for far too long now. Any feeling other than hunger was muted. Feelings were a consideration for a time back when his body had been warm. A time he'd wasted. When he thought of the extent of the crime that had been committed here, and the way they had been used to commit it, the anger consumed him.

"Stop!" he ordered.

IN THE END they'd had to pull Gulag out of the nest of serpents that was Eugene's intestines. Vadim had thought they'd lost him to the hunger, that he would have to be put down, to join Genadi, his friend. At the last moment, however, with a gun in his face, Gulag had returned to them.

BLOOD RAN IN the sink as he tried to wash it off his hands and arms up to his elbows, off his glistening red face. His clothes were utterly soiled. He caught a glimpse of himself in the mirror. He didn't look dead, or not yet. Pale, his features slack, he looked sick. He pulled up his sodden jumper and opened his shirt with the neat hole in it. His wound, his stigmata, was a dry, blood-ringed black hole in white, sickly skin. Jagged black lines grew from it like faults in the Earth. He stared at it for as long as he could, and then back into the mirror at the animal, the monster he saw there.

BY SOME UNSPOKEN agreement, they had moved away from the ruins of Eugene's body. Gulag, Mongol, the Fräulein and Skull stood in a rough circle, unable to look at each other. The shame at what they had done was palpable. They cleaned themselves up as best they could, checked their weapons to make sure they hadn't been fouled and pretended to be soldiers, if only briefly.

Vadim had walked past them and out into the corridor. New Boy was down by the corner leading to the stairwell. Vadim found himself looking down the barrel of the scout's AK-74. He whispered something to Princess, who must have been just round the corner. Vadim was both surprised and impressed that they hadn't run.

"Well?" New Boy asked.

"Can you come back and listen, and *then* make your decision?" Vadim asked.

"Are you asking, or is that an order?"

Vadim gave the question some thought before answering.

"I'm asking you now. If you choose to stay, then you do what I say." He turned away from the door and headed back to the others. It was a few moments, but New Boy appeared in the doorway, Princess covering his back in the hall.

"We're going back home –" Vadim began.

"How?" Mongol demanded. Under normal circumstances the big medic would never interrupt him like that. Vadim could hear the anguish in his voice.

"Nergui," the Fräulein said quietly. Skull put his hand on the medic's shoulder. Mongol's head dropped.

"Why?" Skull asked, black eyes fixed on Vadim.

"To help your loved ones survive, see them one more time, die in the Motherland, whatever reason you choose. When we reach the borders of the USSR we can decide whether to stay together or not. You don't want to come? You stay here, now. If you can't live – exist – in this new world, I'll put you out of your misery right here and now; there's no shame in that." There was a snort of derision from Gulag. "But if you come with me, there are rules." He pointed at Eugene's body. "This never happens again."

"You think this is the first time I ate human meat? I was in a Siberian Gulag. What about you? I've heard about the siege of Stalingrad."

"Shut up, Gulag," the Fräulein told him.

"No, we're going to talk about this!" Gulag spat.

"You come with me you don't eat human meat. You want to feed, stay here," Vadim told him. "You almost didn't come back this time. How many times do you think we have to lose control until we're like those things down in the street?"

"What are we supposed to eat? Rations?"

"We're dead," Mongol told the Muscovite. "I don't think that's why we eat." All of them turned to look at the medic. "I think it's about spreading the virus."

"Can you prove that?" Gulag demanded. Mongol just shrugged.

"Gulag?" the Fräulein asked. Gulag shook his head.

"I'm not making any promises," he told them.

"Disobey me and I'll kill you," Vadim told him.

"I'm already dead, comrade captain."

Skull caught Vadim's eye, his hand on his Stechkin. Vadim gave the slightest shake of his head.

"The second rule," Vadim told them and glanced at New Boy, still in the doorway. "We protect our still-living squad mates, no matter what." He could see the Fräulein nodding.

"Why are *they* so important?" Gulag demanded.

"It's just the same thing it's always been," the Fräulein told him.

"Oh, bullshit!" Gulag shouted. "You know what I see? Meat-on-the-hoof. If they had the slightest bit of loyalty, they'd join us." He made a move towards New Boy. New Boy cleared the doorway, his AK-74 levelled at Gulag. Princess swept into the room, moving to the other side of the doorway, levelling her Dragunov sniper rifle at the criminal. Skull's Stechkin was out of its holster.

"You don't like the boss's rules, Gulag, stay here, or die now," the Fräulein told the Muscovite levelly.

"A big girl like you managing to climb so far up the captain's ass," he said quietly, but he was staring at Princess.

"What's it to be?" Vadim asked. Gulag turned to him and took two steps, stopping nose-to-nose with the captain.

"This is a fucking *war!* This is *the* war! There's no rules."

Vadim opened his mouth to retort.

"This isn't a war, it's a blasphemy," Skull said. Gulag looked over at him, opened his mouth to retort and then noticed the pistol in the sniper's hand. "And I am growing tired of you." Gulag stared at Skull. The sniper held the look. In the end it was Gulag who looked away.

"I'll obey your rules," Gulag told Vadim. "For now." Then he backed off.

"Are you with us?" Vadim asked New Boy and Princess. They glanced at each other. New Boy nodded.

"For now," Princess told him.

"Why are you going back?" Skull asked the captain.

"I am going to find this Major Yurinov and make him tell me what he knows. Then I'm going to hunt every single person responsible for this and make sure they suffer before they die, then I'm going to kill Varishnikov," he told them. Skull nodded. There was even a slight smile on his death's head face.

Eugene sat up.

"What are we going to do with him?" Mongol asked.

"Close the door after us," the Fräulein told him.

CHAPTER EIGHT

2015 EST, 16th November 1987
Corner of Park and 38th, New York City

THEY HAD GONE out into the dark streets, humid with black rain and lashed by winds. The silent cars were bumper-to-bumper, blood stained, their windows broken. Emergency lighting shimmered on the wet streets and in the broken glass that crunched underfoot. All the people had gone. The dead had long since swept out and away from the area, looking for more prey.

Vadim knew there were ports in Brooklyn, so they headed south. Skull was on point, the massive suppressor screwed to his .303. Princess, her own suppressed sniper rifle in her hands, brought up the rear with New Boy, both of them still holding back from their dead comrades. Noise and ammunition were issues; Vadim didn't want the squad to draw attention to themselves unless they had to. If they saw lone zombies, then they would leave it to the two snipers to deal with them, but if they encountered a horde, they would run and hide. They would only use unsuppressed weapons as a last resort.

They had burned through a fair amount of their ammunition during the fire fight in the station. They had switched their weapons to semiautomatic and would only fire when they were sure of a headshot.

Frankly, he was making it all up as he went along, keeping up appearances.

He was taking command out of habit more than anything else. Even the decision to go home, the hunt for vengeance, was little more than busy work. An excuse to keep on existing.

He heard more gunfire in the distance. There was a glow in the sky, to the west. They moved quickly, tirelessly. If Princess and New Boy were struggling to keep up, they gave little indication. The streets were wide, lined with trees and not strewn with rubbish; Vadim guessed that this was one of the more upmarket parts of the city. A fire engine had crashed into a church on the corner of the intersection. The engine's spinning red light was still functional, giving the deserted streets an even more alien feel.

"Boss," Mongol hissed from behind him. Vadim turned around to look at the medic, who pointed to the fire engine. Vadim nodded and signalled the team. They crossed the road quickly and quietly. Mongol slung his RPKS and raised his suppressed Stechkin, and the rest of the squad took up covering positions. Vadim concealed himself behind a small bush as best he could. Mongol wouldn't waste their time. If he wanted to search the fire engine, he had good reason. He didn't even look around when he heard the hushed cough of the medic's suppressed pistol.

Princess hissed and Vadim turned around to look at her. She pointed down the adjoining street and raised a hand, five fingers extended. Mongol stopped climbing out of the fire engine and slid back out of sight, and the rest of them hunkered down into their concealed positions. Vadim could hear footsteps, the creak of metal as the strangers walked over the abandoned cars filling the road. He was more *aware* of them, somehow, even before they emerged into the intersection.

He wasn't sure what he had been expecting: there was none of the shambling his limited exposure to capitalist filmmaking had prepared him for, and nor were they the pouncing animals he'd seen in Grand Central Station. They just walked out into the intersection, almost casually. There were two men and three women, a mix of ages, all from different walks of life, judging by their clothing. It seemed the virus was the ultimate equaliser.

True communism? he mused grimly.

They had a good look around and continued on their way, and he revised his initial opinion. There was something predatory about their movement. Not a pack on the hunt, more like an apex predator: at leisure, but still alert. They disappeared from view, but it was still a number of minutes before Princess gave the all clear. Once, Vadim would have felt some semblance of relief; now, he didn't care. Quiet moments only gave him time with the red hunger.

Mongol climbed out of the fire engine, carrying a pack. It looked like a paramedic's kit, and Vadim almost started laughing at the absurdity of it. A walking dead man carrying medical supplies. They were a bit beyond that.

A louder cough this time, from Princess's Dragunov. On the other side of the intersection, one of the five zombies – a middle-aged man in a business suit – fell in the road, half his face missing. Vadim waited, expecting the others to come back, but none of them did.

2151 EST, 16th November 1987
Off Lafayette Street, New York City

A HOOKED NEEDLE pierced unfeeling flesh the colour of fish skin. Vadim sat on the edge of a display in the camping shop they'd broken into. The window had already been shattered, but there'd evidently been little time for looting. It was a strange place to Vadim's eyes. The equipment all seemed somehow absurdly luxurious for such utilitarian things.

The Fräulein, Skull and Gulag, were keeping watch whilst Mongol patched him up. The medic had already sewn up the rest of the squad's wounds. The Fräulein and Gulag had something of Frankenstein's monster about them. Some of Gulag's wounds, like the bite mark in his neck, just had to be covered with trauma dressings. There was no denying that any of them were dead, but Mongol was hoping to delay the onset of putrefaction, the inevitable rot. It was a good idea, as was stealing functional outdoor clothes from the shop. If he wanted them to act as though they were still human, then they needed to look and feel as human as possible. That was difficult when your flesh was hanging off you.

Vadim hadn't felt very human when Mongol had dug out the bullet that killed him; there had been little of what he would consider pain, just discomfort and an odd feeling of dislocation as Mongol rooted around in his chest with forceps.

"How are you doing?" Vadim asked the Mongol, more for something to say than any good reason. At first he didn't think the medic was going to answer the stupid question.

"I am frightened for my family," Mongol finally said, not looking up as he continued to sew the captain's chest wound shut. The words were a little indistinct; Mongol had had to cut away flaps of skin from the side of his mouth and sew them up, exposing most of his teeth and jaw. Vadim nodded, although it had been a long time since he'd had any family, other than the military. The Nazis had seen to that.

"I don't want revenge, I don't care about that. I just want to go home..."

He left it there, but Vadim had a notion of what he was thinking. Even if he made it home, how could his family possibly accept him like this?

"What will you do?" Vadim asked, and Mongol shrugged.

"I don't know," he said. "Perhaps I can live away from them, but watch over them." He looked up at Vadim. "It may not be an issue. We're going to rot. It's unlikely we'll make it that far, assuming we can even *find* a ship."

"Shh!" said the Fräulein, by the window, and the squad moved into cover. Something shambled past the front of the shop, broken body casting monstrous shadows across the racks of camping equipment, backlit by the few light still burning in the city. He heard New Boy exhale once the danger had passed, just another reminder that some among them still lived. Mongol must have heard it as well. He followed the sound, but instead ended up watching Princess as she changed.

"I don't feel any stronger than Genadi," he said quietly. Then he looked back to Vadim. "I am so hungry."

Vadim nodded. He felt it as well.

"When it becomes too much..."

"I promise," Vadim told him.

"Boss?" New Boy said. Vadim closed his eyes, opened them again and looked up at the scout, who was holding up some rappelling gear. Vadim didn't want to weigh them down with any unnecessary weight, but they had been very underequipped, beyond weapons and ammunition. He considered the climbing gear for a moment, then nodded. They had also taken trail rations for the living, flashlights, boots and civilian replacements for all the equipment they should have had for the mission.

0039 EST, 17th November 1987
Corner of the Bowery and Delancey Street, New York City

THE FRÄULEIN HAD found a map of New York in the camping store. They'd skirted Little Italy, heading for Manhattan Bridge, when they caught up with the mass of the dead. Moving east, glancing south down streets with names like Mulberry and Mott, they'd seen large crowds of what had once been people milling around in the darkness, drifting and eerily silent. If there were people still alive down there, then they were well-hidden and very quiet.

Just past Elizabeth Street they heard the clank of armour, and the almost reassuring sound of tracks on concrete, searchlights stabbing through the darkness of the starless night and grimy rain. Skull signalled a halt.

Vadim glanced down Elizabeth Street. The dead were on the move now, migrating like herd animals at a steady walk, moving through Chinatown maybe four or five blocks to the south. Skull had headed across the street to get a better vantage point. He signalled what he saw ahead: two tanks, two APCs and a jeep. Vadim beckoned to the Fräulein and explained his plan.

"We're going in. I want an APC."

"Why take the risk? We can go around," she said.

"Between us and where I want to go there are a lot of dead people. An APC could make our lives a lot easier." He slung his AK-74, pulled two hand grenades from his webbing and started towards the intersection.

"Vadim!" the Fräulein hissed, but he ignored her.

VADIM TRIED NOT to think about what he was doing. There were other, less risky ways of achieving what he wanted here. Did he *want* to die? Really die, as in stop moving? He was looking at a future of rot, after all. Did he want to be punished?

From where he skulked, he could see a number of bodies lying in the streets: people who had, mercifully, been too badly hurt to reanimate. A few were twitching, but were too broken to move. He was very well aware of what they – what *he* had done to this city. There was no doubt in his mind that if there was natural justice, then death was the very least of what he deserved.

He gave the rest of the squad enough time to get into position and removed the pins from the grenades, but left them hanging from his fingers.

The two M48A5 Patton tanks were two generations old; the boxy, tracked M113A3 Armoured Personnel Carriers were a generation behind the current US military. *National Guard*, Vadim decided. According to the street signs, this was the intersection of the Bowery and Delancey Street. It was clear that the Guard were just doing as they had been told, blocking this particular thoroughfare. It irritated Vadim; whoever had given the order had clearly been working on doctrine and had no real idea of the situation. Things must be pretty extreme.

"Don't shoot!" he called in English as he moved out of the darkness and into the street. A few of the broken, mindless dead cocked their heads and started dragging themselves across the asphalt towards the source of the noise. He raised his hands high, but kept his fists curled around the grenades. The searchlight almost blinded him. That wasn't good, but it was to be expected. There was shouting from the tops of the APCs and the tanks.

"Quiet!" a voice unused to command shouted. "Who are you?" Despite the bright white light, Vadim was pretty sure the voice was coming from the passenger side of the jeep. He'd spotted a manned M60 machine gun mounted in the back of the vehicle.

"My name is Captain Vadim Scorlenski of the armed forces of the Union of Soviet Socialist Republics."

There was some muttering from the jeep.

"A Russian?" the voice asked.

"Just so. Who am I addressing?"

"Lieutenant William Smithson of the 50th Armoured Division." Lieutenant Smithson sounded young, and more than a little nervous. This did not fill Vadim with confidence. In some ways, given the situation, he was impressed that the young officer was holding it together, but nervous people made mistakes. "Can I assume that you're surrendering?"

"I'm afraid not," Vadim said apologetically. "Take the light off me and we can talk." He could hear discussion from the vehicles. Someone referring to the lieutenant as Bill, encouraging him to just 'blow him away'. "As you say, you have me covered, but I have information pertaining to the force that is about to attack you."

"I'm going to send two of my men out to secure you," the lieutenant said, still little more than a shadow behind the lights from the two tanks.

"That would be a mistake," Vadim told him and opened his fists, revealing the grenades. "Lieutenant, please understand, I am trying to save your life." *Is that it?* he wondered. *Is that the reason for this stupid plan, is this just a pathetic attempt to alleviate a tiny bit of my guilt?* He told himself he was just buying time for the squad to get in place.

"I could just shoot you," the lieutenant pointed out.

"Your men in the tanks and the APCs will probably be fine, but I suspect the blast will catch your driver and gunner. Besides, you can see me without the lights and you need them to check your surroundings. I am not the threat, unless you make me one."

"Just fucking shoot him." The voice sounded like it came from the turret of the M48A5 to the right of the jeep.

"That's enough," the lieutenant said. "Take the light off him."

"But lieutenant..."

"Now, Rogers!"

The light was moved off Vadim, leaving bright spots in his sight. His night vision was ruined.

"Did you do this?"

Vadim blinked trying to make out the figure wearing a helmet and poncho in the passenger seat of the jeep. "We brought this to your city, yes," Vadim told him. "We were just..." He was about to tell the lieutenant that he'd been following orders, but he'd heard that excuse before. It was a coward's excuse.

"Son-of-a-bitch!" This was from the gunner stood on the back of the jeep. "Let me kill him, loot!"

"Can you think of a terribly compelling reason why I shouldn't just kill you now?" the lieutenant asked, voice taut.

No, Vadim thought. He would have sighed if he'd had breath.

"Do I look well to you?" he asked.

"No, sir, you do not. We heard rumours of a biological weapon."

"That is correct. It makes people kill in a frenzy," Vadim told them. He couldn't be bothered to try and explain what was actually happening.

"Like rabies?" the jeep's driver asked.

"Yes, only it is much stronger and acts much more quickly."

"Bullshit," the gunner in the jeep said. "Where are the bodies?" It was a good question. Vadim decided to ignore it.

"Lieutenant, you have a force of several thousand frenzied cannibals, probably two or three blocks south of you, in the Chinatown district." Several of the soldiers actually turned around and looked down the Bowery. "You have been sent here to die. You need to put all your men in one of your armoured personnel carriers and leave."

"Why would I put all my men in one of the APCs?" he asked.

"Movement!" This came from the turret of the tank to his left. Still trying to blink away the spots in his vision, Vadim could see the tank's commander had twisted around and was pointing a pair of binoculars back down the Bowery towards the bridge. Vadim wasn't sure, but he thought he might be able to see the darkened silhouette of the bridge at the end of the broad road.

"Because I need your APC," Vadim told the lieutenant.

"I get the feeling you're not asking," he said. Vadim could hear it in the young officer's voice: resignation. He knew he was about to die.

"There's no duty left here, only ruin," Vadim all but pleaded.

"It's an ambush!" the lieutenant shouted. Vadim brought his tired arms down.

The two commanders in the turrets of the tanks died first, shot by Princess and Skull. Vadim threw the grenade in his right hand at the closest tank, the one on the right. It was a lucky throw, dropping through the open hatch. He heard the ensuing panic. With his now-free right hand, he drew his Stechkin and opened fire. The RPKSs opened up from a building on his right, bullets tearing into the jeep and sparking off one of the APCs. He heard cries of pain, but the M60 in the back of the jeep started firing. Tracers flew past him. He heard the sharp *crack* of the near misses as he reached the deceptive safety of cover behind the left-hand tank, just as its turret traversed towards the building Mongol and the Fräulein were firing from. Both gunners on the APCs were firing at the building as well, their big .50 calibre heavy machine guns blowing huge holes through the masonry. Bullets from the M60 sparked off the tank Vadim was hiding behind.

When the two .50 cals went silent and the gunners slumped forward, Vadim assumed his snipers had killed them as well. He heard shouting from inside the closest APC as the rear hatch opened and the infantry squad inside started to debus. Vadim clambered up onto the front of the tank, firing his Stechkin wildly at the M60 gunner in the jeep. He tossed the grenade awkwardly, underhand, at the open hatch of the tank. At first he thought he'd missed, but the hand grenade bounced off the armoured plate and in.

There was a popping noise, a grenade launcher. An explosion in the back of the closest APC. *No!* Vadim thought. They needed one of them. Screaming, the shredded remnant of a soldier staggered out of the back of the vehicle only to be cut down by bullets from an AK-74. The M60 gunner on the jeep slumped, his gun swinging up, tracers shooting into the air like fireworks. The tank Vadim was crouched on bucked as its main 105mm gun fired and part of a building ceased to exist. Vadim's second grenade went off inside the tank and the gunner's torso leapt out of the open turret hatch. A cloud of powdered masonry rose from the building the tank had hit. Vadim hoped that it had been a blind shot, that Mongol and the Fräulein hadn't been anywhere near where the shell had hit.

He heard the staccato of AK-74s on burst-fire. Gulag was advancing on the rear of the APC he'd hit with the grenade launcher, firing into it, finishing off the wounded soldiers. New Boy was doing the same with the far APC, but at least *he'd* listened to the orders Vadim had passed on through the Fräulein, to capture a vehicle with as little damage as possible. The younger man closed with the APC, firing into the hatch; at the last moment, he let the assault rifle drop on its sling, grabbed the sawn-off KS-23 from his back scabbard and fired the weapon, twice, into the APC. Vadim could see the muzzle flash of the shotgun lighting up the carrier's interior through the narrow armoured windows.

"Clear," New Boy said. There was something in his voice; he sounded sickened. There was a low, unpleasant laugh from Gulag.

"Yeah, clear," Gulag said.

"Check the other tank," Vadim said, reloading and holstering his pistol before looking in the tank. It was a slaughterhouse. He tried to ignore his hunger.

At the sound of birdsong, he turned to see Skull on the corner, pointing down the Bowery towards the bridge. Vadim was still seeing spots, and it took him a moment to work out what Skull was pointing at: a vast, dark mass of people about three blocks away, sprinting towards them. They weren't uttering a sound, but now he was aware of them, Vadim heard the thunder of their feet.

"Get the bodies out of the back of the APC!" he shouted. "Grab any spare weapons and ammo to hand, but don't waste any time!" He needed to hope that the Fräulein hadn't been killed. They'd all been trained on various pieces of captured or bought NATO equipment, but only the Fräulein had ever actually driven an M113. To his relief, he saw both Mongol and the Fräulein stagger out into the intersection, though both were covered from head to foot with dust. The Fräulein cast him a look of utter scorn as she ran to the jeep.

Gulag and New Boy were tossing bodies out of the back of the less-damaged M113, stripping them as well as they could of weapons and ammunition. New

Boy kept casting glimpses back at the rapidly closing horde of the dead. Skull ran to aid them; Princess followed, but paused, briefly, to watch the closing horde as well. Even Vadim was finding their silence eerie.

"Captain, help me with this!" the Fräulein snapped at him. She was trying to unscrew the M60 in the back of the jeep. He ran to aid her. "Get the ammo!" She pointed at two ammo boxes as she finally wrenched the gun free. "What the hell are you playing at?" she demanded, quietly enough so the rest of the squad couldn't hear. Vadim was looking at the lieutenant in the passenger seat of the jeep. He was young. The captain found himself wondering if he was a college student. He'd sounded educated. Vadim resisted the urge to apologise. Suddenly Gulag was by the jeep, searching the lieutenant.

"What the fuck are you doing?" Vadim demanded, grabbing Gulag's arm. The gangster threw his hand off and held up Smithson's Colt M1911, and a couple of spare magazines.

"I've always wanted one of these," the Muscovite said, and grinned.

"Come on! We don't have time for this!" the Fräulein snapped and all three of them were running for the APC.

CHAPTER NINE

0046 EST, 17th November 1987
The Bowery, New York City

THE M113A3 ARMOURED personnel carrier was basically a brick on tracks, with a sloping front and a Browning M2HB .50 calibre heavy machine gun mounted on top of it. Given a straight road, the APC was capable of hitting a speed of just over forty miles an hour; and the Fräulein seemed determined to reach it.

"I can smell blood in here," Gulag shouted over the roar of the engine and grinned at Princess. She narrowed her eyes but held her peace. It wasn't just the smell. There was blood sloshing around in the bottom of the vibrating armoured vehicle. The APC had held an entire squad of infantry until they'd been killed and unceremoniously slung out onto the road. Vadim had no idea if they would rise again or not.

He found himself gripping his rifle tightly. The smell of blood suffused his senses. He wanted to launch himself across the cramped interior of the APC and bite Princess, or New Boy, until he tasted flesh; and if he felt like this, the others must as well. It could only be a matter of time before someone snapped. He wondered briefly if this was some kind of delayed adrenalin response from the fight, sluggish biochemistry trying to force its way through a dead body. He had felt nothing during the fight itself, no excitement, no fear. It had been clinical.

"Get ready!" the Fräulein shouted from the driver's seat. They didn't feel the impact – the APC didn't even slow – but they *heard* it: bodies bouncing off the armour, the wet tearing of flesh under the tracks. Through the narrow window slits on the roof, they saw bodies tumble past. Vadim heard something hit the .50 cal. He was staring at New Boy. He knew he was going to attack if he didn't find something to distract himself.

"New Boy!" he shouted, but the scout didn't hear him over the roar of the APC's engine. Vadim reached over and grabbed New Boy's leg. The scout flinched, and almost brought his weapon up. Vadim let go and pointed up at the roof. "When I pass my shotgun down, you pass yours up and reload mine, and keep doing it! Understand?" New Boy nodded. Unsteadily, Vadim pulled himself up and opened one of the roof hatches.

"What the fuck are you doing?" It might have been the closest that Vadim had ever come to hearing the Fräulein actually scream. Straightaway, one of the dead was in the hatch, trying to scrabble into the compartment. Vadim grabbed it by the face, avoiding snapping jaws, and dragged his *saperka* from its loop on his webbing. He jabbed the sharpened edge of the entrenching tool up into the mouth of the struggling zombie; he cried out when he heard a crunch, but continued pushing until the creature went still. He shoved it away, and only then did he realise it was just a torso with arms.

"How come Infant gets to have all the fun?" Gulag shouted, but Vadim ignored him. Despite the Fräulein's protest, he had a purpose. He wanted to save the .50 cal. He had a feeling that they would be needing it.

The Bowery was obviously a less salubrious part of town. There wasn't much emergency lighting, and the buildings were more rundown. The APC's headlights cut through the night, showing the charging horde sprinting at them and bouncing off. The APC mowed them down like wheat. A broken, flailing form sailed over the roof, and Vadim tried to batter it out of the way, but the body slammed into him, throwing him into the edge of the open hatch.

Despite the speed of the APC, some of the dead managed to cling on. Vadim lashed out with his *saperka*, severing fingers and dislodging zombies, but there always seemed to be more of them. Row after row of the horde were disappearing beneath the vehicle. They were sprinting out of the side streets, out of the alleyways, forcing more of the dead into the path of the APC. The press of bodies was horrific. All he could see were what had once been people, filling the street wherever he looked. There must have been thousands, tens of thousands.

Vadim checked behind him and saw a zombie clambering onto the roof from the rear of the vehicle. He jammed his *saperka* into a handhold, drew the sawn-off KS-23 from its back sheath and rammed it, one-handed, against the thing's head. The rear top hatch of the vehicle flipped open, hitting the barrel of the shotgun and knocking it away from the zombie. The weapon discharged into the masses, the muzzle flash illuminating the silent, distorted faces of the dead horde. The zombie practically fell on Gulag as he rose through the hatch; Vadim heard the crack as Gulag rammed his *saperka* into the thing's skull again and again, before heaving it over the side. He swung round to face Vadim.

"Did you just try and shoot me?" he demanded, shouting to be heard over the APC's engine, although he was smiling. *Not yet*, Vadim thought.

"Pay attention!" Vadim cried. Gulag had hold of New Boy's KS-23. He fired, ejected the shell, and fired again. A face ceased to exist in a cloud of matter and bone. He worked the slide and fired again as Vadim turned away. Another zombie was clambering up the sloping front of the APC; Vadim put the shotgun in its mouth and squeezed the trigger, and a headless corpse slid down and under the tracks. Behind him, the muzzle flash from Gulag's shotgun lit up the night once more.

"Reload!" the Muscovite cried, passing the shotgun back down into the passenger compartment for New Boy. Suddenly the APC veered sharply to the right, sending zombies flying into the air. They were heading towards the wall of a building.

"What are you doing?" Vadim cried.

"I can't see!" the Fräulein shouted back.

"Left, left! Forty-five degrees left!" Vadim shouted. He was thrown around again as the APC veered the other way. Behind him Gulag was striking out with the *saperka*. Vadim fired his shotgun twice more, dropped it into the APC and started doing the same. The entrenching tool's blade sparked off the APC's armoured plate as he cut the hand off one of the zombies, and the creature fell back into the press. The night lit up as Gulag fired the KS-23 again. Vadim felt a tap against his leg as his now-reloaded shotgun was passed up to him. From behind him, the sound of an unfamiliar handgun as Gulag fired his new .45 repeatedly into the head of one of the zombies, laughing maniacally. Vadim shouted another course correction to the Fräulein and blew a zombie off into the road, and then they were clear of the horde.

"Yeah!" Gulag cried out from behind him. "Wooh!" Vadim glanced behind. He could make out the dark mass of the horde sprinting after them, but they were getting further and further away. The APC had left lines of gore on the street. He reloaded the shotgun and slid it back into its sheath, wiped the worst of the mess off the blade of his *saperka* with a rag and then slid the entrenching tool back into its loop. He clambered out onto the roof of the speeding APC, holding on tightly to one of the hand rails, and did his best to clean the narrow slit of armoured glass that passed as the APC's windscreen, so the Fräulein could better see the road. Just for a moment, it felt like they were all alone in the city. Just for a moment, it was almost peaceful.

The Fräulein slewed the APC up onto the ramp to the Manhattan Bridge. As the road rose, Vadim could make out what looked like state housing on either side. They were dark and still. Whatever had happened here had happened while they were still uptown. Even so, he wondered at where all the millions of people living in New York City had gone. He envisaged them sweeping away from the city, sprinting as fast as they could, like a viral herd migration. Perhaps the squad had stayed close to each other at Central Station, even as they had succumbed to the mindless hunger, out of loyalty to each other, their own herd instinct.

If the bridge had been a choke point, it had passed. It was deserted now, though thoroughly blocked by abandoned cars, their windows broken, stained with blood, like the rest of the city. The whole tableau was illuminated by a flickering glow from the south and the west.

The APC slowed as its caterpillar tracks clawed its way up onto the roofs of the abandoned cars, crushing them under its weight as it made its way across a carpet of Detroit metal. They passed under an ornate arch flanked by colonnades and out onto the bridge proper on the upper Brooklyn-bound lane.

Looking back down the East River, through the Brooklyn Bridge, past the twin sentinels of the World Trade Centre, he realised that part of New Jersey and much of the Upper Bay was on fire. The Statue of Liberty, tiny at this distance, was almost lost amongst the flames, but somehow she looked unbowed. Between Manhattan Island and the Atlantic, he could see burning ships in the flames. He assumed an oil storage or tanker leak had been ignited by the firestorms. At his back was the now-silenced city, the city they had killed.

"We need to be punished for this," he whispered to himself.

"It's fucking beautiful," Gulag said from behind. It seemed that Gulag was embracing his condition. Vadim tried to ignore him.

Below them, he saw ships making their way up the East River, away from the Upper Bay and the fires. A huge container ship, looking too large for the river, headed towards the Brooklyn Bridge; a coast guard cutter ran alongside it, shining searchlights up at the larger ship. Vadim could hear shouting over a loudhailer, but couldn't make out words. There were people running all over the decks of the larger ship, clambering around the containers, and that was when Vadim realised it was already a ship of the dead. The crew must have tried to help evacuate people and only too late realised that they had the infection on board.

There was the sound of tortured metal as the container ship collided with the coast guard cutter. Vadim saw the flicker of muzzle flashes from the cutter and heard the gunfire moments later as the dead spilled from the larger ship, plummeting to the decks of the boat. The gunfire intensified. The sheer weight of the container ship forced the cutter into shallower water; he heard more shrieking metal and an almighty crash as the cutter hit one of the bridge's supports. Then the container ship ran aground as well, sending the dead tumbling into the river. Meanwhile, a smaller container ship was trying to slowly pick its way past the colliding craft without running aground, and without getting too close to the larger ship and its cargo of zombies.

Seeing his vague plan of hijacking a ship from one of the Brooklyn Ports going up in smoke, Vadim turned to look over the bridge to the Brooklyn side, hoping for inspiration. That was when he saw the dead running at them from Brooklyn, scrambling across the carpet of abandoned cars. He looked down at the smaller container ship. There were people on the decks, more than would be needed to crew a ship that size, but they weren't running around trying to eat each other. He pounded on the roof of the APC.

"Stop! Stop!" he shouted. The APC lurched to a halt. Vadim checked behind him, looking towards the Manhattan side of the bridge. He wasn't sure, but he thought he could see dark figures sprinting towards them from that direction as well, the horde from the Bowery catching up. He turned to Gulag and gestured towards both groups of the dead. "Man the .50," he told the Muscovite, "but don't fire until I tell you to."

Gulag nodded and crawled out of the rear hatch across the roof as Vadim sank down into the APC, moving out of the way so the gangster could stand on the gunner's pedestal. The rest of the squad were all looking to him.

"Switch off the engine," Vadim told the Fräulein, and she did so. "We have forces closing in on us from both ends of the bridge. There's a container ship going by under..." The thunder of the .50 cal overhead drowned him out as Gulag fired a short burst, and then another. Hot shell casings rained down into the APC. "Gulag, cut it out!" Vadim shouted. Gulag laughed, but didn't fire again. "Gulag, Fräulein and myself will cover; New Boy, you rig a rope and drop it over the side. Everyone gets into harness and rappels down onto the ship. Understand?" They all nodded. New Boy kicked the rear hatch open and threw out the duffel bag full of climbing gear he had taken from the outdoors shop.

"Can I fire now, Infant?" Gulag asked insolently.

"I want the whole belt gone before we leave," Vadim told him as he looked around at the weapons they had taken from the National Guard squad. He grabbed the M16/M203 combination assault rifle and grenade launcher, along with ammo for both weapons, and followed Princess out of the APC. As she stepped out she fell forward, hitting the ground. He saw an arm reach out from under the vehicle and a zombie – one leg missing, the other a crushed, mangled mess – pulled itself out from under the APC and tried to climb up her. The roar of the .50 cal atop the armoured vehicle drowned out any warning cry. Vadim's hands were full, nothing readied. He was about to drop the assault rifle and reach for his *saperka* but Princess used her boot to ram the zombie's head against the lip of the rear hatch as she drew her pistol. There was a *crack* as powerful leg muscles broke something in her attacker's spine. Then Vadim flinched away, more by instinct than anything else, as she fired two rounds into its head, perilously close to where he was standing. Then the torso was still. Princess didn't even look at him. She just stood, holstered her pistol and grabbed the M16 she'd taken.

Vadim quickly pulled the climbing harness on, securing it in place. The APC's tracks – the whole lower half of its body – were caked in dripping gore. He then moved a little way away. Gulag was firing towards Brooklyn, every three-round burst sending one bright tracer arcing lazily into the mass of the dead. Vadim loaded a fragmentation grenade into the M203 grenade launcher mounted underneath the M16's barrel. Gulag didn't need a head hit with the .50 cal. A limb hit would destroy and probably remove the limb, the hydrostatic shock of a centre mass torso hit could pop the head off. *Just like Pavel*, he thought. There was an explosion as one of the API rounds from the .50 ignited a fuel tank, blossoming into flame over the bridge; in the red light, the dead looked like ants swarming from a nest.

Mongol fixed a second belt of ammunition to the first in the M60 the Fräulein had taken off the jeep. The big East German woman lifted the large weapon to her shoulder like an oversized rifle and started laying down fire towards the Manhattan side of the bridge, Skull feeding the belt into the machine gun. Vadim saw targets taking hits; the 7.62mm round did significant damage, but the zombies kept moving until they were utterly destroyed.

Skull and Princess both had M16s and were aiming carefully, firing single shots and taking aim every time. Both were probably good enough to reliably make head shots from that distance.

Vadim fired the launcher, sending a fragmentation grenade into the masses coming from the Brooklyn side. Then he reloaded and fired towards the Manhattan side. He saw dark figures torn apart, flung into the air, but some of them kept on crawling when they landed.

"Ready!" New Boy shouted, flinging the rope over the side of the bridge. Vadim glanced over and saw that the ship was almost below them.

"Go!" Vadim shouted and New Boy disappeared over the side of the bridge. "Princess, go!" Vadim ordered, firing another grenade towards Brooklyn. Princess was shooting down into the lower level of the bridge, where the subway lines and extra car lanes were.

"They're below us!" she shouted before dropping the M16 and sprinting for the line, attaching her descender to it and following New Boy over the edge. Looking down, Vadim could see more of the dead moving through the lower levels. He fired a high-explosive grenade into a mass of them. It detonated, throwing cars into the air. There was a second explosion as another fuel tank went up, fire blooming up through the bridge.

"Skull, you're next," Vadim called. The bow of the container ship was now under the bridge. Skull fired a few more shots down into the lower levels of the bridge and then dropped his M16 and made for the line. Vadim loaded another fragmentation grenade and saw the last few bursts from the .50 cal tear zombies apart.

"Empty!" Gulag shouted from the APC.

"Mongol, go!" Vadim shouted. Mongol abandoned the Fräulein as she cut loose with a long burst of fire from the machine gun. Vadim was firing the M16 now. They were close enough. Three-round burst, shift, three-round burst, shift, fire again. The fire from the gas tank that Gulag had hit had spread; a tanker truck exploded, blowing burning cars off the bridge and into the East

River. Vadim heard a clang as car bounced off the side of the ship below. It looked as though the fireball had consumed a number of the zombies, but they just came sprinting out of it a moment later, on fire.

Gulag didn't wait for an order. He pulled on a climbing harness, attached his descender and rolled over the side of the bridge. Vadim heard gunfire from below; it didn't sound like anything carried by his people.

"Liesl, go!" Vadim shouted. The dead from the lower level were starting to clamber up towards them. Vadim was firing the M16 and backing towards the riverside edge of the bridge. His magazine ran dry. He ejected it as three of the dead climbed up onto the upper level. Vadim grabbed the last magazine he'd taken for the weapon and slammed it home as they charged him. The long burst from the M60 sent the zombies staggering backwards, the rounds churning up their unliving bodies as they tumbled back into the lower levels. The Fräulein dropped the M60 and ran to the line. Vadim fired his last grenade towards Manhattan and then turned towards Brooklyn, firing the M16, illuminating the bridge one more time before dropping the weapon, and attaching his descender to the line. Charging zombies from both sides were almost upon him, several of them on fire, reaching for him. He clambered over the railings and tried to kick off, but there were already people on the rope below him, holding it taut, and he slid down, battering himself against the superstructure. The dead just threw themselves off the bridge at him, grabbing at him as they plummeted by. As he slid past the lower level, he saw more of them sprinting along the subway lines to throw themselves out over the river, whether to try and get to him or the container ship, he wasn't sure. He slid below the lower level into open air. The bridge castle of the ship was beneath him now. He saw Gulag on top of it, removing himself from the line, the Fräulein just about to touch down. Gunfire sounded from the tops of the containers and the decks running along either side of the stacks, answered by fire from the bridge castle and the stern.

Vadim was trying to make sense of the situation as he rappelled towards it, when a shadow fell across him. He looked up in time to see one of the dead falling towards him, its chest cavity glowing from within. The zombie half-landed on him, and he half-caught it. At first he thought it was one of the burning zombies, but realised it had one of the .50 cal API rounds lodged inside it. The round must have passed through a number of vehicles, slowing it down, before it had hit the zombie, but the incendiary was still burning.

The zombie had hold of one of the straps on his climbing harness, and seemed to be simultaneously trying to climb him and claw at him as they swung around beneath the bridge. The creature managed to wrench its hand free and started to fall, but Vadim grabbed its wrist, not wanting to add another zombie to whatever was happening on the ship below. He pulled his knife from its scabbard and rammed it down again and again onto the top of the struggling, glowing creature's head. The awkward angle of attack meant that the knife was mostly scraping off the thing's skull. Finally, however, with a sickening crunch, Vadim managed to get a solid enough blow to pierce the skull and the zombie was still. Then Vadim let it drop and bounce off the ship. He continued sliding down the rope, conscious he was about to run out of ship.

He could see the stern of the vessel. A man he didn't recognise was standing by the rear edge of the bridge castle, firing a Heckler & Koch G3 with a distinct lack of expertise. Behind him, Vadim could see a limp-legged zombie dragging itself across the deck towards the man.

Vadim tried to rappel even faster, but the rope jammed in the descender. The ship was about to disappear beneath him. He cut the rope and fell through the night air.

CHAPTER TEN

0059, 17th November 1987
The East River, New York City

THE EDGE OF the ship's stern was rushing up to meet Vadim. Cold fingers stretched out for it. The flames of the burning bridge glittered in the dark waters. Dead flesh touched metal, slipped. His right hand found purchase. He slammed into the hull, hard, and almost let go. He spent a few seconds hanging in space, finding an odd moment of peace. Then he felt his fingers starting to slip and reached up with his other hand to pull himself onto the deck.

The short podgy man with the G3 rifle stood at the aft corner of the tower; he still hadn't noticed the dead woman crawling across the deck towards him. Vadim swung his AK-74 forward on its sling, raised the weapon to his shoulder and squeezed the trigger, blowing the top of the woman's head off. The sailor jumped and started to swing round, and Vadim caught the barrel of the G3 and wrenched it out of his hands. The man looked terrified. Vadim wondered just how dead he looked right now.

"Do you have people on deck?" Vadim demanded in English. The man just gaped at him. "Answer me now!" He slung his AK-74 again and checked the G3 over. The man was nodding, but seemed to be struggling to speak. "Ammunition," Vadim ordered. The stranger handed over two more twenty-round magazines for the rifle. "Okay, you need to listen to me and do exactly as I tell you if you want to live, do you understand me?" The man just nodded again. Vadim could hear the cracks of single shots from various directions around the ship. "Get all your people inside." Vadim patted the superstructure of the bridge castle. "Anyone bitten, wounded, you leave them out here, understand me?"

A hatch in the side of the bridge castle opened, and another man in uniform, also carrying a G3, stepped out onto the deck. Vadim aimed his own rifle at the man.

"Don't move!" he shouted, and the man froze, his back still to Vadim. The report of an AK-74 sounded, nearly on top of them, and the top of the man's head exploded.

"No!" The podgy man found his voice, as his shipmate toppled to the deck. Vadim risked looking up. Gulag was standing atop the bridge castle, rifle pointing down.

"Just target the dead!" Vadim shouted. "Tell the others!" Gulag disappeared from view, and Vadim turned back to the podgy sailor. "Get your people inside, now!"

"You'll shoot me!" the man protested as Vadim knelt over the corpse, searching him, removing two more magazines for the G3 before taking the weapon itself. Even wanting to preserve their own ammunition, he was carrying altogether too many weapons.

He didn't answer the man; after all, it was a distinct possibility. He could hear the Fräulein shouting in Russian from the roof of the bridge castle, and saw muzzle flashes light up the night as she fired a short burst from her RPKS-74. This was not a good situation. They were spread out across the ship; there were zombies on board, though presumably damaged from the fall; and they had a civilian crew wandering around. Ideally, Vadim didn't want to kill the civilians, but they were armed. "Fine," Vadim finally said. "Go ahead and hide, your friends can take their chances." He looked up at the man. He was pale, almost as pale as Vadim, and coated in a cold sweat. He nodded. He would help. "Stay behind me."

"Wait," the sailor said. Vadim opened his mouth to say something harsh, but the man had pulled out a radio handset and was speaking into it in German. He hooked the radio back on his belt. "Okay."

Vadim moved forward along the narrow walkway next to the bridge castle, heading towards the stack of containers along the long flat front of the ship.

Cranes fore and aft of the cargo area cast long shadows over the stacks. Vadim saw the spark of a muzzle flash from the fore crane, heard the boom of Skull's .303 and assumed that something or someone had just died. He reached the edge of the bridge castle and found himself face to face with a young black man in a police officer's uniform, pointing a pump-action shotgun at him.

"Freeze! Drop the weapon!" the police officer shouted. Vadim kept his G3 levelled at the man. He was young, late twenties at the oldest. Short, with neatly-cropped hair, he looked in good shape. He had a plain honest face, wracked with strain.

"Put the gun down," Vadim said evenly.

"Are you Russian?" the police officer demanded.

"I'm trying to keep you alive..."

"Please, officer," the German sailor said from behind him. There was more gunfire from above, on the stacks of containers.

"You did this!" the police officer said. Vadim saw the pain on his face, and knew he was going to have to kill him. There was a soft whistle from behind the officer, and Princess stepped out of the shadows, her AKS-74 levelled at the back of the police officer's head. Then the shadows at his feet shifted and pulsed, as if something overhead were –

"Move!" Vadim shouted. The officer, sensing movement, looked up at the dead man plummeting towards him. A shot echoed as the police office threw himself to one side, and the zombie hit the deck with the top part of his head missing. Princess lowered her rifle and calmly resumed aiming at the police officer.

The policeman was staring at the corpse in disbelief. In fairness, Vadim couldn't quite believe it either. G3 levelled, he moved to stand over the officer.

"Don't force us to kill you," Vadim told the police officer, and lowered his gun, looking beaten. "Leave your weapons. You are going to go with this exceptionally dangerous woman." He nodded towards Princess. "You're going to send any of your people back to the bridge castle and tell them to lock themselves in. You leave anyone wounded out here for us to check, understand me?"

He was just shaking his head and mumbling to himself. Vadim couldn't really blame him, but it wasn't terribly useful.

"Officer!" he snapped. The man looked up at Vadim. "You have a responsibility; people still need your help." The policeman nodded and stood up, leaving the shotgun on the deck. "Your revolver as well." He removed the weapon from its holster and laid it on the deck as well. Vadim passed one of the G3s to Princess, who slung her AKS-74.

"I'm not a mule, you know," she told him. She had a point, but they needed to conserve as much of their own ammunition as possible. He passed her two spare magazines.

"Where are the others?" he asked. He'd worked out most of their positions, but wanted it confirmed, the blanks filled in.

"Fräulein and Gulag are on the roof of the bridge structure. Skull is using the crane forward as a sniper's nest. Mongol's up on the containers and I don't know where New Boy is," she told him. The sailor and the police officer watched them talk in Russian with fear and suspicion on their faces.

"Okay," Vadim said, nodding. "Fräulein, Gulag, Mongol, can you hear me?" he shouted. The Fräulein and Mongol answered; he assumed Gulag could hear him too. "Fräulein, cover us from the bridge castle. Gulag, Mongol, I want you on top of the containers. We're going to sweep forwards. Check everything! I don't want any surprises. We do not target civilians! If they're not already dead, then do not fire unless defending yourself! Mongol, shout to Skull, tell him what we're doing, tell him we're going to be working forward on either side of the deck. We'll announce ourselves, but he needs to check his shots." He heard the Mongol relay his orders. There was a high-pitched electric squeal that put Vadim on edge and even made Princess tense for moment, as the PA system came to life.

"*This is the captain speaking,*" the voice was calm, used to authority, German accent. "*All civilian personnel must make their way aft to the bridge castle. If anyone is injured, leave them where they are for the military personnel to deal with. It is imperative, for your own safety, that you do this now.*"

Gulag appeared out of the shadows above them, leaping from the bridge castle to the top of the container stacks. Vadim pulled out a flashlight he'd taken from the outdoors shop. He had his AK-74 slung across his back, the G3 slung down his front. He pushed the police officer's revolver into his webbing belt, switched on the flashlight, checked the officer's shotgun had a shell chambered and then held the flashlight to the weapon's slide as he shouldered it. He felt overburdened, but he didn't want to leave weapons lying around.

"Let's go," he told the German sailor, making for the narrow walkway that ran down the port side of the ship. Princess and the American made for the starboard side.

He heard movement as soon as he reached the corner of the containers. He came wide around the corner, to find a huddled group of civilians, faces scared in the torchlight.

"Please don't shoot!" An American accent.

"Are any of you armed? Injured?" Vadim demanded. There were three of them, all reasonably big; Vadim supposed they were longshoremen. They just shook their heads.

"Please, go back into the crew quarters," the sailor said, gesturing towards the bridge castle. Vadim saw movement past them.

"Down! Now!" he snapped, and they flattened themselves against the deck and crawled past him.

Vadim saw the barrel of a rifle, and shone his light in New Boy's face. He immediately dipped it again, so as not to further damage the scout's night vision.

"Good to see you, boss," said the younger man, lowering his weapon. Vadim wordlessly passed him the G3 and the two spare magazines, and the scout slung his own weapon and readied the G3. He glanced at the frightened-looking sailor, and without saying anything, fell in behind them both.

Vadim moved along the narrow walkway on the edge of the cargo area as the ship slid through the water. They were rounding a bend in the river: Vadim could just about make out a park on the Manhattan side, another bridge spanning the river ahead. New Jersey was still a glow to the west. He shone the torch into the narrow gaps between the stacks of containers, checking them thoroughly. He heard a scrabbling noise in front of him and shone the light along the deck. A man in pyjamas and robe, legs shattered, was dragging himself surprisingly quickly towards them. Vadim aimed his shotgun, tracking the corpse's progress. He heard a gunshot from the other side of the containers, the deep boom of Princess's G3, but did not fire.

"Boss?" New Boy asked. *Patience isn't a virtue of the young*, Vadim thought. The zombie surprised him, using his arms to launch himself at him. The shotgun blast lit up the side of the ship, echoing out across the river and into the darkened city. The corpse slumped to the deck, its head hollowed out by buckshot. He worked the slide, ejecting the spent, smoking casing and chambering another.

Another gunshot, then a second from atop the containers: Gulag's AK-74. Vadim checked another gap between the stacks and found a hissing zombie jammed in it, clawing at a refrigerated container.

"Gulag, Mongol, call out!" They answered. They weren't near him. "Firing up!" He aimed carefully and then fired into the gap. Some of the buckshot sparked off the container, but enough caught the trapped zombie in the face, and it slumped and was still.

Skull's .303 boomed, and something fell off the top of the containers, bounced off the railing and splashed into the river. "Careful, Skull!" Gulag cried, sounding less than happy.

Someone was staggering towards them, holding their neck. Vadim shone the flashlight straight in their face. The blood running through their fingers from the wound looked black in the harsh light.

"Please don't shoot!" the man cried, voice heavily accented. Vadim assumed he was crew.

"Stay where you are!" Vadim commanded as he continued moving forward. "How did you get hurt?"

"It bit me!" the man howled.

"That's..." the sailor started, but was cut off by the shotgun. "No!" Vadim helped the body over the side with his boot.

"That was –"

"Shut up!" New Boy snapped in English.

"Clear!" Mongol shouted from ahead. *Like fuck it is*, Vadim thought.

"Work your way back, check the gaps between the containers!" he shouted. "Use your flashlights!" He was still moving forwards, but had allowed himself to become distracted in his irritation. The zombie lunged out of a gap between containers; it must have been the one that attacked the crewman he had just killed. Vadim threw himself out of the way, almost going overboard.

"Down!" New Boy shouted, stepping on the back of the sailor's knees and sending him face first down on the deck. The zombie was flailing in the gap. Vadim heard flesh ripping as it tried to tear itself free. There wasn't enough room to bring the shotgun up, so he dropped it. The G3 fired, throwing everything into negative, and Vadim grabbed for the revolver stuffed through his belt. New Boy's bullet took the dead woman in the shoulder, almost severing her arm, and Vadim put the revolver to her head and pulled the trigger twice.

"Boss!" Mongol shouted from atop the container stacks.

"We're good!" Vadim shouted back. He checked the zombie was dead and then picked up the shotgun. New Boy was chuckling.

"What?" Vadim demanded, more annoyed with himself than anything else. *Stupid old man!* The sailor was whimpering on the deck his hands over his head.

"Just like a cowboy, boss."

"Skull!" Vadim called from the forward corner of the container stacks. "Three of us at the port corner; don't shoot!"

"Understood!" Skull called back. Moments later, Princess was shouting something similar from the starboard side. There had been a few more gunshots, but it sounded like Princess and the police officer had encountered more civilians without shooting them. They checked the bow of the ship in the shadow of the forward crane but found nothing else. The sailor sat down, his head in his hands. New Boy leant against the crane's support and visibly sagged.

"What's wrong with you?" Vadim demanded; it was only then he realised he'd been on the go for forty-eight hours with little sleep, and running and fighting for at least ten of them. The boy was drenched with sweat. He barely felt it now – he was dead, after all – but New Boy and Princess had to be exhausted.

There was an island in the river ahead of them, with another bridge running across it.

"What's that building?" Princess asked, nodding toward a high, slab-shaped building on the Manhattan side of the river. The police officer evidently didn't speak Russian, but he saw what she was looking at.

"That's the UN building," he told them.

Tonight, to Vadim, it looked like a tombstone.

"Boss," New Boy said.

They had been making their way back along the deck, past the containers, towards the bridge castle, with Princess and the two civilians. Vadim was less than pleased that Gulag had joined them.

They had left the others on overwatch; between them they could cover most of the ship. Vadim turned to see what New Boy wanted. The scout was pointing his flashlight at the deck. The rain had stopped, ash and dust was falling from the dark sky in big flakes, settling on the ship like snow.

"It's blood," Vadim said. He'd seen so much of it in his life. New Boy played the torch along the trail of blood, following it to the hatch. The sailor Gulag had killed was still lying on the deck in front of it, but judging by the body's position the blood hadn't come from him. Vadim turned to the sailor. He looked ashen and was shaking like a leaf. "What is your name?"

"I am First Officer Gerhardt Colstein," he managed.

"Gerhardt, it looks as though someone has taken a wounded person in here. I need you to contact your shipmates and find out what the situation is." The first mate nodded and started speaking into the radio in German. Vadim turned to the police officer. "Is anybody inside armed?"

The American pointed at New Boy and then Princess. "They look okay" – he pointed at Vadim – "but you don't look well." Then he pointed at Gulag. "And *he* looks like Frankenstein."

"What's he saying?" Gulag demanded in Russian.

"He thinks you're pretty," Princess told him.

"I fucking hate the militia," Gulag muttered.

"Are you breathing?" the police officer asked Vadim.

"What's your name, officer?" the captain asked him.

"Harris. Montgomery Harris," the officer told him after a moment's consideration.

"Do you know what we are?"

"Fucked-up walking corpses," he spat. He glanced at Princess. "Some of you, anyway."

"Beyond that?" Vadim persisted.

"Russian special forces?" he guessed.

"What do you think will happen if there's any armed resistance?" Vadim asked. He leaned in close, and Harris shrank away. "I've had my fill of killing civilians today, but rest assured I will have not a single compunction in doing so if you force my hand, do you understand me?" Harris stared at him. "Are there weapons inside?"

"Yes," Colstein said in English. "There are more rifles. I have spoken with my captain. He said if you wish access, then you need to turn your weapons over to me."

Gulag was following the exchange, though it was doubtful he understood much of it.

"Fuck this," he muttered and went to turn the wheel to open the hatch.

Vadim cursed, but cleared Harris and Colstein out of the way, so they could cover the Muscovite.

The wheel didn't budge. Gulag looked less than pleased. "Let's kill this black pig," he said, nodded towards Harris. "See if that makes them more reasonable." Vadim ignored him and turned to Colstein.

"I think you know we're not going to surrender. If you don't let us in, two things are going to happen: if you've got any infected in there, then they could turn and kill everyone inside. Even if you don't, we'll blow the doors off here, probably end up fighting on the bridge, kill a lot of your people and possibly shoot something critical to the ship's operation." Threatening to blow the doors was a bluff; they didn't actually have the tools.

Colstein stared at Vadim for a moment, and then relayed the message over the radio. This time Vadim listened. His German wasn't nearly as good as his English, but it was passable. Colstein passed on his message almost word for word.

There was a lot of static from the radio. He assumed the interference was the result of atmospheric ionisation from the New Jersey nuclear detonations. He suspected any attempt at long-range radio communication was a waste of time at the moment.

"What are we doing with them?" New Boy asked, nodding towards Colstein and Harris.

"Keep an eye on them out here until we know the situation inside."

New Boy nodded and shifted both the civilians to one side as the wheel on the hatch started to turn, his G3 at the ready. Princess and Gulag raised their guns as the hatch opened. A frightened-looking man in a thick jumper looked up at them.

"Move back," Vadim told him. He hadn't brought the shotgun up to his shoulder, although it was now reloaded, and Harris had given him spare ammunition. The man backed away, his hands up, and Vadim stepped over the lip of the hatch.

A corridor stretched out in front of him, lined with cabins on either side. Crew quarters, at a guess. It was packed with people, spilling out of the cabins. They weren't all crew. There were two men waiting for them: an older man, big but running to fat, and a youth in oil-stained overalls, thin, with a pockmarked face. Both of them were pointing G3s at Vadim. That was less a problem than how nervous they looked. Nervous people and guns were a poor mixture. The kid was practically shaking.

"You need to lower your weapons before you're killed," Vadim told them, deciding directness was the way forward. He didn't like how their fingers were curled around the triggers. He stepped into the corridor proper. To his left were metal steps, both up and down. He moved towards the armed crew members, trying to look as nonthreatening as possible for a walking corpse bristling with weapons.

Then Gulag stepped in behind him, and the older one panicked. The sound of the G3 in the cramped corridor was deafening. Vadim felt the bullet pass close by him and heard a grunt from Gulag. Another gunshot from behind him, the bullet passing close by on the other side. He went deaf in one ear. The young man's head snapped backwards, spraying the wall behind him as his legs buckled.

"No!" Vadim shouted, interposing himself between Princess, who'd just killed the mechanic, and the sailor who'd just shot Gulag. He grabbed the barrel of the man's G3 and pushed it up, his ears ringing, as it fired again. He slammed his elbow into the man's face, breaking his nose, and wrenched the rifle free of his grip. Then he heard the screams.

"I'm going to fucking kill him!"

Vadim turned to face Gulag, who was missing most of his left ear. Vadim got in his way and shoved the G3 into his hands.

"Stand there and shut up!" Vadim said. Gulag's eyes went wide. There was madness in them, and Vadim had no time to deal with it; if Gulag pushed now, he would put a bullet in his head.

The Muscovite managed to master himself, and Vadim took one of the biggest risks of his career and turned his back on him. The sailor who'd shot Gulag was on his knees.

"I'm sorry, I'm sorry, I'm sorry..." he muttered, rocking back and forwards. Vadim levelled the shotgun at his head.

"The wounded! Where?" he snapped. The man had wet himself. Vadim knew just how much of a monster he must appear to these people. *How much of a monster you are.* He shook his head; the thought had come unbidden.

He was suddenly aware of the life all around him. The smell of their meat suffused the corridor. Shaking, the shooter pointed at the closest cabin. Vadim was salivating as he followed the direction. It felt like he was wading through noise. Someone got in his way; he swung the butt of the shotgun into their face and they were gone.

There were two wounded in the room, in bunks. Both men. The one on the bottom bunk was trying to push a screaming woman and child away. They were throwing themselves over him, pleading with Vadim. He could see their mouths moving, but he couldn't make sense of their words through the roaring in his ears. They were dragged out of the way.

The man looked up at him, his face a mask of terror. Then the face was gone.

Vadim tried not to open his mouth as the blood spattered him. He stared down at the ruin of the man's head, wanting to sink his mouth into it. He didn't even notice the body on the top bunk sit up. The blast of the G3 in the close quarters of the cabin brought him suddenly back to his senses, as the zombie in the top bunk collapsed back onto a pillow.

Vadim turned. Gulag stood in the cabin's doorway, lowering his G3. Suddenly Vadim had to get out of this blood-stinking cabin. He pushed past Gulag and made it out into the ash-filled humid night.

CHAPTER ELEVEN

0146, 17th November 1987
Upper East River, New York City

HAD VADIM STILL been alive, he would be taking deep breaths, trying to calm himself, trying to get rid of the roaring in his head. Instead he was just staring at the riverside. He could see fires in Manhattan now, some of them up high, skyscrapers burning like candles. He heard distant gunfire; there were still people living in the city, fighting. He wasn't sure whether he wished them well or just wanted it to be over for them quickly. A wide road ran down the side of the river, jammed with abandoned cars. He could see figures running over the tops of the cars, silent: the dead. The plague was spreading as fast as the tireless could run.

"Boss... Vadim?" New Boy asked from the doorway to the bridge castle behind him. *Of course it had to be New Boy*, he thought. *One of the living ones*. He could smell the scout's life from where he stood. He wanted to take it, steal it, consume it, hope that it would satisfy the hunger he felt, even just for a moment or two. "Are you okay?"

"Get away from me!" Vadim snapped. His voice carried on the humid night air, flakes of ash still falling from the sky. His voice didn't sound right, even to himself. Some instinct, honed by years of healthy combat paranoia, told him that he was being watched. He looked up to see the Fräulein on the edge of the bridge castle five decks above, looking down at him. He turned back to the city, gripping the rail, squeezing his eyes shut so he didn't have to look at the destruction he'd wrought on this city. It wasn't far enough. Vadim couldn't be around the living. Maybe when he was calm, but not like this. *Stop making excuses! Are you in control of yourself or not?* He turned back to New Boy.

"Let's go and see the captain," he said.

THE BRIDGE CASTLE was also the crew quarters: it was filled with people, their fear – of Vadim's appearance, his squad and the situation – a palpable reek in the air. He wasn't sure how many, but he figured at least a hundred, possibly twice that number. It was the still-terrified first mate, Gerhardt Colstein, who led Vadim and New Boy up the metal stairs. They passed through four decks of cabins, a mess area, bathroom facilities – heads, as Vadim was sure nautical types called them – and the larger staterooms for the officers. Judging by the sound of clanking machinery echoing up the stairwell, the stairs also led down to the engine room.

The bridge was on the fifth deck of the castle, surrounded by glass on three sides, backed by the smoke stack, with a catwalk running around the outside of it. Two officers sat in comfortable-looking chairs in front of a number of screens and instruments. Another sailor was scanning the surrounding area with binoculars, and two more were poring over paper charts spread over a high table.

The older of the two men at the map table was probably of an age with Vadim, maybe a little older; he had weathered skin, and a thick but well-kept silver beard with a few streaks of black still in it. He was a little fleshy, but looked in reasonable shape for his age. He glanced at Vadim with dark eyes and then went back to concentrating on the charts. Vadim was pretty sure that this was the captain. He looked less afraid of having well-armed commandos on his bridge than irritated.

"I am Captain Scorlenski of the…" Vadim stopped. "My name is Vadim, and I am afraid that we are in command of your –"

"Captain Scorlenski." The captain spoke with a German accent. "Rest assured that I appreciate the realities of the situation, but, gunfights notwithstanding, we are currently charting a navigable but unfamiliar and unforgiving passage along this strait using charts that I suspect are out of date. That is going to take all my concentration, and that of my bridge crew, for the time being. So unless you have something particularly pertinent to keeping this ship from running aground, I'm afraid that your threats, your establishment of dominance and the general pushing us around with guns may have to wait until we reach Long Island Sound."

New Boy glanced at Vadim, clearly worried about his response. Vadim chuckled and looked out the window. He could see Mongol patrolling the top of the containers. He didn't like how exposed his medic was. He glanced at the fore crane. He couldn't see Skull, but he hadn't expected to.

"And you are?" Vadim asked. The ship's captain looked up from his charts again, irritated.

"I am Heinrich Schiller, captain of the *Dietrich*, and I am of an age where I have seen bully boys with guns before." He narrowed his eyes as he studied Vadim's appearance. "Have you brought some disease onto my ship?" he demanded.

"I don't want to kill any more of your crew," Vadim said, ignoring the question.

"I will order them to cooperate and not to resist your act of piracy. Now please, get off my bridge and let us do our job."

Vadim didn't move. "I need some of your crew."

"As I explained, my crew are busy."

"A number of the walking dead made it on to your vessel. We think we've dealt with them, but we need to search every inch of it, and for that we need people who know the ship. That is assuming you don't want the virus loose on board."

Schiller stared at him for a moment before turning to Colstein and speaking a few words in German. The first mate nodded.

"Herr Colstein will see to your requirements." Schiller went back to the charts. Vadim couldn't shake the feeling that he'd been dismissed.

VADIM HAD TO force himself not to hurry away from the stink of frightened refugees in the crowded corridors of the ship's crew quarters. When he made it back out into the night air, a breeze was freshening up the air, blowing around the ash, making it feel a bit less like a sweaty summer's day and more like November. *And hopefully blowing the fallout west, away from us,* Vadim thought. Though that was more of an issue for New Boy and Princess than it was for him.

He heard gunfire echoing out across the river, and crossed the deck.

The river had opened up a little. He could see an airport on what had been the Brooklyn side of the river. It looked as though it had been built on reclaimed land. There were still lights on in the airport buildings, but he was too far away to make out much detail. He could, however, see a passenger jet taxiing to the end of the runway. Several hundred people were sprinting towards the aircraft as it started down the runway. At first Vadim thought all the running figures were zombies, chasing the living in the plane, but then he saw some of them being taken down. The mindless dead, feeding on their prey. The roar of jet engines filled the night and Vadim willed the plane to make it, but as it clawed its way into the air, he wondered if they were just putting off the inevitable.

He heard gunfire again and turned his attention to the large island to port. It looked like a prison. People were firing from the towers at the hordes gathered outside the walls. In a situation like this a prison was as good a defensive position as a castle, at least until your supplies ran out. He turned away and called the others to him.

SKULL WAS NOW up on top of the bridge castle, which gave him the best command of the entire ship. They had turned east, though both sides of the now much broader river were still very built up, and still dark. There was another bridge ahead of them, and beyond that, what looked like more rural areas.

The rest of the squad had assembled just outside the starboard hatch to the bridge castle. First Mate Colstein and three other anxious-looking crewmembers were also present. Gulag was sitting on an equipment locker whilst Mongol cleaned and sewed up the ragged mess that was the Muscovite's left ear. There was little blood coming from the wound.

"Princess, New Boy, you stay here and keep an eye on the passengers, secure any other weapons, okay." Gulag and the Fräulein had the other two G3s they had taken from the crewmembers. "Don't antagonise any of them – they're just civilians – but if they act up, take whatever actions you deem necessary." There was a reason he wasn't asking Gulag to do this; in fact, he didn't want any of the dead anywhere near the refugees, if he could help it. New Boy and Princess nodded. He turned to the others and pointed at Colstein. "We're going to search the ship from top to bottom. We're looking for zombies. We find them, kill them, throw them overboard."

"I just need to find the guy who shot me first," Gulag told him. Vadim withheld a sigh.

"Just leave him alone," Vadim told him.

Gulag frowned. "It wasn't your fucking ear he shot off! In fact, what were you doing, getting in the way of Princess's shot?" he demanded.

It was a good question. "There was no need for him to die," was the best Vadim could manage. "He's a civilian."

"He's an enemy combatant with a gun," Gulag spat. "So I'm going to fucking kill him, and then get on with my day." He turned away from Vadim and reached for the hatch.

"You're going to do what I tell you to, do you understand, Gulag?" Vadim said. It was extremely rare that ever had to drive home an order like this. To his mind, it was a failure of leadership. This wasn't a conscript motor rifle regiment, after all.

Gulag stopped, and the rest of the squad shifted uncomfortably. The gangster spun back to face Vadim.

"Or what, Infant?" Gulag demanded. He turned to the rest of the squad. "Why are we still listening to him? What has he ever got us, but dead?" Then to Vadim again: "I mean, aren't you supposed to be second-in-command of a whole company? Where are they, old man?" He leaned in close. "They're all fucking dead! *We're* fucking *dead!*" Out of the corner of his eye, Vadim could see *Dietrich*'s crewmen flinch. Gulag pointed at Princess and New Boy. "Two people. Two, out of an entire company. I don't think we're taking orders anymore. So I'm going to find that fat German fuck, and kill him. If you're lucky, I won't eat him, *do you understand?*" Gulag turned away from him.

"You're going to follow my order, Gulag," Vadim told him as the Muscovite reached for the hatch.

Gulag swung round again. "You've got nothing!" he howled.

"How far do you want to take this?" Vadim asked.

"That it?" he asked. He nodded towards the bridge castle. "One of them over one of us?"

"He doesn't need to die."

"He's just meat! They're all *meat* now!" Gulag shouted. New Boy shifted uncomfortably, and Princess moved to better bring her weapon to bear.

"That's enough, Gulag," the Fräulein said. "You have your orders."

"Why don't you just crawl up his arse?" Gulag asked her, but didn't take his eyes off the captain. Vadim held his stare.

"You're right," Mongol told his friend. "The captain's led us into the mincer time and time again, and everyone's dead, but I think if it hadn't been for him, it would have happened a lot quicker."

"And he gave us the opportunity to defect," New Boy pointed out.

Gulag turned on him. "Who gave you permission to speak? Think you'd be strong enough to come back from the dead, boy?"

"You keep threatening me and one day I'll have to take you seriously," New Boy said. Gulag opened his mouth to retort.

"Gulag, New Boy's all right," Mongol told him

The Fräulein caught Vadim's eye and shook her head. This wasn't good

"I am sick of your whining," Princess said quietly. Suddenly it went very quiet. Gulag's face was contorting. Perhaps it was the sum affect of all his injuries, but the rage made him look more than ever like a monster. Vadim's hand was on the butt of the revolver he'd taken from the police officer. The others were getting ready to intervene. Vadim was sure that if Gulag made a move, Princess was going to kill him.

"Yeah, but you're still alive, aren't you, *bitch!*" he spat. Princess didn't say anything. She just looked at him with calm, cold eyes.

"Gulag!" The voice came from above. They all looked up. Skull stood on the edge of the bridge castle's roof, .303 in hand, looking down at them. The silence stretched out. Neither Gulag nor Skull said anything.

"Okay, that's enough," the Fräulein finally snapped, breaking the silence. "We have things to do."

Gulag turned to her, his grin rendered monstrous by his wounds.

"Sure, Fräulein," he said.

"Gulag," Vadim said. "Nothing happens to your guide, understand me?"

Gulag crossed the distance to Colstein and laid his hand on the trembling first mate's shoulder.

"Sure, Infant, I'm not even hungry anyway." Colstein blanched and wobbled a little, as if his knees had gone weak, but he managed to hold it together. It was a lie, of course; if Gulag felt anything like Vadim did, he was hungry all the time. "Lead the way," he told Colstein, and the pair headed towards the containers. Mongol took his guide and made for the starboard side of the ship. New Boy turned to Princess.

"Go on," she told him. "I'll catch up with you." The scout opened the hatch and went into the bridge castle. Princess looked to the Fräulein, but it didn't look like the big East German sergeant was going anywhere.

"I messed up, boss," she told Vadim. He was hoping she didn't mean by standing up to Gulag. "The wounded that got inside: they came past me, I didn't check. No excuses, it was my fault." Vadim just nodded. She was making mistakes because she was tired. *She's tired because she's still alive*, Vadim thought. He was worn out, mentally, but not physically tired. But even by Afghanistan standards, it had been a busy few hours.

"Okay," Vadim said. "We're going to do this sweep and see about rest." There was no need to say anything else. Princess knew what she had done, and would take the steps to remedy it. She would be a lot angrier with herself than anyone else was. She nodded and followed after New Boy. Vadim turned to the Fräulein.

"Are you still running this squad?" the Fräulein demanded. Vadim felt like he'd been slapped.

"Did you not just see..."

"I watched you and Gulag measure your dicks, but seems to me Skull's is the biggest."

"Are you remembering who's the sergeant and who's the captain here?"

"Do you?" the Fräulein demanded. She leaned in towards him. "I know what's happened is bad, but if we're doing this – if we're still a squad, a family – then you need to be back in charge. Gulag's always been an insubordinate arsehole, but he spoke to you like that because you're just going through the motions. That stunt you pulled with the National Guardsmen... who did you think you were, Clint Wayne or something?"

"It's Clint Eastwood," he told her, smiling. His smile wasn't returned.

"You looked like you were trying to get yourself killed," she told him, and his smile disappeared. "And you know what? Gulag was right. I talked to Tas, you walked right into her field of fire."

"He didn't need to die," Vadim told her. "You weren't there."

"They pull a gun on us, they die," she said, glancing back at the two increasingly nervous-looking crew. "The rules of engagement. We start second guessing ourselves and we hesitate; and then we die..."

"We *are* dead, and we've done a lot of harm. And we'll do more." Now Vadim looked at the sailors. He blanched. "I have no more stomach for killing civilians. We've done enough of that." He turned back to her. Her expression had softened.

"Vadim, I'll back you to the hilt, but you have to prioritise. What's done is done."

"Keep Tasiya and Orlov alive, keep the civilians on this ship safe..." he started, surprised at how important it suddenly was to him.

"That's guilt talking," she told him.

"Can we not do something right for once?" he asked her.

"There *is* no safe," she told him.

"Then we do what we can!" Both the waiting sailors jumped at his suddenly raised voice. He pointed back towards the city, towards the glow of New Jersey burning. "And we find the architects of this and remove them from humanity."

"What about the rest of us?"

"We're already dead," he repeated. The Fräulein just watched him warily. "Can you accept that, Liesl?" She considered for a few moments, but finally nodded. She snapped something in German at the crewmember waiting for her, and both of them disappeared into the bridge castle. There was no denying it, he reflected: his masters may have been deranged psychopaths, in the end, but life was much easier when someone told you what to do.

It was clear they were no longer in the river. The water had grown rougher, and they had picked up considerable speed. The banks of the estuary were more rural, though Vadim could still see the odd town with its own electricity. No fires or gunshots in evidence. He guessed the dead hadn't got that far yet.

As he climbed the steps up to the bridge, he wondered if they needed to worry about the US Navy. The Russian submarine wolfpacks would have concentrated on hunting NATO subs rather than surface fleets. The ballistic missile launching submarines were, after all, the biggest threat. The big naval bases would have been targets for nuclear weapons, as would carrier groups. The American navy probably wouldn't be too interested in a ship like the *Dietrich* fleeing the country. He guessed what remained of them would be too busy with humanitarian aid.

"Captain Schiller," Vadim said, as he walked onto the bridge. The captain sat in one of the chairs facing the instruments. He looked tired.

He spun the chair round to face Vadim.

"Captain Scorlenski," he said. He *sounded* tired, as well. The reactions of the rest of the bridge crew ran from nervous disgust to borderline terror, judging by their expressions. Schiller, despite the obvious fatigue, remained impassive.

"I trust you understand what happens if you call for help, captain?" Vadim asked. Schiller sighed.

"I suspect the coast guard and the navy have more important matters to deal with at the moment, and besides" – he nodded towards the radio – "we can't raise anyone long range at the moment; too much interference. I can only assume it is some side effect of the nuclear weapons. Perhaps it is a side effect of the gates of Hell opening." There was a collective held breath on the bridge. Vadim wasn't sure whether it was supposed to have been a joke or not. He'd met religious people before; he didn't understand them, but it could provide them with a great deal of strength. It could also make them crazy. But he understood why people would see the current circumstances from a religious perspective. Most religions seemed to have their end-time myths.

Captain Schiller stood up. "Well, I suppose, since you've gone to all the effort of hijacking my ship, I should at least pay you the courtesy of a conversation." He exchanged a few words in German with one of the bridge crew and walked past Vadim for the stairs.

SCHILLER POURED HIMSELF a very large glass of brandy and offered Vadim one. The other captain was tempted, but had no idea what it would do to him in his current state. He suspected it would just be a waste. He shook his head.

Schiller's cabin was bare, but for a picture Vadim took to be of the captain's family. There was a woman of an age with the captain, and two younger families with five children between them: presumably the captain's children, their spouses and grandchildren. There was also a crucifix on the wall and a bookcase, mostly nautical texts or biographies. The captain sat on a wooden swivel chair at a narrow desk.

Vadim found himself looking at the cross.

"I wasn't being serious about Hell, in case you were wondering," Schiller said. "I suspect that whatever made people crazy is just another technological horror, like the nuclear weapons. We are more than capable of making our own hell."

Vadim turned to face the captain.

"I am dead, and so are four of my squad. You need to come to terms with that," he told him. "Whether it's supernatural, or science –"

"I thought Communists do not acknowledge the supernatural?" Schiller asked. Vadim didn't answer. "What do you want, captain? I am assuming you want us to take you somewhere."

"The Baltic –" Vadim started but Schiller was already shaking his head.

"We're a feeder ship, we don't have the fuel."

"Captain, if you're lying..."

"Enough," Schiller said, and leaned forward. "I will deal honestly and fairly with you at all times, because my paramount interest is the safety of my crew and my passengers, and I don't want you threatening either of them."

For what it was worth, Vadim believed him. He put the police shotgun down on the bunk, then the revolver, which was digging into his stomach. He unslung the AK-74 and laid that down on the bunk as well. The captain watched with something approaching amusement.

"Are you sure you don't need any more guns?" he asked.

"We had to keep taking them from your crew. *Are* there any more?" Vadim asked as he sat on the edge of the bed. Then the fatigue really hit him. He wondered if he could still sleep. The more he thought of sleep, however, the more it scared him. It felt like it would be a loss of control, like he would wake up one of the mindless dead.

"We have six rifles in total, standard ship's complement. I have no idea if the passengers are armed or not."

"Where can you get to, with the fuel you have?"

"Most of the people we took on are American. I think we should make for one of the ports further north, or perhaps even Canada. Are you at war with Canada?"

Vadim nodded; he assumed that they were at war with all of NATO and Iran, at the very least.

"America is gone," Vadim told him. "The entire continent."

Schiller chuckled. "My countrymen learned some forty years ago not to underestimate the Americans."

"This attack was part of a coordinated strategy. The release of the... chemical weapon in cities, nuclear weapons for infrastructure. Create chaos, and then remove any chance of a coordinated response to it. The continent will be a wasteland for however long it takes the corpses to rot. You take those people back to America and you guarantee their deaths."

Schiller was staring at Vadim, open disgust on his face. "I trust you know that's monstrous," he finally managed.

"Even by German standards," Vadim told him. "Fuel?"

"Greenland," Schiller suggested, clearly trying to suppress his anger.

"Europe," Vadim insisted.

"Spain, Portugal..."

"Too far south."

"Ireland, maybe the UK."

"Britain," Vadim said, nodding. He was sure the USSR would have invaded the island nation. They wouldn't have made the same mistakes the Germans made during the last war, allowing what amounted to a huge staging post to go unconquered that close to Europe. "Supplies?"

"Surprisingly, we have enough food. We were shipping beef up from Galveston. We also have several containers of tinned fruit. Potable water will be the issue."

"How many of the containers are refrigerated?" Vadim asked.

"Just over a hundred, I believe."

"We can scrape the ice out, melt it."

"It will be filthy."

"We can show you how to purify it."

"And when we get to Britain, then what?" Schiller asked. Vadim's smile was without humour.

"Then you all learn to become good communists."

"And live in a socialist utopia? I'll leave it to you to break this to our American passengers." It wasn't a conversation that Vadim was looking forward to.

"What happened?" Vadim asked, after a few moments of silence.

"You mean after your despicable attack?" Schiller asked. He took a sip of his brandy. It looked as though he was trying to wash a bad taste out of his mouth. "We saw the flash. A wall of flame. I can only imagine the Upper Bay and the Hudson served as a firebreak, though it sent banks of scalding steam across the water. The pressure wave almost capsized us."

"The people?" Vadim asked quietly.

"There was anarchy. Many people in Red Hook made for the docks. We were trying to find out what was happening when the... well, the things like *you* attacked the crowds. We took as many on board as we could."

Vadim looked down and nodded.

CHAPTER TWELVE

1142 Coordinated Universal Time (UTC) -4, 17th November 1987
The *Dietrich*, North-West Atlantic

WEAPONS HAD BEEN collected. Princess and New Boy had been installed in the crew quarters, given the smallest berth to themselves. After consultation with Captain Schiller, Vadim and the dead Spetsnaz had taken up quarters in a half-empty container towards the bow of the ship, much to Gulag's vocal disgust. Vadim, however, wanted them as far away as possible from the living passengers and crew. It was cold, but they didn't really feel that, and Mongol was of the opinion the cold would slow down the rot as their bodies started to putrefy.

They had all gone through pallor mortis, becoming pale and drawn. Algor mortis also: Mongol had checked their body temperatures and they appeared to match the ambient temperature. Rigor mortis, the stiffness of the limbs, fortunately did not seem to affect them. Vadim had, however, noticed that much of his lower body was covered in patches of purple and red, as the blood started to settle. The agent that they had been infected with seemed to have slowed down the stages of death a little, but decomposition seemed inevitable.

He was making his way aft past the containers towards the bridge castle, accompanied by the Fräulein, for a task that he wasn't looking forward to. He'd managed some rest and even drifted off to a fitful sleep full of red dreams.

He'd been jerked awake by the motion of the ship. There had been a moment's disorientation, and then he remembered what he had become and what he'd done. At least sleep hadn't caused him to give into the mindless hunger, however.

Out in the Atlantic, the weather was much worse: gone was the radioactive humidity of New York, to be replaced with driving Arctic winds and rough seas. The sun hadn't come up, either. The thousands of tonnes of dirt, dust and ash thrown up into the sky by the nuclear detonations were blocking it out. If he concentrated, he could just about make out a dull glow above the solid, dirty cloud cover. Then it had started to snow. The snow was as black as the ash had been.

Vadim and the Fräulein entered the bridge castle. It smelled of vomit, brought on by seasickness, and food odours from the overworked galley as it tried to cope with all the new passengers. Vadim was thankful that the stench made him considerably less interested in feeding on any of them. People were sleeping in the corridors, the crew having done the best they could to supply them with blankets, or at least some kind of cover, and something soft to lie on. The refugees stared at Vadim and his second-in-command with expressions ranging from naked terror to borderline fury. He couldn't blame them.

He mounted the stairs to the second level, where more refugees lying in the corridor, struggling with the motion of the ship, had to move out of their way. He hammered his fist against the door of the cabin that Princess and New Boy had been assigned, and then opened the door. They were both in there, sound asleep.

"Wake up," Vadim called. Tired eyes opened, hands moved towards convenient weapons.

"You need to lock this door," the Fräulein told them. She didn't need to say it was in case the refugees turned on them. The wooden door wouldn't stop them, but it might give them enough time to grab weapons.

"I thought I had," a sleepy New Boy said.

"Can you speak English?" Vadim asked him. He knew Princess could, from her time on the VIP squad, but of the two of them, New Boy was more diplomatic. Princess liked to keep communication to a bare minimum, where possible.

"Not well, boss," he said shaking his head.

"You'd better not just be wanting extra time in bed," the Fräulein snapped.

"I swear," he told her.

"Princess, get up, get dressed, you're coming with us. Sidearm only, we don't want to scare them any more than we already have," Vadim told her. He and the Fräulein were only carrying their Stechkins and knives. Princess grumbled, glared at New Boy and then started to drag her clothes on.

VADIM AND THE Fräulein stood at the front of the room. A bored, sleepy-looking Princess sat on a table pushed against the wall in the cramped mess area. Captain Schiller was there, along with a crew member that Vadim didn't recognise. The *Dietrich* had been docked at Red Hook in Brooklyn, and the majority of the refugees came from there. There was no place on the ship large enough for them to assemble, so Schiller had asked them to choose representatives to speak with the Spetsnaz commandos on their behalf. Vadim wasn't surprised to see Officer Harris among them.

"My name is Captain Scorlenski –" he managed to begin.

"We are citizens of the United States of America, you have no right to hold us against our will." The speaker was a slightly fleshy man in a rumpled, oversized suit, with glasses and an odd, floppy haircut.

"Commie bastard," added a large, red-faced man dressed in rugged clothes and boots. Possibly a dock worker, Vadim decided.

"Look that's not going to help –" Officer Harris started.

"Yeah? You already gave up your weapon," the red-faced dockworker said. "What are you, a collaborator or something?"

"Fred, let them talk." This from a Hispanic woman, in her late twenties or possibly early thirties, dark-haired, with an accent so thick Vadim struggled to make out what she was saying. A young girl of about seven or eight, presumably her daughter, clung desperately to her.

"Why don't you leave this to the menfolk, Maria?" Fred suggested. "Maybe do something useful, like go and help out in the kitchen?" Princess laughed and earned a glare from Fred, which she gave no indication of having noticed.

"You need to turn this ship –" the man in the suit started.

"Shut up!" the Fräulein snapped, in her drill-sergeant voice. Even Vadim was tempted to obey it. The little girl jumped and started to cry. Maria tried to comfort her.

"Thank you," Vadim said. "I'm afraid there are some undeniable realities to your situation here. America has been subject to both a nuclear and chemical attack. To all intents and purposes it has been rendered uninhabitable. Even if the ship had the fuel to take you back and still carry us to our destination, it would be kinder for us to just put a bullet in your head and throw you overboard. Kinder to you and easier for us."

"You bastards!" Fred shouted.

"If he does that once more, I'm shooting him," Princess said in Russian.

"What did she say?" Fred demanded.

"Why don't you ask her?" the Fräulein suggested, not bothering to hide her irritation.

"Have you radioed the navy, the coast guard?" the man in the suit asked Schiller.

"This is Eric," Schiller gestured to the other crewmember, a thin, nervous-looking man, although everyone looked nervous at the moment.

"Short-range radio communication is problematic due to the effects of" – he swallowed – "nuclear detonations. Currently long-range communication is impossible."

"If you attract the attention of the navy, then we will have to fight, and nobody wants that," Vadim pointed out.

"So we're a human shield, then?" the man in the suit asked.

"That's what I figured," Fred snorted. "These guys are pussies, not capable of a stand-up fight. They just wanna pick on civilians."

"I suspect that the navy and the coast guard will have more pressing issues to attend to," Schiller interjected, possibly to try and forestall a confrontation.

"You are responsible for this?" the man in the suit demanded of Vadim.

"We took part in the attack, yes," Vadim told him. Maria looked up from comforting her child. He had their attention now.

"You monsters," the man in the suit said. Vadim said nothing.

"We're going to nuke you back to the Stone Age," Fred told them.

"There's no 'we,' to do the nuking," Vadim explained.

"You won't get away with this," the man in the suit said.

"Obviously we didn't," the Fräulein muttered.

"Why?" Officer Harris asked his voice trembling.

"I could speculate, but we're not part of the decision-making process, as I'm sure you can imagine."

"Fucking communists!" Fred spat.

"So now what?" Harris asked. "You taking us to Russia so we can all become good Marxists?"

"I can assure you that we're not going to Russia," Schiller told them. "We don't have the fuel."

"The UK," Vadim told them.

"England?" the man in the suit demanded. "My family and I aren't going to England, that's ridiculous. Canada, take us to Canada, they'll have an embassy. We can find out the truth of all your commie terrorist propaganda!"

Vadim turned to look at the man. "What is your name?"

"Why do you want to know?" he asked suspiciously.

"Tell him your fucking name!" Princess snapped, losing her patience and making him jump.

"Carlsson, Davis Carlsson," he told her.

"Well, Mr Carlsson," Vadim began. "The only question you need to ask yourself is whether or not you wish to survive. It's that simple."

"Hey," Fred said. Vadim ignored him. "Hey, I'm talking to you!" Vadim looked up. "When the US military catches up with you, they're going to hang you high, you understand me."

Vadim crossed to the big man. Part muscle, part fat. Vadim knew the type, using his size and strength to intimidate and bully. The longshoreman blanched at his approach, going almost as pale as Vadim was himself.

"Would you like to check my pulse?" Vadim asked quietly.

"What are you going to do with us?" Maria asked. Vadim looked over at her, and Fred backed away.

"We have no interest in you," Vadim told her. "We wish you no ill."

"Yeah?" Fred demanded. "Tell that to Will Foster, and that other poor kid."

"Not to mention the two crew members they killed," Carlsson added. Vadim glanced at Schiller, but he remained impassive.

"The crew deaths were unfortunate –" Vadim said.

"And in self-defence," the Fräulein added.

"Foster?" Vadim asked.

"The two wounded that you killed in cold blood," Maria told them.

"They were wounded?" Princess asked. Nobody answered. The sniper chuckled.

"They were infected..." Vadim started.

"With the same thing you have?" Maria asked. Her little girl was staring at Vadim.

"Yes," Vadim admitted.

"Gonna do us all a favour and kill yourself?" Fred demanded.

"Give it a break, Leary," Harris told the longshoreman. Vadim figured they had history.

"Fuck yourself, collaborator," Leary snapped. Vadim tensed, ready to intervene, but the police officer just sighed.

"I'm not collaborating, I'm listening," Harris said. "Y'know, so I can learn stuff."

"Can I shoot the big loud man?" Princess asked in Russian.

"No," Vadim told her.

"What did she say?" Leary demanded. "Why doesn't she speak American?"

"Because there's no such language," Vadim pointed out. "And she asked if she could shoot you."

"What did you say?" Leary sounded a little worried.

"That I hadn't decided yet," he said, and then to Maria: "As far as we're concerned, you just happen to be on the same ship as us. We'll even help you survive. But if anyone acts against us, they will die. If all of you act against us, then you all die."

"Has England been occupied?" Carlsson asked.

"My honest answer is I don't know," Vadim told him.

"And if you were to guess?" Officer Harris asked.

"Probably."

"So you're going to have us enslaved by your commie masters, then," Leary spat.

"I don't know what you think communism is about..." Vadim started.

"What about the... disease. Is that in the UK?" Maria said.

"We don't think so," Vadim told her, thinking longingly about military life, where people just did what you told them without having to discuss it. Well, except for Gulag.

"Except you... we'll be bringing it," Maria said.

"We're not contagious," the Fräulein told her, though Vadim had no way to be sure it was true. From what he had seen and what Gulag had theorised after initial infection, the virus, or whatever it was, was transmitted by bite.

"That's it, isn't it!" Leary shouted, and Vadim sighed. "You're going to keep us alive to infect us and then release us on England!"

Princess was looking at him. He shook his head. "There would be much easier ways," he pointed out.

"We need to speak to people, okay?" Harris said. Vadim nodded. The officer cast a glance at Leary, trembling in impotent fear and rage, and then left. The others followed until finally only Maria and her daughter were left.

"Fred had family in Red Hook," Maria told him. Vadim nodded. She seemed to be deciding whether or not to say anything. "Gloria was with me in the office," she told him. "I couldn't get a babysitter. If she hadn't been with me, I wouldn't have gotten on the ship." She made for the door but stopped again. "Maybe the US military will catch up with you, or maybe things are as bad as you say; but one thing I do know. God will judge you."

"I'm afraid I don't believe in God," Vadim told her.

PRINCESS HEADED BACK to her room and Vadim exchanged a few words with Schiller before leaving with the Fräulein. As he made his way downstairs he heard more and more crying, presumably as word of the reality of their situation circulated. Tear-filled accusatory eyes watched them as they passed.

On the main deck level of the bridge tower, he saw Carlsson arguing with an angry-looking woman and a well-fed teenaged boy that Vadim took for his wife and son. A young girl probably a little bit older than Maria's daughter was looking on, tears in her eyes. As he watched, Mongol came in through the door on the port side, at the opposite end of the corridor from where Vadim stood. The girl turned at the sound of the door opening and let out a scream, and her mother swept her up into her arms.

Mongol squeezed by. Dead or not, he was visibly devastated at the child's response.

The big medic reached Vadim at the bottom of the stairs, glancing up at the Fräulein a few steps up from the captain.

"You okay?" Vadim wasn't sure what made him ask this. It seemed ridiculous, in the circumstances. Mongol glanced back at the family.

"We've done all sorts of bad things, I can't tell if it was for the right reason or not anymore." He turned back to Vadim. "But none of that mattered when I got back home. That" – he nodded back towards the Carlsson girl – "is how my nieces, my nephews, my younger cousins are going to look at me, if we ever make it back. That's assuming the shamans don't just have me killed out of hand." He pushed past Vadim and the Fräulein, heading up the stairs.

"Worried yet?" the Fräulein asked when she was sure the big medic was out of earshot.

"Proud of yourself?" a woman all but shrieked. Vadim looked back along the corridor to see Mrs Carlsson cradling her crying daughter and staring at him.

"This is a powder keg," the Fräulein said in Russian. Vadim turned to look up at her.

"Do you want to kill them all?" he asked.

She didn't answer.

"Give me an alternative."

"Gulag is supposed to be on patrol with Mongol," the Fräulein told him. Vadim just closed his eyes. It was a problem he was going to have to deal with sooner or later. For a moment he wondered why he couldn't have just died when the transit cop had shot him beneath Grand Central.

THE SEA HAD grown ever rougher and they had to cling to the rail on their way back along the main deck. White-capped waves broke across the ship, sluicing water all over the deck. They would have to be careful to protect their weapons from salt-water corrosion; Vadim wasn't sure how long their gun oil would last.

He was pleased to discover that, in his newfound condition, he no longer suffered from seasickness.

They could hear Gulag shouting before they reached the container.

"There is no God!" he screamed. Vadim and the Fräulein exchanged glances. At a guess, the Muscovite was trying to pick a fight with Skull. Vadim wasn't sure that anyone had ever done that before. The Fräulein hauled the door to the container open. Electric lights provided dim illumination, pallets kept them and their weapons off the wet floor. Their beds were made of packing material. Vadim had no idea where Skull had found the prayer mat. Gulag was standing over the sniper as he performed the *Zuhr* afternoon prayer. "You're a fool!"

"Gulag!" The Fräulein sounded genuinely angry. Gulag looked up at them both.

"What? Aren't we fucking communists?" He pointed at the ruins of his face. "I think we know for sure that God doesn't exist now."

Vadim was less sure of that. The virus may have been created as a weapon, but it made no sense in terms of what little he knew about biology. If ever there was proof of the supernatural, this horrible disease would seem to be it.

"Leave Skull alone," Vadim told him as he stepped into the container. Gulag pointed down at Skull as he bowed down, chanting the words of the prayer.

"Isn't that against army regulations?" Gulag demanded. Vadim marvelled that Skull could ignore all the shouting.

"Since when did you give a fuck about regulations?" the Fräulein demanded. "When did *any* of us, for that matter?"

Gulag screamed, startling Vadim, simply because it hadn't been what he expected. The Muscovite turned away and banged his arms against the side of the container.

"Does this not seem fucking mad to you?" he demanded. "I mean, now, in this situation?" Vadim and the Fräulein were staring at him.

"Skull's always prayed," Vadim finally managed.

"The world's ended," Gulag said much more quietly. He said it as though he were looking for understanding.

"So what do you want to do?" Vadim asked.

"Other than not attend to your duties and support your comrades?" the Fräulein muttered.

Gulag threw his hands up in the air. "Something," he managed and turned away, pacing like an animal in a cage. If Vadim didn't know better, he'd assume that Gulag had taken some kind of stimulant.

"We have a purpose," Vadim reminded him. Gulag swung round to face him again.

"*You* have a purpose!" he snapped.

"*We* have a purpose. The captain has said that you do not have stay with us if you do not wish to," the Fräulein reminded him through gritted teeth. She'd clearly had more than enough of Gulag.

The Muscovite looked affronted. "See that?" He pointed at her. "You accuse me of disloyalty – have I not been loyal ever since you found me in that pile of corpses, Vadim?"

"You have been loyal in your own insubordinate and deeply aggravating way," Vadim admitted.

"Exactly," Gulag said.

"So what is troubling you so much you feel the need to scream at Skull as he prays?" Vadim asked.

"What are we doing?" he asked.

"Could you be more specific?"

"With these people, on this boat? One of them *shot* me."

"We've all wanted to do that," the Fräulein pointed out.

"Think about what we've done to them! We're the architects of their misery. They'll turn on us, and the absolute best we can hope is that we waste a lot of ammunition on them. That's assuming they don't catch us with our guard down."

"For example, when we're supposed to be patrolling the ship?" the Fräulein asked.

Gulag ignored her and stared at Vadim, who was still trying to work out where the Muscovite had picked up a phrase like 'architects of their misery'.

"So you want to kill them all?" Vadim asked. It was a stupid question; of course he did.

"No," Gulag said. Vadim almost missed it over Skull's prayers.

"No?" Vadim asked, surprised.

"We need to feed on them," he told them. "For our own good."

They both stared at Gulag. Skull continued his devotions. Vadim was impressed that the Muscovite had somehow managed to find something worse to contemplate. They had done so many things in the service of their masters, even before the atrocity in New York, and now here was Gulag trying to outdo that. Vadim was tempted to deal with him now before he did something awful. He could, after all, do a lot of damage on his own.

"Our own good?" Vadim asked instead. It was difficult to get the words out of his suddenly very dry, dead throat. He felt the Fräulein tense next to him. Skull still seemed oblivious.

"We need the crew, I understand that. The rest of are just so much meat. We aren't *people* anymore! We're denying our own nature. Nothing good ever comes of that, it's moral cowardice."

Vadim laughed, and Gulag's face hardened. The Fräulein's hand inched towards her sidearm, and suddenly Vadim wished he'd taken one of the G3s with him to the meeting. He could see them leaning against the container. "We're something new," Gulag continued. "Something perfectly fitted for this world. You want to have revenge on those that have done this, and I understand that, but we could do whatever we want. We could carve out kingdoms in our own image."

"With you as the king?" Vadim asked. Gulag smiled and shook his head.

"Oh, I don't want the crown," he said. He pointed at Vadim.

Vadim started laughing. He was a little worried that he wouldn't stop. It was so absurd, the bloody imperial fantasises of a petty, violent thug. Revenge might not have been any better, but at least there was a sense of natural justice to it, in Vadim's mind.

"Don't laugh at me," Gulag said, which just made Vadim laugh harder. "*Don't laugh at me!*" he was screaming now. "We've burned villages! How is this different, except we won't be doing it for masters no better than the psychopaths who run the *Bratva*!"

"Has it occurred to you that if we feed, then we end up on a ship full of the mindless dead, which at the very least narrows our chances of keeping the crew alive?" the Fräulein asked, while Vadim managed to get himself under control. Gulag just glared at her.

Something occurred to Vadim. "Princess and New Boy?" he asked.

"We bite them," he said. "Princess is strong enough, she'll be one of us. New Boy is weak. I can crack open his skull with my *saperka* if you want."

At the mention of Princess, Vadim had felt the Fräulein stiffen next to him.

"So you've thought it all out, then?" she said with low menace.

"Do you know how I know Allah is real?" Skull asked from his knees. All three of them turned to look at the sniper as he stood up. "It is because I have become a creature of Shaitan, a *ghūl*. How can there be an adversary if there is no God?" He turned to Gulag. "To deny our base nature is not moral cowardice, it is far from weakness, it is what separates us from animals. We are at war between our savage selves and our higher selves. That is why I carry a Koran as well as a rifle. I hope that one day I may redeem myself to the point that I will be allowed back into His presence." Gulag opened his mouth to retort, but shrank back as Skull leaned towards him. "And if you attack one of us you attack all of us; even you, my friend." He straightened up and turned to Vadim. "With your permission, I'll go and find Mongol." Vadim nodded. Skull grabbed a G3 and made to leave the container, but paused. "I apologise if my praying bothered you, Gulag. I shall endeavour to do it out of your presence in future." He turned back to face the Muscovite. "If, however, that is not possible, do not ever try and disturb me again, do you understand?" Gulag stared at the sniper. Skull staggered to the rail of the violently pitching boat and started making his way aft.

"You want to go your own way when we get to Britain, you may do so," Vadim told the Muscovite. "Carve out your kingdom if you want. Start here and we'll ki – destroy you." He locked eyes with Gulag, and the other man broke contact first. Then he staggered out of the container and headed aft as well.

"He's going to do something bad, isn't he?" Vadim asked. The Fräulein nodded. The problem was he was still one of them until he wasn't.

"Or Skull is," the Fräulein said slowly.

Vadim turned to stare at her.

"He's changed. He scares me."

CHAPTER THIRTEEN

1400 UTC -2, 22nd November 1987
The *Dietrich*, North Atlantic

IT HAD BEEN six days since the end of the world.

The sky burned red. Vadim wasn't sure if it was the result of all the crap the nuclear detonations had thrown up into the atmosphere, the ionisation, something to do with radiation, or another atmospheric effect, but it wasn't the red of sunset. It looked deeply unnatural. The first time Vadim saw it, he'd wondered if he was just looking at everything through a filter of blood. Was he seeing the sky as the meat he craved so much?

It was still snowing black. It fell from the sky like ash, covering the ship. Vadim was heading aft past the containers, Mongol behind him. Two members of the squad were always on patrol, though it was busy work and they knew it. They also always made sure that someone was in the container to look after the weapons. The patrols were meant to keep the refugees cowed, but their greatest ally had been the rough crossing: most of the living had spent the previous five days hanging on to the ship for dear life and trying not to vomit on each other. It was difficult to stage a revolt when you were struggling to keep your meat and tinned fruit down.

Everyone was sick of meat and tinned fruit.

He had hoped that teaching them how to boil the impurities off the ice they had chipped out of the refrigerator containers would go some way towards improving relations; in retrospect, that had been naïve. He'd been instrumental in murdering their city and had helped kill their entire continent. It was difficult to make amends for that, even with clean water. His approach still silenced whispered conversations when he walked around the castle bridge.

They'd lost around twenty people. Some may have slipped on the icy decks and gone overboard, though he suspected most of them had been suicide. He wasn't sure how he felt about that. He despised suicide as weakness and cowardice except in the most extreme circumstances, but suspected this brave new world qualified. He quietly investigated where Gulag had been whenever people went missing. On the other hand, he'd overheard a number of the refugees talking of Britain as some sort of Promised Land.

He suspected that they were going to be disappointed as well.

For the most part, the refugees had come together and cooperated with each other and the crew of the ship, but some had behaved with surprising entitlement and selfishness. He had largely left it to the refugees to police themselves, only allowing his people to get involved if it was going to turn nasty. What surprised him most was how little their behaviour seemed to take in the actual circumstances. He smiled grimly as they kicked their way through the icy slush. He suspected that in the USSR, the most selfish ones would have ended up as senior party members. Arseholes were arseholes the world over.

Most of the refugees had been dressed warmly enough for a cold November in Manhattan. They were going to struggle if the temperature kept dropping the way it had, however. *That's not your problem,* he told himself. *They're on their own once you make Britain.*

Gulag had surprised Vadim and the Fräulein by not doing anything particularly unpleasant beyond goading some of the refugees; assuming he wasn't responsible for any of the disappearances. Of more worry was Skull. They had seen little of him over the past few days. He turned up for patrol, but he rarely spent time in the container, preferring the cab of the forward crane, where he'd made a sniper's nest. Vadim had been putting off speaking to him about that. Part of the point of them all staying in the container was so they could keep an eye on each other, make sure they didn't lose control of their appetites.

Vadim turned the wheel on the starboard hatch to the bridge castle.

Mongol watched on, his peeled and stitched mouth giving him a permanent, obscene smile, but it seemed more and more like the big medic was sinking into despondency. This was understandable; there was little keeping Vadim going beyond loyalty, and fantasies about wrapping his corpse hands around Premier Varishnikov's fleshy neck. Though deep down, he knew it was just that: a fantasy. The best he could hope for was that Varishnikov had died in a radioactive flash. If not, he would be buried deep in some luxurious bunker.

Vadim pulled the hatch open and stepped over the lip into a stinking miasma that even his dead nostrils couldn't ignore. The worsening stench of unwashed humanity, constant vomit and overused head facilities almost blunted his appetite.

Almost.

Part of the corridor had been cleared and the Carlsson girl – Vadim was pretty sure she was called Serafina – was trying to play marbles with Maria's daughter, Gloria, using ball bearings. Their mothers were standing a little further down the corridor, talking to each other. The girls looked up as Vadim and Mongol stepped in, closing the hatch behind them: Serafina blanched, but Gloria just watched them, expressionless. There was something about the child, Vadim decided. She had an old soul.

"Hello," Mongol said, leaning forward. Gloria still didn't move, but Serafina screamed, making her mother jump. The child scrambled away and wrapped herself around her mother's legs.

"What the hell do you think you're playing at?" Mrs Carlsson demanded. She was a handsome woman, Vadim thought, but the enforced voyage was not doing her any favours. Her features looked slack, there were bags under bloodshot eyes, and her clothes, which looked more suitable for a coffee morning than an ocean voyage, weren't holding up too well either.

"I'm sorry, we were just –" Vadim started. She spat in his face.

"Anna!" Maria gasped. She had scooped Gloria up. Vadim stared at Mrs Carlsson, more surprised than angry.

Maria tried to hustle the other woman away, but she continued glaring at Vadim. "Anna, this is no good, you have to come away." She succeeded in pushing Mrs Carlsson to the stairs on the port side of the bridge castle. When Mrs Carlsson had gone from view, Maria came back, making sure that she was between them and Gloria at all times.

"Thank you," Vadim said, wiping the spit off his face.

"Don't thank me, I'm not your friend. You killed everyone I ever knew, but you're not going to take my daughter –"

"I wouldn't –" Vadim started.

"You go near her and I will kill you. I don't care who or *what* you are, understand me?"

"We weren't –" Vadim started again, but she was walking away from him.

"I'm not a monster," Mongol said. He sounded unsure, pathetic. And he was wrong. Of course they were monsters.

Laughter from the starboard stairwell; it sounded like wet gravel shifting. Vadim turned to look at Gulag, sitting halfway up the stairs.

"That was beautiful," he said.

"What are you doing in here?" Vadim demanded. He was trying to keep the dead away from the living as much as possible. Gulag stood up and raised his hands in surrender, before coming down the stairs and leaving the bridge castle. Mongol was still staring after Mrs Carlsson.

VADIM HAD CLEANED the spit off his face in the bathroom and spent some time looking at his pale reflection in the mirror. There was little doubt he was a corpse now, just from the colouration. Some rigor seemed to be setting in; it wasn't affecting his movement, but he was sure his face was becoming more rigid.

After the patrol with a very quiet Mongol, he had left Gulag annoying the Fräulein in the container. He'd put off talking to Skull for too long.

Despite the gloves he'd taken from the camping store, and his own cold flesh, he still felt the cold of the ladder's icy rungs as he climbed up to the operator's cab on the forward crane. The higher he got, the more he felt the rocking of the ship. The still slightly choppy sea reflected the blood red sky, far above.

Skull didn't even look at him as he climbed into the cab. It was a bit cramped, but there was just about room for both of them. The sniper sat in the seat, the stock of his .303 resting on his thigh, pointing up, nearly touching the roof of the cab. He was scanning the horizon.

"A latter day crow's nest?" Vadim asked, resting his back against the windscreen. Skull chuckled. "It's like another planet. I keep on expecting to see some kind of exotic beast poke its head out of the water."

Skull didn't say anything. The silence stretched out enough to become uncomfortable.

"Skull, are you okay?"

Skull turned to look down at him. He looked different; beyond the obvious. Vadim was sure his eyes were darker, almost a black mass now. He didn't like the hint of a smile on the sniper's lips either.

"Should I be?" he asked.

"It's a stupid question, I know. I guess I mean something specific; something – I don't know – personal. You're spending a lot of time up here."

"Because I can't trust myself," Skull told him, his eyes back on the horizon. Somehow the red light seemed warm in here, despite the temperature.

"None of us can. That's why we're in the container. We can keep an eye on each other."

"I wonder," he said. "It didn't help us in Eugene's apartment. And I can't help but think that the mindless dead operate in packs. Perhaps we reinforce that kind of behaviour in each other."

Vadim gave this some thought. He had to admit that Skull had a point. He noticed a copy of the Koran atop the crane's controls. He picked it up.

"Does this help?" Vadim asked.

"It is providing me with guidance, much of which I choose to ignore" – he lifted his rifle – "but little comfort."

"Why no comfort?" he asked. Skull seemed to sag a little in the operator's seat.

"Because I think Gulag may be right. That *Yawmuddin*, the Day of Judgement, has come and gone and I was found unworthy because of my service to the infidels. Perhaps we are a part of this new world and we should do as Gulag suggests and embrace it, embrace our punishment."

"Infidels? You think we are 'infidels'?" Vadim asked. He was starting to get a little angry.

"No, I think you are like me: a tool, a weapon. But swords can cut their wielders as well."

Marx's teaching notwithstanding, Vadim's opinion was that other people's religious beliefs were none of his business. What he was uncomfortable with was how Skull's beliefs seemed to be influencing his interpretation of their predicament.

"I don't want you to turn fundamentalist on me," he told Skull.

Skull looked at him again. Vadim could not make out his expression. The sniper's now-pale skin caught the red light.

"Fundamentalist? I think part of the point of many religions is to be a better person in service to your god. It's sad how quickly that part seems to be forgotten."

Vadim wasn't sure he was getting the answers he wanted, or indeed *any* real answers.

"So how are you doing, up here on your own?" he finally asked.

"I still want to kill," Skull answered. He had gone back to looking out to sea. Suddenly Vadim had an image of Skull sighting his rifle on members of the crew, the refugees, even the squad.

"Us or them?" Vadim asked.

"Which would be better, do you think?"

"I think I may be getting sentimental in my old age," Vadim told him, "but I can't help but think that they might need us."

Skull gave this some thought.

"That's not sentimentality, my old friend. That's a guilty conscience."

ONLY THE FRÄULEIN was in the container when Vadim returned.

"Where's Gulag?" he asked. It was becoming a common refrain, though he had been better since their confrontation five days earlier. This was the first time since then that he hadn't shown up for duty. Vadim knew the Muscovite was bored – they all were – but it was no excuse.

"Last seen drinking with some of the refugees," the Fräulein said. She sounded less than pleased. Gulag was like a child pushing boundaries.

"Drinking? Can we even do that?" Vadim asked. They had taken no food or drink since they had changed... other than 'the' meat. The very idea of anything else repelled him. The others seemed to feel the same way. If their biology was effectively frozen, he couldn't see how alcohol would affect them. The Fräulein just shrugged.

"Where'd he get it from?" Vadim asked, and the Fräulein shrugged again. It was a stupid question. *Never underestimate the ability of a soldier, particularly a Russian one, to find alcohol*, he thought. "Who's he drinking with?"

"Some of the workers from the dock. The loudmouth from the meeting."

"Leary?" he asked, and the Fräulein nodded. Vadim shook his head. He couldn't see how Gulag could be drunk but he didn't relish the idea of dealing with him if he was. They would probably need to lock him up somewhere until he sobered up.

"Mongol?" Vadim asked.

"I don't know."

"You're supposed to be my –" he started.

"I was looking after the weapons," she said, testily.

"Okay," Vadim said. It wasn't, but she was right, the ordinance couldn't just be left hanging around. "I'll go and get Skull to look after the weapons, and we can go and find the others." He turned towards the door just as someone knocked on it. Vadim and the Fräulein looked at each other. Nobody ever really bothered them at this end of the ship. Vadim's hand was inching towards his Stechkin.

"I don't think they'd knock," the Fräulein said. She was right, though she'd still picked up one of the G3s. Vadim opened the container door, one hand on his sidearm. Harris stood out in the black snow, looking very cold.

"Officer Harris," Vadim said in English.

"Can I speak with you?" he asked. Vadim nodded and stepped outside. He didn't think that the policeman would want to be stuck inside the container with the hungry dead.

"I'll go and get Skull," the Fräulein told him in Russian. Vadim nodded and moved out of her way. Harris was silent until he was sure she was out of earshot.

"What can I do for you?" Vadim asked. Harris turned round to look at him. Unlike many of the refugees, he did a good job of hiding any feelings of disgust, anger or fear when speaking to the squad.

"I was getting some fresh air," he said. "It's getting a bit much in there at the moment. Though it's not much better out here. It's like a summer day in Manhattan, when the smog's heavy. It catches in your throat. Doesn't make much sense when the weather's this cold." The police officer sounded like he was talking for the sake of it.

"It's ash and dust in the atmosphere," Vadim told him. "Is this a social call, then?"

Harris didn't answer him.

"Are you afraid of something I might do, or of your fellow countrymen seeing you as a collaborator?"

"They asked me to come out here and speak to you," he said.

"I see," Vadim said. He heard the sounds of boots on cold metal, and frowned when he saw the Fräulein coming down the crane's ladder alone. Harris opened his mouth to say something, but Vadim held up a hand.

"Skull's gone," the Fräulein told him in Russian, glancing at the police officer. It was probably just poor timing, Vadim told himself, but he couldn't shake the feeling that something was going on. He wondered if Harris had been sent here to distract him.

"Gulag, the one with the tattoos –" Vadim started.

"The criminal?" Harris asked.

"Any idea where he is?"

"The last I saw of him, he was in the mess with Leary and some of the other longshoremen, drinking and making everybody uncomfortable," Harris told them. "Everything okay?" The young man sounded utterly guileless, but then, Eugene had taken them in as well.

"Find the others and bring them back here," Vadim told the Fräulein, again in Russian. "Tell Princess and New Boy they have the patrol. I'm sick of this."

"The black man?" the Fräulein asked, tilting her head at Harris.

"I'll deal with him," he said, "I think I'll be pretty safe."

"Discipline problems?" Harris asked, after the Fräulein had left them.

"What can I do for you, Officer Harris?"

"I understand there was something of a misunderstanding with Mrs Carlsson earlier today."

"If by misunderstanding you mean she spat in my face, then yes."

"Look, she didn't –" he started, but Vadim held his hand up.

"I understand her feelings. I've been spat on before, and worse."

"Her kids...?"

"I – *we* meant no harm, but I will order my people to stay away from them, even the living members of my squad." And then more softly: "I understand her concerns."

"Any children yourself?" he asked, and then winced as if he regretted it.

"No." Vadim said. "No family at all. Well, except them." He nodded towards the ship, meaning the squad. He wasn't sure why he'd said it.

Harris was regarding him thoughtfully. "Somebody hurt your family, didn't they?" he asked.

"How did you end up on board the *Dietrich*, officer?" Vadim asked, changing the subject. He had time until the Fräulein came back, after all, and he couldn't leave the weapons unattended.

Harris hesitated, as if deciding what to say.

"My partner," he finally said, his voice tight. "Gallagher, big Irish guy, so fat it took him about five minutes to get out of the patrol car. He drank all the time, even on duty, crooked as the day was long, racist as well. At least I thought he was; should've heard the things he called me."

"You thought he was?" Vadim asked, intrigued.

"I don't know, maybe it's how those guys relate to each other. I'm not sure they always mean it how it sounds. Anyway, I thought he hated his 'nigger partner' but he started inviting me to the bars, to meet his family. He was respectful when he met my ex..." Something caught in his throat. "When it happened, he... I don't know, somehow he knew what to do. I mean how do you know what to *do*, in a situation like that? Fucking nuclear bombs going off, Jersey's burning, we're hearing that you've invaded, fighting in Manhattan.

"Anyway, people have panicked, there's a near-riot on the docks as they try to get onto ships. A lot of the crews have been given rifles, and things are going to turn bad any minute. Then there's this big, fat, permanently-drunk Irish cop calming everyone down, getting them organised, nose-to-nose with armed sailors."

He stopped to wipe his eye. "And then the dead came. I mean, you could see them at the back of the crowd. They were pouncing on people. It was like one of those nature documentaries, or something. We saw some panic, but Gallagher's getting people on the ship, and shooting the dead. Just buying us enough time. He told me to get on board, to look after them." Harris sniffed and wiped his eyes again. He wasn't talking to Vadim because he liked him. He just needed to talk to someone. "Big-ass ugly cracker." He looked at Vadim. "'Course, I didn't think I would be going to England." He took a deep breath. "Tell me something, is there racism in the USSR?"

"You wish to become a good Soviet?"

"I was kinda happy being an American, most of the time," Harris told him. "That all really gone?"

"For now. And yes, there is racism in the USSR."

"So much for your communist utopia," Harris said. "You think we deserve this world?" He was looking around at the black snow.

"I think the people that created this world deserve it. The rest of you? I think most people just want to look after themselves and their loved ones. Get on with life."

"We're supposed to be a democracy, you're supposed to be about the people. Somewhere along the line we let this happen. We've got to take some responsibility, right?"

Vadim tried to think about the question, but it was too big. The forces at work that brought them to this point were too monolithic, somehow. To stand in their way would be like lying under the tracks of a tank. And yet at the end of the day it was all decisions made by humans, and just over forty years ago he had seen the difference individuals could make.

"I don't know," he finally told Harris. He could hear staggering footsteps moving along the deck through the snow towards them. Laboured breathing. "I'm just a soldier."

"Fucking pinko collaborator!" a very drunk Leary spat as he staggered around the corner. Harris sighed. Vadim turned to look at the big longshoreman. There was something about the way that this was going down that was making Vadim very suspicious.

"Jesus, World War Three happens and I'm still having to deal with a drunk Leary," Harris muttered. "All right, Leary, let's go and find a place for you to sleep it off before you do something particularly dumb."

"Fuck you, nigger!" he shouted before turning on Vadim. "You think I'm fucking frightened of you?"

"Only enough to get really drunk before confronting me," Vadim suggested, but he suspected that Leary wasn't really listening. Harris was watching, distaste on his face. Vadim wondered if, after the last bit of namecalling, the policeman would be happy for Vadim to handle Leary.

"I'm not afraid of you! I'm a fucking American!"

"Well, this is embarrassing," Harris muttered.

"We might be down, but we're not out." Leary was in Vadim's face. There was a lot of pointing going on as well. "We're going to turn your country into a smoking fucking crater!" Every word came with a blast of rancid, alcohol-laced breath. "You fucking Satanic abomination!" But through the breath, Vadim was very much aware that even someone as repellent as Leary was made of meat. The longshoreman poked him in the chest. "Not so tough now, are you?" Vadim was trying very hard to control himself, to let Leary live.

"Leary..." Harris said. He sounded nervous now. He'd clearly seen something in Vadim's face. Leary rounded on the police officer.

"See, that's the problem with you people! No fucking gratitude, no fucking loyalty! I never liked you, Harris!" He was pointing at Vadim again. He thought about eating the finger. "Do you know what he did?" There were tears rolling down Leary's face. "*Do you?*" he screamed. Now he was weeping. "He killed my family!" He staggered over to one of the forward crane's support struts and sank down into the black snow.

"Why didn't I go back for them?" he moaned, powerful sobs wracking his body, his head sinking down in shame. Harris knelt down next to him.

"You panicked, Fred; we all did." Then he was holding the longshoreman as he cried. Vadim took a moment to reflect on just how confusing and complicated people were. Then he heard the shouting. Someone was making their way along the deck towards them, as quickly as possible. Maria appeared, gasping for breath. Shivering, not even wearing a coat, a stricken expression on her face.

"Serafina Carlsson has gone missing," she said.

CHAPTER FOURTEEN

1621 UTC -1, 22nd November 1987
The *Dietrich*, North Atlantic

VADIM GRABBED HARRIS'S shotgun and locked the container behind him. Maria and Harris joined him as he made his way quickly back along towards the bridge castle, gripping the rails as the ship surged up and down in the still-choppy ocean. The castle bridge looked perfectly calm in the ship's lights, but something wasn't right. He tried to tell himself that it was nothing, just a coincidence that he didn't know where Gulag, Skull and Mongol were and now a child had gone missing.

He opened the hatch to the castle bridge and the three of them stepped inside, Harris closing the hatch behind them. Mr Carlsson was comforting his wife, who looked close to hysteria. She turned on Vadim as soon as he entered.

"*Where is she? What have you done with my little girl?*" she screamed, advancing on him, clawed hands outstretched towards him. Mr Carlsson had to physically interpose himself.

"Where did you last see her?" Vadim tried, but Mrs Carlsson wasn't listening and her husband was too busy trying to stop her attacking him. "Calm down!" Vadim put every last bit of command he had into those words, to no effect. More refugees were taking an interest now, standing in the doorways of the overpopulated bunkrooms.

A slap rung out. Mrs Carlsson went quiet, staring at Maria, who seemed surprised that she'd struck the older woman.

"I'm so sorry, Anna," Maria told Mrs Carlsson. "Serafina needs you." Mrs Carlsson stared blankly at the other women for moment; Vadim was worried that she was about to go into shock. Instead, she nodded slowly. Something about the Carlsson girl was trying to push its way into Vadim's brain.

"We saw the girls playing marbles," Vadim said. "They were using ball bearings. Do they ever go down to the engine room? The stores?"

"No, we told them not to," Mr Carlsson told him.

"In my experience, that doesn't always work with children," Harris said, earning himself a glare.

"We've got good kids, officer –" Mr Carlsson began.

"I found Gloria exploring down there yesterday," Anna suddenly said.

"Let's look," Vadim said, pushing past the Carlssons, but stopped at the sound of running feet.

The little girl was too fast for him. She ran by him, arms outstretched, reaching for her father, jumping into his arms.

His screams didn't begin until his daughter's teeth sank into his neck.

Vadim grabbed the girl, tore her off her dad and rammed her against the wall, the shotgun held lengthways against her neck, but dropped her when Mrs Carlsson hit him with the full weight of her body. The girl leapt for her shrieking mother next, and Vadim grabbed Mrs Carlsson and spun her round him, kicking her down the corridor. The shotgun roared, deafening in the cramped confines – again – and two members of the Carlsson family hit the floor.

"No!" a bleeding Mr Carlsson screamed from behind him and charged Vadim. Vadim rammed the butt of the shotgun back into Carlsson's face, then grabbed the man and dragged him away from Harris and Maria. The shotgun roared again, another shell casing tumbled to the floor.

"Everyone out, now!" he screamed, moving towards the port side, the direction Serafina had come from. The refugees who had come to see what the screaming was about had dived back into their cabins when the gunplay had started. Now they were starting to peer out through the doorways again. "Out, behind me, now!" Vadim tried again, and they started to obey. Then the first of the engineers appeared at the top of the port stairs, looking for meat.

"Contact!" Vadim screamed at the top of his voice, hoping some of the squad were close enough to hear him. The engineer raced up the stairs to the next deck; a fresh round of screaming started. Another zombie tried to leap over the rails into their corridor, and Vadim's shotgun blast took him in the face in mid-air. "Out! Out! Out!" he screamed, backing away from the stairs as people scrambled to get out the starboard hatch. "Fräulein!" Vadim shouted, hoping against hope she was somehow in earshot. "Get everyone up to the bridge!" There were two lockable metal hatches between the fourth and fifth decks.

He pushed the refugees out towards the starboard hatch as he backed towards it. They spilled out of the tower and onto the main deck. He heard screaming from behind him. One of the engineers had run up the starboard stairs from belowdecks and jumped on one of the refugees.

"Move! Move!" Vadim shoved people through the hatch, trying to make his way through the press. He kicked the zombie and its struggling victim back down the metal stairs, took a few steps down and fired the shotgun twice more, emptying it. Already he could see other zombies leaping onto the stairs.

He turned and shoved the few remaining people in the corridor out through the hatch. There were screams behind him in the corridor now. He stepped out onto the main deck and slammed the hatch shut, and something hit it hard. At this point it didn't matter whether it was zombie or victim, he had to lock it down. He spun the wheel and slammed the locking lever in place. "Hold that shut!" he ordered two of the burlier refugees. They jumped to obey him. "Harris, with me!"

Vadim ran down the narrow alley between the bridge castle and the container stacks, under the aft crane. It was too late: he watched as one of the zombies ran past the end of the alley, heading forward.

The boom of Skull's .303 high above him came as a comfort. Vadim reckoned the sniper was on top of the bridge castle. Two more zombies ran into the alley ahead of them, and Vadim threw the empty shotgun at Harris, drew the Stechkin and snapped off four shots in rapid succession, laying both to rest. He continued moving around the tower.

The port hatch was wide open; he saw newly-made zombies sprinting up the stairs away from him. Sensing movement, the zombies feasting in the corridor turned bloodied faces towards him and charged the hatch as he tried to slam it, knocking it open. Vadim thumbed the selector on the Stechkin with his free hand and fired it on full automatic through the gap, not troubling to aim. It had the desired effect. The zombie fell back and Harris added his weight to the hatch, allowing Vadim to close and lock it.

"Get two more men here, big ones, to hold this closed!" Vadim ordered Harris, taking the shotgun back, and the officer ran back to the starboard side. They called the dead mindless, but Vadim had no idea how intelligent they actually were. Could they unlock hatches and turn wheels? He didn't want to find out. He put his back against the hatch and holstered his now empty Stechkin. That had been his last magazine. *So much for conserving ammunition*, he thought.

"Skull!" Vadim called as he slid new shells into the shotgun. The sniper's answering call was drowned out by several shots from New Boy's KS-23, accompanied by a Stechkin; the dead had evidently reached Princess and New Boy's cabin. "Did any get away?" Vadim called up to Skull.

"None onto the main deck!" Skull shouted down. Then there were several shots from a pair of AK-pattern rifles. Two large, terrified-looking men ran around the corner and Vadim barely kept himself from shooting them; they turned out to have been sent by Harris, to hold the hatch lock in place. Vadim moved away from the hatch for them.

It was all happening too fast. The mindless – no, *predatory* – dead moved too quickly. He backed away from the bridge castle, looking up as portholes were painted red and agonised cries echoed out across the ocean. *Think, damn you, think!* The chatter of light machine guns added to the noise, sounding like it was coming from the bridge. The Fräulein and Mongol, Vadim assumed.

"What's happening?" Leary asked as he huffed up to Vadim, who ignored him. Then someone was charging him. Instinctively he brought the shotgun up, catching Maria under the chin and knocking her to the ground. Assuming she'd been bitten, he took aim at at her face.

"Stop!" Harris said, pushing the barrel out of the way. Maria had tears pouring down her cheeks.

"Gloria's in there!" the woman shouted at him. Vadim turned to look at the castle bridge. Frankly, he didn't think there was much chance for the girl.

"What happened?" Leary asked, appalled. Again, everyone ignored him. Vadim tried to think, but he didn't like any of his options. They would have to go in there and clear the tower, room by room. It would be messy. He looked away from the bridge and found himself looking at the containers. A plan was starting to develop.

"We need to get in there!" Maria cried.

"Maria, please," Vadim said, and despite the panic, she fell quiet. Glass smashed, somewhere above them. Vadim looked up. Princess had squeezed through a porthole out onto the wide ledge running around the third deck. She poked her AKS-74 back through the porthole and fired a string of three-round bursts into the room. Vadim could hear New Boy's AK-74 from inside the cabin. Princess stopped firing and let her weapon drop on its sling; New Boy thrust his head and torso through the porthole, but was yanked back in. Vadim's heart sank.

"Aah! Get off me! Get the fuck off me!" New Boy howled as he fought, half out of the porthole. Even down on the main deck, Vadim could see the fury on Princess's face as she changed her Stechkin's magazine, pushed her hand into the porthole and fired off the entire magazine. New Boy cried out in pain and Princess dragged him through the porthole.

"Has he been bitten?" Vadim shouted up.

"No!" Princess shouted down.

"Are you sure?" It had definitely sounded like he'd been bitten.

"I hit him in the leg," Princess cried, New Boy echoing the message in more plaintive tones. That would do for now; Vadim couldn't see Princess having any compunction about putting a bullet through the young scout's head – or anybody else's, for that matter.

He noticed the Fräulein's and Mongol's RPKS-74s had stopped firing.

"Liesl!" he tried shouting.

"Here, boss!" It came from the bridge. Briefly he wondered where Gulag was. "We have about fifty up here..."

The Fräulein was interrupted by a shot as one of the dead tried to climb through the hole from which Princess and New Boy had come out. It appeared that Princess's plan was to plug it with bodies.

"We've locked off the hatches, but we're stuck up here!" Only fifty? That wasn't good. Even allowing for the few he'd got out, there could be as many as a hundred humans – potential zombies – in the bridge castle.

"My daughter!" Maria shouted up. "Gloria, she's only eight, is she up there with you?"

It took some moments for the answer to come.

"No!" the Fräulein shouted down. Maria looked stricken, but she held it together. Vadim turned to Leary and pointed up at the aft crane.

"Do you know how to work that?"

*   *   *

THEY DUMPED THE containers into the sea, leaving a sinking trail of them in the ship's wake as they cleared the two aft-corner stacks. The longshoremen and the other civilians outside with Vadim emptied the contents of two of the forty-foot containers over the side. Skull and Princess leapt from the bridge castle to the top of the container stacks. Princess had left her Dragunov in her cabin, so she went to retrieve a G3 from the container.

He had a problem. His plan called for at least two shooters, but he also needed bait. New Boy would have been the best choice, but he was leg-shot. It looked like Vadim himself would have to replace Princess as one of the shooters, but he really needed to be on the main deck, co-ordinating. Besides, they would also need a gunner on the main deck, which was why he was now carrying Princess's AKS-74 and the two spare magazines she had managed to grab from her cabin.

"I'll do it," Harris said. Vadim looked over at him, frowning. If Harris was prepared to do this, he must have been desperate. It was a deeply flawed plan.

"Do what?" Maria asked.

"He doesn't have enough guns down here and he needs bait," the police officer said. Maria looked at Vadim.

"Me too," she said.

Leary, who'd proven adept with the crane, was currently lowering the first of the forty-foot containers into place. He had lifted it out of its guides and left it straddled across the starboard walkway, effectively cutting off the aft of the ship, though one of the forward-pointing doors had been left open.

"They move very fast," Vadim warned Harris and Maria.

"My child is in there," Maria said. She was clearly on the edge of hysteria, and with good reason: if Gloria wasn't on the bridge it was extremely unlikely that she was still alive. This didn't seem to be a good time to tell her that. "Besides, I used to run from the police all the time." She glanced over at Harris.

"This is going to happen very quickly," Vadim said, drawing his knife. Harris stared at the blade.

"Well, if it worked for Wile E. Coyote..." he muttered.

ONE OF THE forty-foot containers was suspended in the air about twenty feet above the port side of the ship. All the longshoremen and the rest of the civilians were inside the starboard container. Vadim was lying down on top of it. Harris and Maria were the only two people left on the main deck.

It had been Harris's idea for Maria and him to smear blood from the deep cuts Vadim had made in their hands on one of the port-side container stacks. The police officer had described it as 'street sign.'

It had taken every last bit of resolve that Vadim had not to sink his teeth into the wound.

Harris started somewhat cautiously, but Maria strode to the port hatch and wrenched it open.

"Zombie freaks!" she shouted into the bridge castle. They needed to make lots of noise; a shouted conversation with the Fräulein suggested that the majority of the dead were up on the fourth deck trying to get into the bridge. Had there been a zombie on the other side of the door this would have all been over very quickly.

"Come on, dead men!" Harris shouted. They quickly descended into a stream of obscenities that seemed very American, and to Vadim's limited knowledge, very New York in their colour and variety.

"Movement!" Vadim shouted from atop his container, spotting dark shapes behind the portholes on the second deck. "Here they come."

Maria and Harris looked ready to bolt, but to their credit, they stayed where they were until the last moment.

"Go!" Harris shouted and they were off at a sprint, heedless of the movement of the ship. The blood-spattered dead poured out of the bridge castle after them. They looked very close behind Maria, who was just behind Harris; too close for comfort. Maria and Harris disappeared behind the port container stacks as they ran along the side of the ship. More and more of the creatures came out of the bridge castle. As far as Vadim could tell, all of them took the bait, but his view was obscured.

The echoing boom of Skull's .303 rolled out over the ocean. He was covering the port side, tasked to shoot any of the zombies that got too close to the runners. The .303 fired again and again, as fast as Skull could work the bolt; Vadim was worried.

It seemed to take forever, but finally the stream of zombies dried up. He signalled Leary in the operator's cab of the crane. He lowered the other forty-foot container down across the portside walkway, blocking their way back aft.

Vadim hammered on the top of his container. The longshoremen came out of the rear doors. Eight of them hovered behind the doors while the ninth ran through the narrow alley between the stacks and the bridge castle, underneath the crane, towards the port hatch of the castle. If any of the dead were still waiting, he was done for.

Vadim heard gunfire from the stacks: Princess's G3. The dead were on the starboard side of the ship now.

Watching the longshoreman run to the port hatch, Vadim wasn't sure he'd ever seen a middle-aged, overweight man move so quickly. He heard the hatch shut and lock. The longshoreman poked his head around the corner and gave Vadim the thumbs up.

Vadim turned to face towards the bow of the ship. He could see Harris sprinting for all he was worth, occasionally staggering with the movement of the ship. Behind him, Maria was doing the same; and behind her, in the narrow walkway, were all the dead. As Vadim watched, several of the zombies were pitched overboard by the sheer press of their numbers.

Princess was leaning over the container stack, shooting down into the dead closest to Maria. They went down, took others with them, were trampled into the deck. Vadim brought the AKS-74's folding stock to his shoulder, but held fire; there was too much of a risk of hitting Maria.

And then Maria went down. Vadim didn't hesitate. The AKS-74 thumped into his shoulder as he fired again and again. Afterwards, he was sure it was some of the finest shooting he'd ever done. Princess was firing even faster from the tops of the stacks. One after another, the zombies dropped. Maria was back on her feet. Harris was running under Vadim now, into the container. Vadim let his weapon hang from its sling. Maria was sprinting, the outstretched fingers of the dead practically touching her.

She was in the container. So were the zombies.

Shouting from behind him, as eight Brooklyn dockworkers tried to slam the rear doors shut. He heard panic and what sounded like metal hitting metal. More and more of the dead were sprinting into the container, adding their strength to the press against the rear door.

"Close the door, you weak American bastards!" Vadim roared from the top of the container. It seemed to take forever, but finally he heard the locking lever clang into place.

"It's shut! It's shut!" one of the longshoremen shouted. Vadim watched as more and more of the zombies ran into the container.

"We're out here! Come and eat us!" The longshoremen were shouting and banging on the closed rear doors, trying to keep the zombies' attention, but Vadim could see them slowing down. One even came back out the open front door.

"Signal Leary! Signal Leary!" Vadim shouted. The smart zombie, hearing the noise, tried to jump up, so Princess shot him. Vadim held on for dear life as the crane lifted the front of the container sharply, and he heard the zombie cargo slide towards the back of the container. Vadim grabbed the open front door slightly awkwardly with one hand, holding on to the roof with the other, pulling with all his might, trying to give gravity a guiding hand. The open door teetered and then slammed shut on the container, and Vadim clambered forwards, leaning down the front and slammed the locking lever into place. He pushed himself back onto the roof.

"Tell Leary to drop it!" he shouted to the longshoremen, and moments later the front of the container dropped back down into place. He stood up and ran back to the other side of the container.

There were still zombies milling around the walkway; he heard the odd gunshot as they tried to climb the stacks. He climbed down, noticing a red smear down the rear door of the container. An arm lay on the deck. The *saperka* he'd lent to one of the longshoremen was red. Harris was bent at the waist, gasping for breath. Maria sat in the black slush, the back of her sweater torn. She looked up at Vadim.

"Now we have to do it again, for the rest of them," he told her.

"Did you just call us weak American bastards?" one of the longshoremen asked him.

"I apologise, it was the heat of the moment," Vadim said, and for some reason, they were all laughing.

VADIM CHECKED THE deck behind their ad-hoc blockade to make sure that none of the dead had gone the other way, but it was clear. Then they pulled the same trick again. It was easier the second time: there wasn't so many of them, and Maria and Harris didn't have to get so close. They didn't quite get all of them into the containers, but Vadim, Princess and Skull accounted for the stragglers between them.

Then they turned their attention to the bridge castle. After a shouted conversation, the Fräulein agreed to stay on the bridge with Mongol and guard the refugees and the crew. Mongol threw down the bridge's first aid kit to New Boy, but he was out of action for the time being, so Vadim and the two snipers would clear the bridge castle, level-by-level and room-by-room. Maria insisted on coming with them; she eventually had to be restrained by Harris and several of the longshoremen.

They cleared belowdecks first, finding a zombie trapped in one of the pistons. Princess killed it with her *saperka*.

They found Gulag in a bunkroom on the second deck. They had to force the door; the cabin was full of bodies. Vadim entered first and almost fired before he recognised his comrade, covered head to toe in blood.

Vadim could see he was still sentient, though. He knew this because he was looking down the barrel of the man's Stechkin.

CHAPTER FIFTEEN

1653 UTC -1, 22nd November 1987
The *Dietrich*, North Atlantic

"WHAT DID YOU do?" Vadim asked, his finger curled around the finger of Princess's AKS-74 as he looked down the barrel of Gulag's Stechkin.

"Don't you point your gun at me," Gulag said quietly. He had a dripping *saperka* and knife in his off-hand. There were shell casings all over the floor. Vadim stepped into the room and to the side, letting Skull in behind him; Princess remained out in the corridor, watching their back.

"Couldn't control yourself," Vadim said, not bothering to hide his disgust, though the charnel stenches of the bridge castle were making him salivate.

"You've never liked me, have you? Why didn't you just leave me in the pile of bodies you found me in?" Gulag hadn't lowered his weapon.

"Lower your weapon, now," Vadim told him.

"Make it easier for you to shoot me? I don't think so."

Vadim started to squeeze, feeling the resistance of the trigger against his finger. It would be *so easy*, and one less problem.

"Boys?" Princess said from the corridor.

Gulag had caused this, somehow. Vadim had to kill him. He was aware of the movement amongst the bodies down on the floor. He saw Skull shift, knew the sniper would handle it; he could concentrate on Gulag's execution.

"Boss," Skull said quietly. Vadim didn't take his eye off Gulag, but he was aware of Gloria, Maria's girl, covered in blood, wriggling out of the bodies. At first he took her for one of the zombies – expected Skull to kill her – but she wriggled free, took a few running steps to Gulag and wrapped her arms around him. Gulag put his arm round her, careful not to cut her with the knife or the *saperka*.

They heard sobbing from the pile; Skull kicked some of the bodies away and found the Carlsson boy, now the last survivor of his family. Skull reached over and pushed Vadim's weapon down, and Gulag lowered his pistol.

"Skull, disarm Gulag and take him and the kids down onto the main deck. I want him down on his knees, facing a bulkhead, hands laced behind his head, you covering him at all times..." Vadim said. The children notwithstanding, he was far from convinced that Gulag didn't cause this.

"Boss..." Skull started.

"Do you understand me?" Vadim growled, not taking his eyes off Gulag. Skull nodded.

"Him?" Gulag asked, turning to Skull. "Where were you?" Skull didn't answer, and Vadim didn't want to think about it right now. He started removing Gulag's weapons from him.

He finished clearing the bridge castle with Princess. There were no more zombies. Even from deck three, he heard Maria's reunion with her daughter.

ON THE LEDGE on deck three they found New Boy. Vadim checked his wound and – squashing the impulse to sink his teeth into it – confirmed it was a graze from a bullet rather than a bite. The young scout elected to stay where he was until their sweep was finished.

On deck four they found a carpet of dead bodies and a multitude of shell casings. It looked like Mongol and the Fräulein had lain down a lot of fire, covering the refugees so they could get to the bridge.

Eventually Vadim found himself stepping over the bodies on the stairs to the bridge, accompanied by Princess. He banged on the hatch, and a grim-looking Fräulein opened the door for them. He could hear weeping.

"Is it over?" she asked. Vadim nodded and stepped in.

There were two bodies lying in the corner. Even in the now cramped confines of the bridge people were trying to give them some room. "They were wounded on the way in," the Fräulein offered by way of explanation.

The resentment and fear that Vadim had seen in the refugees' eyes had given way to naked fear. They flinched when the squad walked by.

He caught sight of Mongol. Even dead, despite the sutured skin twisting his mouth into an obscene grin, Mongol looked sick.

Vadim felt eyes on him, and turned to find Schiller staring at him. The captain didn't have to say anything; it was Vadim who had brought this onto his ship.

"Can you still sail this ship?" Vadim asked Schiller.

"Are my engine crew all dead?" Schiller asked. *Yes, but we have them all locked in a container.* The thought came bubbling up unbidden and with it the urge to start laughing and possibly never stop. Instead he nodded, screaming at himself internally.

"Colstein, you have the bridge," Schiller told his first mate, walking past Vadim. He looked pale, drawn and exhausted. Vadim couldn't think of anything useful to say to the man.

"Boss?" the Fräulein asked.

"Mongol, I want you to check New Boy's leg wound, okay?" Vadim said. Mongol nodded. Vadim turned to the Fräulein. "Get everyone downstairs, we need to find out what happened."

IT WAS SNOWING black snow again, but the sea wasn't too rough and the cold didn't bother the dead. The zombies in the containers seemed to have quietened down. He could hear them shuffling around and bumping into each other.

Mongol had properly cleaned and dressed New Boy's leg wound. The scout had looked less than happy about this, keeping his pistol in his hand the whole time. It took a moment for Vadim to realise Mongol was salivating, dripping from his exposed jaw.

Gulag was down on his knees, hands behind his back, Skull standing a little way behind him. Vadim doubted the gangster would have done that for anyone else on the squad; perhaps the Fräulein, but he doubted it. Vadim could never make up his mind what Gulag thought of Skull. Did he fear him, hate him, respect him, a mixture of all three? He certainly seemed to believe that Skull would shoot him if the Muscovite gave the sniper any trouble.

The Fräulein was watching Gulag and Skull unhappily. Princess was dressed in a great deal of warm clothing and leaning against the bridge structure's bulkhead in the shadow of the crane.

Maria was still there, with Gloria, trying the best she could to clean the child's face. The Carlsson boy was there as well. Someone had brought them warm clothes. Vadim suspected Maria was loath to take her daughter back into the slaughterhouse that was the bridge castle. He was also sure that the Carlsson boy was going into shock. Both children kept glancing at Gulag.

Harris was also watching Gulag, but thoughtfully. Leary was leaning against one of the legs of the crane he had piloted. He looked more dazed than anything else; Vadim was pretty sure the longshoreman was also going into shock.

"Is that the guy who did it?" Harris asked, pointing at Gulag. He'd also found warmer clothes. Vadim ignored him.

"Captain!"

Vadim turned around to stare at the police officer, but all he saw was a sack of meat. It took him a moment to remember that it had been he, along with Maria, who had acted so bravely to help resolve the situation.

"Do we have a stake in this, or are we just your hostages?" It didn't sound like a demand.

"We don't know who did this yet." It was the Fräulein who answered, in English. Then she looked at Vadim. "It's what we're here to find out." He had the feeling that she was talking to him rather than Harris.

"You have a stake in this," Vadim told the police officer. *It was your people who got slaughtered. Again.* "And you are not hostages." The three civilians had earned their place. "Princess, I want you to translate for the Americans."

Princess looked less than pleased but didn't complain.

"Where were you, Gulag?" Vadim asked.

"I'm standing up," Gulag said, starting to move.

"If he stands up, shoot him," Vadim told Skull. Gulag stopped.

"That would make things easier for you, wouldn't it?" Gulag said. "Easy to blame old Nikodim."

"You said you saw them as meat," the Fräulein pointed out. Princess was translating it all as Leary, Maria and Harris looked on.

"Son-of-a-bitch," Leary muttered under his breath, though his anger seemed to have subsided with his bluster.

"I still didn't do it, Infant," Gulag said.

"Infant?" Harris asked, once Princess had translated, much to Vadim's irritation. It wasn't as though it was important right now.

"Do you know why they call him Infant?" Gulag asked. Princess translated. She seemed to be taking some kind of perverse pleasure in this. "Because he's killed more people than the infant-mortality rate." Gulag started laughing at his own joke.

"You bastards!" Maria spat after she'd heard the English version. Her voice caused more bumping and moaning from the containers.

"That's not why they call me Infant," Vadim muttered in English, which Princess helpfully translated into Russian for Mongol, Skull and Gulag.

"Can you let him face us?" Harris asked. Vadim shot him a questioning look. "I'm police, it helps to see people's faces, to get an idea if they're telling the truth or not."

"Gulag, turn around, keep your hands behind your head," the Fräulein told him. Gulag did as he was bidden, but he was staring at Skull.

"So cool, Skull, but I know. Despite all your bible bullshit, you like killing just as much as me," he said. The sniper didn't respond. "Where were you?"

"Yes, where were you?" the Fräulein asked the sniper. "How did you end up on top of the castle bridge?"

"I went for a walk," Skull said.

"Where?" Vadim asked. Gulag's grin made him want to kick him in the teeth.

"Along the stacks. Then I climbed the other crane, from there onto the roof of the bridge."

"Anyone see you?" Harris asked. Princess didn't even bother translating.

"He wouldn't be much good if they did," she told him, and then to Vadim: "Boss, Skull didn't do this, you know that."

"How would you know?" Gulag asked from his knees. "See, I know *I* didn't do this, because I know where I was and what I was doing. I'm pretty sure Princess and New Boy didn't do it, because they're the prey, not the hunters anymore." Princess bristled. "As for the rest of you..." He turned to Princess. "See maybe the old Skull wouldn't. Though frankly I think he was a sick bastard as well. But that corpse" – he pointed at the other sniper – "that you think is your daddy isn't the same creature he was. You don't know what goes on in our heads, you don't know how we see stringy sacks of flesh like you, the thoughts we have when we smell your raw meat."

Princess wasn't translating anymore; she was just staring at Gulag. Harris was watching Gulag very carefully.

Princess turned to Vadim. "I want to put him out of my misery."

"Not just yet," the Fräulein told her. Vadim was watching Skull, but if there was a reaction to Gulag's words, he couldn't see it.

"He's not acting like he's guilty," Harris said, nodding towards Gulag. "An arsehole, but not guilty."

"Not translating anymore?" Gulag asked Princess.

"He said you're an arsehole," she told him.

"So Fräulein and I were together until Officer Harris joined us..." Vadim started.

"Excuse me, captain," Leary said. His most recent brush with death had done wonders for his manners. "Nik was with me." It took Vadim a moment to work out that Nik was Gulag.

"Yes, winding you up to send you after me," Vadim said, "as a distraction."

"You'd be surprised how little excuse people need to get pissed off with you," Gulag told him.

"Are you saying you didn't send him after the boss?" the Fräulein asked. "Then why were you talking to him?"

Gulag didn't answer.

"Because he wanted to feel human again, like a real person," Mongol said quietly. Everyone turned to look at the big medic. Gulag had squeezed his eyes shut. Vadim couldn't quite read his expression. Anguish, maybe.

"Glory, no!" Maria suddenly shouted as her daughter wriggled out of her arms and ran across the snowy deck and threw herself into Gulag's blood-stained arms. Gulag hugged the girl fiercely.

"It's all right," he told her. "It's all right, you're safe now," he whispered in a language she couldn't possibly understand. Vadim couldn't believe what he was hearing. Nor was he sure he could have maintained that level of self-control. Most telling was Maria, who seemed almost unconcerned.

"It was you, wasn't it?" Harris said. Vadim turned, to see the policeman looking straight at Mongol.

The truth was written all over the big medic's face.

"Nergui...?" the Fräulein said. Vadim could hear the heartbreak in her voice. Even Princess looked appalled.

"No," Gulag moaned, his eyes still closed tight, still hugging the girl.

Mongol leaned his RPKS against one of the containers and stepped away from it.

"I need to let you go now," Gulag told Gloria, his eyes open again. He started to prise her arms off him, but she didn't want to let go. Eventually her mother had to come and remove her. "I'm standing up now," he told Vadim, who just nodded numbly. He climbed to his feet and turned to Mongol. "I'm sorry man," he said.

"I wouldn't have let them kill you," Mongol told him. Gulag nodded.

"You tried to put it on Skull!" Princess spat, clearly still angry at Gulag. Gulag shrugged. Skull didn't seem particularly bothered, but Vadim wondered if the sniper intended to deal with this at a later date.

"What happened?" Harris asked. Still glaring at Gulag, Princess translated. Mongol tried to speak a few times.

"I – she reminded me of my cousin..." His words trailed away. Then he shook his head and looked down. "No. We're trapped in these rotting bodies." Then he looked straight at Vadim. "Can't you feel it?"

Right then, more than ever, Vadim could.

"Life, warmth, belonging, that's what my family means to me. I didn't mean to hurt her. More than anything, I just wanted to talk to a child. They are the antithesis of what we are, so full of life." Mongol was trying his best not to look at either of the children present. Maria hugged Gloria more tightly, tears in her eyes. "She screamed, she was frightened." His hand rose up to touch the rictus grin of his face. The Carlsson boy was staring at Mongol, terrified, transfixed. Vadim was worried that they would lose the boy. "She screamed. After that, I don't know, I can't remember..." He squeezed his eyes shut, clenched his fist and screamed, making Maria, Leary and the children jump.

"It's not true. Her fear, her blood. I lost control, but I remember everything, every morsel. By the time I managed to control myself, it was too late."

"Okay," the Fräulein said. "You've fucked up, but we can..." she faltered.

"Do what?" Maria asked as Princess translated. She stood up, holding Gloria close to her, moving the Carlsson boy behind her. "You are monsters; we keep saying it, you seem to acknowledge it, but nobody wants to *do* anything. You're the worst of both worlds: zombie cannibals and well-trained commandos. You're like every normal person's worse nightmare."

"I think they saved our lives in New York," Harris said quietly.

"Or brought the dead with them," Maria said. "But even if they did, maybe if we'd died, it would be better than living on this knife edge. Waiting for them to kill the rest of us."

"Better your child had died?" Princess asked. Maria glanced at her and then looked back at Vadim.

"If you ever had even the slightest regard for humanity, you need to kill yourselves right now," she told him. Vadim was pretty sure she was right. Except that seemed too easy. Except there were people he didn't think should live longer than him.

Or you're just afraid.

"What about him?" Harris asked, nodding towards Gulag.

"He's..." the Fräulein started. The gunshot made all the civilians jump. A neat hole appeared in the middle of Mongol's head. He toppled backwards into the black snow. The Fräulein and New Boy were both staring, appalled, Gulag looked away, shaking his head, even Princess looked shocked.

"He was *one of us!*" the Fräulein screamed at Vadim. She had never spoken to him like that before.

Neither of the children were crying. They'd seen far too much now.

Vadim lowered his weapon.

"We don't kill the living," he said simply. Then: "We need his ammunition," as he turned and walked away.

CHAPTER SIXTEEN

0823 Greenwich Mean Time (GMT), 24th November 1987
The *Dietrich*, The Irish Sea

THEY WERE SKIRTING the coast of north-western England, east of the Isle of Man, looking for a place to anchor, if not dock. Not that you could tell they were off the coast of anywhere through the thick fog that had enveloped them.

Since his reanimation, and in the solitude imposed on him by the squad since Mongol's death, it seemed to Vadim that his imagination had gone into overdrive: the dark, red sky gave the thick clouds a strange otherworldly feel. It was easy to imagine that the ship had sailed into Hell.

Colstein had slowed the ship right down; apparently they were picking their way through the Irish Sea using marine radar. Colstein was in charge of the bridge now, with Schiller spending most of his time belowdecks. It seemed the captain had worked his way up the ranks from the engine room, and with the help of some of the more mechanically-minded longshoremen was keeping the ship running. They were, however, perilously low on fuel. They would need to find a port, and soon; but since entering UK territorial waters, they had been completely fogbound.

What Vadim didn't understand was, where was the navy? Either the Soviet Navy *or* the Royal Navy? They had picked up very little radio traffic, and most of that had been a garbled mess.

It had been an unpleasant thirty-six hours for everyone. Mongol had been well liked, and between losing him and Genadi, it seemed like the squad had lost its glue. The two snipers had always been distant; snipers had to be. New Boy was too new, Gulag was an arsehole, and the Fräulein, though respected, and liked to a degree, was still a senior NCO.

As for Vadim himself, informal as the Spetsnaz might be, he was still in command, and had to make the difficult decisions. Like shooting Mongol. Even dead, even with everything but the hunger muted, Vadim still saw the hole appearing in Mongol's head, the shock on the medic's face, every time he closed his eyes. It had been Farm Boy and Mongol who had provided the squad's sense of camaraderie. Their friendship with Gulag had gone a long way to keeping the criminal in line.

The Muscovite's scorn, never far from the surface, had become more obvious. Princess was even more standoffish, to the point of monosyllabic; and it was anybody's guess what Skull thought about the whole affair. New Boy was the least affected by Mongol's death – he'd known him the least – but even the scout was looking at Vadim differently. But it was the loss of the Fräulein's trust that was the hardest to bear. She continued to carry out her duties, but regardless of Mongol's crimes it was clear that she felt the execution was a monstrous betrayal.

Nor had it been easy for the refugees. Harris and Maria had very much become their spokespeople. They had been honest with the refugees about what had happened, and the response to the outbreak. When the commandos walked by, even the living ones, they were looked at as though they were overseers on a slave galley. The ever-present gore hadn't helped, but with so little fresh water it hadn't been possible to clean the castle bridge. They'd done their best with fire hoses and seawater, but with the heating on, the place stank, and flies were starting to gather. If they didn't get off the *Dietrich* soon, disease could become a real issue. And Vadim didn't like how the charnel stench made him feel.

He was standing in the port walkway towards the bow of the ship, staring into the fog towards unseen Britain. Even looking back along the ship, the sternward crane was just a shadow, and the castle bridge was little more than an apparition.

The fog did odd things to sound. He could hear the muffled thumps and moaning from the containers, in the top level of the stacks now, locked between other containers. Even secured like that, nobody was happy about their presence: not the squad, not the refugees, not the crew. It had been the only time Captain Schiller had become openly angry with him.

Vadim had seen the containers they'd dropped off the ship, bobbing in the waves, and had had a horrible vision of the zombies washing ashore and spreading their disease to a new continent. The soldier in him wanted to make sure that the contents of the containers were destroyed. Now he realised that it was a mistake. The middle of the Atlantic Ocean might not have been the perfect place to get rid of them, but it had undoubtedly been their best choice.

He heard footsteps shuffling through the snow towards him and looked up to see the Fräulein approach. She was looking fixedly ahead, trying to ignore him.

"Liesl?" he said as she drew level with him. She stopped and didn't quite stand to attention.

"Yes, comrade captain," she said through gritted teeth. He'd been trying to think of something conciliatory to say, but the attitude irked him. He expected better of her.

"Two rules!" Vadim said. "I had two rules. We don't eat the meat, and we protect the living."

"We protect *our* living," the Fräulein said stiffly.

"Mongol broke that rule, and killed over a hundred people!"

"Not *our* people!" Now the Fräulein was shouting.

"Well then go and finish it off!" he shouted, pointing through the fog towards the castle bridge. "What fucking difference does it make?"

The Fräulein stared at him.

"We need them to steer the ship," she finally said.

It was Vadim's turn to stare.

The Fräulein smiled and then sat down on one of the equipment lockers. "More than anything else, it was the way you just walked off. He was our friend, Vadim."

And then he saw it. She *knew* he'd done the right thing, but she couldn't get past it because Mongol was her friend.

"I had to walk away," Vadim told her. "I liked Mongol as well, but I made a promise to him in New York. Liesl, he killed a child."

She sighed. "He didn't," she said quietly. "That gnawing, screaming thing inside us did it."

She turned to look at Vadim. "I think maybe the Spanish girl was right," she said. "We should kill ourselves."

He was surprised; out of all of them, the Fräulein had seemed to be handling this the best.

"Well what do you want to do?" he asked. "Because Liesl, I need you." She met his eyes, and he couldn't read her expression.

"There can't be any give in your two rules, can there?" she asked. He didn't answer because she already knew. "That includes *you*, right?"

He nodded.

"I'm with you, Vadim."

"Then I need you to get the squad back in li –" he began.

"Boss?" Both of them looked up. New Boy was standing a little further along the walkway. Neither of them had been aware of his approach, which worried Vadim. "The captain wants to see you up in the bridge." Vadim frowned. If Schiller was back in the bridge, it had to be pretty serious.

VADIM AND THE Fräulein leaned over the marine radar's display with Schiller. The captain was wearing oil-stained overalls; his face drawn with fatigue. Princess was leaning next to the starboard hatch and the Fräulein had sent New Boy to fetch Gulag and Skull as well.

"There," the uncomfortable-looking radar operator said. Vadim saw a blip on the screen. The image looked distorted, unclear, but it was definitely a ship.

"Are you having problems with the radar?" the Fräulein asked the operator.

"It works on radio waves," the operator told her. "Heat from the fireballs, or beta particles from the blast, can turn the air opaque to the waves. That's how they got so close. Frankly, I'm surprised it's working this well." The ship was less than two miles south of their current position.

"Does that mean that Britain's been hit?" Vadim asked. The operator turned to look at him, unhappily.

"Almost certainly," he said.

"Any idea what kind of ship it is?" the Fräulein asked. The radar operator shook his head.

Schiller straightened up. "What do you want to do?" he asked Vadim.

"What do *you* want to do?" Vadim returned.

"Find the safest port possible," he said. "But I suspect that will require time we just don't have. Liverpool and Manchester are the closest large ports, but there is every chance they've been destroyed by nuclear weapons. There are other, smaller ports. Barrow-in-Furness, but there's a naval shipyard there..."

"Find me a smaller port that was unlikely to have been a target, and head towards the coast. Let's see if it follows."

"With patchy radar, in fog, these waters are very treacherous," Schiller warned. Vadim opened his mouth to ask for a better suggestion but the radio crackled into life. After a few seconds of static and garbled words, it gave way to heavily accented English.

"*To unidentified ship running north of us, this is the* Ushkuinik. *Please bring your vessel to a full stop and prepared to be boarded.*" Oddly, there was laughing in the background. The accent was Russian. The captain turned to Vadim.

"Fräulein, give the refugees back their weapons. Assemble the squad with a full combat load, as much ammunition as we have left."

The Fräulein didn't move.

"We're going to fire on our own people?" Princess asked, an edge in her voice.

"My mother was in Berlin in 1945," the radar operator said. "I do not want to be turned over to the Red Army."

Princess ignored him. Vadim turned to Schiller.

"Captain, you need to run from that ship," Vadim said.

"I agree with Hans, but isn't this what you wanted?" he asked.

"Captain, there's no way there is a ship in the Soviet Navy called the *Ushkuinik*," he said.

"You can't know that," Princess said.

"The Soviet Navy does not name ships after twelfth-century Viking pirates," he told the sniper.

"They're still our people," Princess insisted. Vadim turned on her.

"Our own people did this!" he roared at her, pointing at his own deathly pallor and making the bridge crew jump. Princess looked angry and opened her mouth to retort as the radio crackled into life. This time it sounded much clearer.

"Please line up all female crew and passengers ready for inspection," the voice said. There was more laughter in the background. The radio went quiet. Everybody stared at it for a moment or two and then started moving. Schiller issued orders and the *Dietrich* began turning towards the coast.

"It's picking up speed," the radar operator said. "Twenty knots, still increasing."

"A ship that size? It's military," Schiller muttered. "We can't outrun it."

"I'm going to need some of your people," Vadim told him, outlining his plan to the captain and the Fräulein. Schiller's face became graver and graver, but at length he nodded. Vadim made for the hatch, Princess a little ahead of him.

"I'm sorry I shouted at you," he said as they made their way down the stairs.

"I'm not made of crystal, captain. I've been shouted at before," she said as they turned the corner onto the next flight of stairs. "Tell me, would you be apologising to Gulag, or New Boy, if you'd shouted at them?"

"I was once told by a defecting Contra that the CIA death squad members that trained them had advised them to target female combatants first when fighting the Sandinistas, because –"

"They'd worked harder to get there," Princess muttered, splitting off on the third deck and heading for the cabin she shared with New Boy. "And have to put up with patronising nicknames!" she shouted over her shoulder.

THE *USHKUINIK* PUT a shot across their bows, the large-calibre gun echoed over the sea. Vadim didn't see the shell itself, but he saw the eddies it left in the fog. It was Schiller's cue to cut the engines and slow down; Vadim felt the thrum of the engines die beneath him, where he was lying on top of a container. They had one advantage and one advantage only: that the crew of the *Ushkuinik* wouldn't be expecting six highly trained and experienced commandos on board.

They couldn't afford to hold back, although they were getting very low on ammunition. They had given the crew and Harris back their weapons, but frankly that was a last resort. The civilians were barricaded in the bridge castle. Everything else was in the other ship's favour.

The *Ushkuinik* glided out of the fog, the low, sleek, predatory shape of a *Burevestnik*-class frigate. He was no expert on naval weapon systems, but it looked like their surface-to-surface missile launchers and torpedo tubes were empty, which just left the four 76mm guns behind the bridge castle; and of course the men now lining the deck of the frigate. Some wore naval uniforms, though they carried weapons against Soviet Navy rules. More worrying were the Naval Infantry among them, a well-trained conventional force with an excellent reputation.

The frigate was slowing down, coming alongside. Vadim could see someone in a second-rank captain's uniform he suspected the man hadn't earned. He was shouting at them through a loudhailer, demanding they prepare to be boarded and bring out the booze and the women. Vadim waited until they were nearly level. Then, as one, he, Gulag, New Boy and the Fräulein rose to their knees. The snipers – Princess on top of the bridge castle and Skull on the forward crane – began killing. Suppressed, nearly silent subsonic rounds targeted anyone on the frigate with heavy weapons: RPGs, machine guns, grenade launchers. The pirates hadn't even realised the fight had started; their comrades just started falling over. Vadim, Gulag and New Boy threw grenades down onto the frigate's deck and brought their AK-74s up. *Let's see if you can still shoot, old man*, Vadim thought, aiming at the man with the loudhailer. He squeezed the trigger; the loudhailer exploded and the pirate fell back.

He heard the whoosh of the Fräulein's RPG-18. He'd been sure the rocket was going to be useless against the ship's armour, so the Fräulein aimed the weapon at the window of the bridge. He felt the heat and pressure wave from the explosion as the 64mm high explosive anti-tank warhead impacted with the frigate's bridge. Then their fragmentation grenades started to explode. People were torn apart by the shrapnel, flung into the air by the force of the explosion, some of them over the side.

Vadim and his team capitalised on the sudden chaos, firing into the enemy crew. He heard the chatter of the Fräulein's RPKS-74. He was trying to pick individuals off, but found that, his first shot notwithstanding, his marksmanship wasn't as good as it needed to be at this distance, firing between moving ships. He switched the selector on his rifle and started firing three-round bursts into groups of people. He'd leave the detailed work to the snipers. The other crew hadn't even started to return fire yet.

The cranes started to move, lifting two of the forty-foot containers up into the air. Leary was on the sternward crane, another longshoreman on the fore. The cranes' booms swung out over the other ship just as the return fire finally started. Vadim moved back as bullets sparked off the edge of the stacks and shifted position, leaning over the containers and firing again and again. New Boy and the Fräulein were doing the same. There was an explosion as Gulag fired a grenade from the launcher mounted under the barrel of his rifle. Then came the boom of one of the frigate's 76mm guns. Vadim watched in horror as the forward crane was hit. The operator's cab ceased to exist. The force of the explosion knocked Gulag flying across the top of the containers and took Vadim off his feet. The crane toppled towards the deck. Skull leapt from the boom, falling some twenty feet onto the top of the stacks and crying out as he hit a container, hard.

Vadim crawled to the edge of the stacks. He heard a machine gun firing, saw tracers striking the cab of the aft crane that Leary was driving. Vadim reached the edge of the stacks and risked a peek: the boom of the destroyed forward crane, still holding the container, hit the edge of the *Dietrich*, bounced off the frigate with a deafening clang, and much to Vadim's relief plummeted into the Irish Sea. The main deck of the enemy frigate was lit up by muzzle flashes. The *Dietrich*'s stacks were wreathed in sparks. He found the machine-gunner shooting at Leary's crane and fired his own underslung grenade launcher at him; the grenade exploded and the gunner was no longer there. A bullet ripped into the dead flesh of his left arm and he rolled back from the edge. He grabbed another hand grenade, removed the pin and threw it over the edge of the stacks. He heard it explode as he switched magazine, his second-to-last one.

Further along the stacks, closer to the bridge castle, he saw the Fräulein pull the last drum mag out of her RPKS-74 and replace it with a forty-round magazine. Her head snapped back as she was hit, but she barely seemed to acknowledge the wound as she started firing again. Just a graze. Not nearly enough to kill her.

Skull was pulling himself towards the edge of the stacks, his left leg at an odd angle. Gulag finished reloading and started firing again, roaring at the crew of the frigate. Vadim rolled up onto his knee to fire, and noticed that one of the rear guns seemed to be pointing straight at him. Leary must have hit the releases on the container his crane was holding, as it dropped like a bomb onto the deck of the frigate. The 76mm gun fired. Vadim was running. The force of the blast hit him in the back like the hand of an angry god. Containers went tumbling into the air.

HE WASN'T SURE if he'd lost consciousness or not. He was lying face down, still on top of the stacks, looking at the forward crane. The glass on the operator's cab was holed and bloody, but he could still make out Leary slumped forward, clearly dead, over the controls. Over the ringing in his ears, over the gunfire, Vadim could just about make out the screams that always followed when the living met the dead.

He pushed himself up onto all fours. The dead had spilled out of the container Leary had dropped onto the pirates' deck. They had rigged the containers with grenades and cords, and Harris and Maria – watching from concealed positions down on the main deck – were supposed to pull the pins, exploding the grenades and blowing the locks. In theory. There was a lot that could have gone wrong with the plan, but Vadim watched as something that had once been a Brooklyn dockworker took down a deserter from the Soviet Naval Infantry, biting a chunk out of his screaming face. Leary had done it. He had probably saved them all.

The crew of the pirate frigate had turned their attention to the zombies amongst them now. Vadim saw the top of another infantryman's head come off: he assumed Princess had shot him for being too efficient in dealing with the dead. He looked back along the stacks to see where the rest of the squad was. Where the frigate's gun had hit it looked like someone had taken a bite out of the containers. The Fräulein was still kneeling, firing into the frigate below. He couldn't see the others.

There was the awful shriek of tortured metal as the frigate collided with the *Dietrich*. Vadim was flung forward. He grabbed the edge of the stacks and found himself hanging one-handed, forty feet above the main deck. A shadow fell across him and suddenly he was looking up at Gulag. The Muscovite wasn't exactly pointing his weapon at the captain, looking down at him as though thinking, weighing up a decision. Vadim remained silent. He didn't think anything he could say would help his predicament. He also gave serious thought to just letting go, but for the moment he looked up at Gulag. Finally the gangster seemed to come to a decision, kneeling down and dragging Vadim back up onto the top of the stacks. Vadim heard the boom of Skull's .303 as he rolled onto the top of the container. The sniper was still alive and presumably didn't feel there was any further call for stealth. Vadim could see New Boy wandering around on top of the stack as well. The scout looked dazed. Vadim pushed himself back up onto his knees. The *Ushkuinik* was drifting away from them. The screaming and the gunfire had fallen off. They had fought dirty and won. Vadim wasn't sure that 'winning' was a label you could apply to a situation like this, but his squad were all still moving around.

The harsh squeal of the PA actually made him jump.

"This is your captain speaking. Abandon ship. I repeat: abandon ship."

CHAPTER SEVENTEEN

1130 GMT, 24th November 1987
Morecambe Bay, North-West England

THEY'D HAD A bit of time to gather what supplies they could, while listening to the fading screams of the pirate crew. Eventually the red fog had swallowed the frigate, and they'd heard no more.

There hadn't been enough lifeboats for everyone, but the *Dietrich* had also come equipped with rafts. The rafts were overloaded, the refugees piled on top of each other, but they just about kept everyone out of the freezing water. Had the sea been any less calm, it would have been a different story.

When Vadim had last seen the *Dietrich,* it had started to tilt and slide into the water. They paddled as hard as they could, the lifeboats wallowing as they towed the rafts, to avoid being pulled under. The ship disappeared, still sinking in the fog.

As they paddled towards land, Vadim was troubled by two thoughts. If the Red Army was in charge of the UK, what would they do with the squad and himself? They wouldn't want the virus anywhere near Europe, their prize. And what of the dead he'd used against the pirates? He didn't know much about tides and currents, but all it would take was for the frigate to run ashore and the zombie plague would come to a new country. One more atrocity for his atrophied conscience.

Vadim had no idea where they were. He was aware it was cold only because of the shivers of the living. They had run lines between the lifeboats and rafts in the hope that they wouldn't get separated in the fog. Vadim was in the lead boat with Princess; Captain Schiller was up by the prow with his compass, directing them north-east towards mainland Britain – not that you'd know it through the banks of fog around them.

It was quiet, but for the lapping of the paddles dipping into the still water, the sound of teeth chattering and the occasional sob. Uncharitably, Vadim found himself bothered by the sobs. He didn't see what they would accomplish.

He caught occasional glimpses of the other boats through the freezing fog. The Fräulein was keeping an eye on Gulag in one, and Skull was with New Boy in another. Skull had broken his leg jumping from the crane to the top of the stacks. There was little that they were able to do for him beyond splint the leg and wrap it in duct tape. He said it was uncomfortable, that he could feel the bones rubbing together but he could walk. Somehow Vadim couldn't see it healing.

Princess looked cold. She was hugging herself, wearing a lot of the clothing they had taken from the outdoors store in New York. She was shaking, her teeth chattering. Hypothermia was becoming a real threat. They would need to find food and shelter quickly.

Vadim was down to his last magazine for the rifle. He had no more ammunition left for the Stechkin, eight shells for his sawn-off KS-23 shotgun, a few hand grenades, and some grenades for the GP-25 Kostyor launcher. The squad were in similar state.

Do you care? he asked himself. He felt the bump of the boat hitting something, and he brought his AK-74 up, struggling slightly in the cramped quarters.

"Land." Schiller sounded surprised. Vadim pushed through the press of shivering, frightened, refugees. He wasn't sure what he was expecting, but this flat, black plain wasn't it. It took him a moment to realise he was looking at a beach covered in the black snow, more of which was fluttering gently out of the sky.

"Is this right?" he asked. Schiller didn't answer immediately, and Vadim turned to look at him. The captain had always given the impression of complete competence, but now he looked old, haggard and tired. He seemed to be marshalling his thoughts.

"I think so," he finally said. Vadim didn't like the uncertainty in his voice. "There are mudflats, sandbanks..."

"Are they tidal?" Vadim asked, and Schiller nodded. If they got off the lifeboats and tried to walk to shore, they could still be caught by the tide and drowned. To say nothing of dangers like quicksand.

"So do we get off the boat or not?" Vadim asked him.

"I don't know exactly where we are. I'm not even sure of the tide," Schiller said. Vadim watched the tired old man for a few moments. He'd initially assumed Schiller was roughly the same age as him, but having spent time with the man, he was sure that the captain was older, perhaps by as much as ten or fifteen years. It was clear that Schiller'd had enough, for the moment at least. He needed someone else to lead the way.

Vadim stepped out of the boat. The water came up to his ankle. The ground shifted underfoot, but gave way to hard wet sand just under the surface; another step was rewarded by the crunch of snow as he stepped onto a sandbank. He could see the other lifeboats coming up alongside them.

Further up the sandbank, New Boy pulled one of the rafts in as Skull held their lifeboat steady.

Vadim reached out and did the same with his boat. He wanted it as close to dry land as possible; the last thing he wanted was any of the living getting wet. He had considered sending New Boy and Princess out to scout first, but he needed to get the refugees moving before they froze to death.

"We're going to continue on foot from here."

With a murmur of assent, people began moving. Schiller looked relieved.

THERE WERE JUST over sixty refugees and crew from the *Dietrich* left alive. Many of them wore blankets wrapped around them for extra warmth. New Boy was carrying the Carlsson boy on his back. Princess carried Gloria and walked next to Maria.

They moved in a straggling column across the near-featureless black plain. Vadim was at the head of the column; Schiller, with his compass, followed just behind him. Gulag and a limping Skull flanked the column on either side, and the Fräulein brought up the rear. Nobody spoke. The refugees and crewmembers were each locked in their own private freezing hells, concentrating on putting one foot in front of the other.

They found frozen pools and channels of seawater under the snow, but other than that and the odd rock nothing broke the monotony of the sandbank.

Vadim heard a hiss from Skull, and turned back to see the sniper signalling them to stop, and for silence. Instantly Vadim and the rest of the squad were alert, looking all around them. New Boy slid the Carlsson boy off his back and pushed him gently back towards the refugees. Princess handed Gloria back to her mother and unslung her AKS-74. Harris, and the crewmembers with G3s, were readying their weapons as well.

"What is it?" Schiller asked.

"Quiet," Vadim hissed. He was sure he'd heard something. He moved forward a little, coming alongside Skull. He was aware of the others doing the same, though New Boy stayed with the column. Then he heard it: the crunch, crunch, crunch of many people running on fresh snow. Running silently. He remembered Mongol telling Eugene he didn't understand how viruses work; just because the KGB and the Politburo wanted the virus to remain in the Americas didn't mean it would. The virus seemed to strike quickly, but perhaps they'd used a strain with a longer dormancy period to infiltrate the missile silos, NORAD, the White House; perhaps someone with that strain had made it onto a plane. All of these thoughts hit him in the moments between hearing the sound and seeing the mass of zombies sprint out of the red fog straight for the refugee column.

"Run!" Vadim screamed and his rifle kicked back against his shoulder. A zombie fell. They'd gotten so close, concealed by the fog, that he could barely miss. "Princess! New Boy! Stay with the refugees! Cover their backs! Get them to shore! Go!" He fired again and again. With every shot another zombie dropped, but they came on, closer and closer. Gulag was firing, aiming and firing again. Skull was doing the same, but more rapidly. Every shot had to count. He heard the Fräulein firing three-round bursts from her RPKS.

"Grenade!" Gulag shouted, firing his grenade launcher into a knot of the charging dead. They were showered in sand as zombies were flung into the air, shrapnel from the fragmentation grenades tearing into their corpses. Vadim did the same, his hand darting forward of the AK-74's magazine to squeeze the GP-25's trigger. Another knot of zombies thrown into the air, many of them losing limbs. A disturbing number kept moving, dragging themselves through the snow towards the squad. Vadim continued firing his rifle, dropping those closest to him.

"Reloading!" Skull shouted, and a moment later the Fräulein shouted the same from the end of the line. A tracer shot out of Vadim's rifle, a zombie fell with its phosphorescent tip still burning in his skull. He had three rounds left, and still the zombies were closing.

"Empty!" Gulag shouted. "Grenade!" The blast – a hand grenade – was much closer, spraying them with melted snow and hard wet sand. Shrapnel whistled past Vadim's ear as he fired his last shots. Two more zombies fell, Vadim cursing the hurried shot that had only winged its target.

"Empty!" he shouted, letting the AK-74 drop on its sling. "Grenade!" It was his last grenade, but it was too close. The blast almost took him off his feet, the sand blinded him; something tore into his shoulder, spinning him round. He felt nothing that could be considered pain from the impact. He spun back to see one of the zombies nearly upon him, and dragged his shotgun from its back sheath. The first round was hurried, badly aimed, catching the zombie in the shoulder, severing its arm, knocking it back. Giving Vadim enough time to work the shotgun's slide and fire again. This time he aimed. The buckshot hollowed out the zombie's head.

He heard Gulag firing his Stechkin rapidly.

"Empty!" Skull called. A moment later he was firing his sidearm as well.

"Empty!" the Fräulein cried and then her Stechkin was added to the noise, zombies dropping even as they reached the commandos' extended line. Vadim fired the KS-23 twice more and then that was empty and would take too much time to reload. He slid the shotgun back into its sheath and drew his *saperka* with his right and his knife with his left. He felt the impact run down his arm as the edge of the sharpened entrenching tool split the skull of the closest zombie. The firing had stopped from the others. In his peripheral vision he was aware of the other three grabbing for their knives and *saperkas* as well.

"Come on, you cunts!" Gulag screamed. Vadim squared up to the next zombie and it ran straight past him, utterly ignoring him. The next one tried to do the same, but Vadim opened its skull.

More had run past; it was clear they had no interest in them whatsoever. They wanted only the flesh of the living.

VADIM SPRINTED AFTER the dead. They ignored him, or recognised him as a brother. The Fräulein was following a little way behind. Skull was much further back, almost lost in the fog as he struggled to keep up on his splinted leg. Vadim watched as Gulag swung his *saperka* and took a chunk out of a zombie's head at full sprint, sending it tumbling to the ground in an explosion of black snow. The Muscovite had barely broken stride. Vadim swung out at another and almost went down, the sharpened entrenching tool grazing the thing's skull. Gulag tried to stab one in the head with the knife in his left hand. It scraped along the dead man's skull, but didn't penetrate far enough. Gulag and the zombie tumbled into the snow. Vadim couldn't risk slowing. He heard the knife bite home, the crack of steel piercing bone. Gulag swore and Vadim heard a collision behind him. He glanced behind him to see the zombie who'd just tripped over Gulag having his skull stove in by a s*aperka*.

It was obvious, really. Every single time the dead had attacked them they had been among the living. On reflection, even the one that had leapt on him as he'd rappelled down from the Manhattan Bridge onto the *Dietrich* had just seemed to get caught on his gear. It went some way to explaining how Gulag had survived trapped in the bridge castle with the rampaging dead. He got close enough to another zombie to swing his *saperka*, the blade biting deep. He staggered as he ran by, wrenching the entrenching tool out of its skull.

Vadim looked around for another target amongst his fellow dead. It was ridiculous, he'd known what he was since he'd opened his eyes at Grand Central Station. Had it driven home when they'd fallen on Eugene like a pack of carrion eaters. But even then, he'd still been in denial. Still been pretending to be alive. Now, running tirelessly with his dead brothers and sisters as they hunted for meat, he could deny it no longer. Men and women of all ages, moving as fast as their frames and builds would allow, unhindered by physical limitations like fitness and comfort. All of them dressed differently, from all walks of life, among them soldiers in both British and Soviet uniforms. The Red Army was on this island, or had been.

He faltered and almost stopped running when he heard the deep rumbling bass of the tank engines. He knew the sound. It was the stuff of nightmares, accompanied by the sounds of screaming, explosions and gunfire from his childhood. He'd grown used to it through his life, but this wasn't a Russian T-80 or a British Challenger; it was the unmistakeable sound of a German Panzer, a Tiger, of the kind they had used during World War II. The tanks that had helped destroy his home and his childhood, that he'd seen run over his terrified sister. It had no place here, now, in the modern world. Except that this was Hell, so maybe it belonged here after all. He didn't understand. He was struggling to make sense of it, even after everything that had happened.

Somehow this was a step too far, and he didn't know what to do other than keep running.

Headlights cut through the fog: he could see the shadow of higher ground; dunes, perhaps. He saw the blocky shapes of the Tigers, two of them. The lights silhouetted the sprinting refugees as the zombies gained on them. The tanks advanced onto the beach.

Suddenly Vadim's feet went out from under him. He hit the ice of a frozen channel between sandbanks, sliding across it on his front. Some of the zombies fell with him, but others didn't. Vadim managed to scramble to his feet as Gulag slid past. The refugees had reached the Tigers. There were two trucks and a half-track on the beach behind the tanks. Vadim could hear shouting. He was sure that some of it was in German. Then bullets were flying through the mist, making eddies in the water vapour, the lazy arc of tracers curving down towards them. He recognised the chatter of the MG 34 machine guns, another sound from his youth as he dived into the snow. The bullets sought out the mindless dead running past him, making them dance as they fell.

Vadim felt something slam into his side, and looked down to see his midriff glowing. It took him a moment to work out that he had a burning phosphorous-tipped tracer bullet lodged in his dead flesh. He could just about smell rotting meat cooking. He rolled onto his back, drawing his knife, and cut away at his clothes as bullets flew by overhead. He could hear other weapons now: MP-40 submachine guns, Mauser rifles, both of which had been carried by the *Wehrmacht* in the last war. He could also hear other more modern rifles – FNs, he thought, like the ones the ANZACs had carried in Vietnam. He dug the knife into his pale flesh. The steel blade was cold, but that was all he could feel as he dug the still glowing bullet out of himself. Bullets were digging up the snow and sand all around him.

The Fräulein landed next to him, her Stechkin held in both hands.

"Do you have another mag?" he asked, nodding towards the pistol.

"What have you been doing, *eating* the bullets?" she shouted, handing a magazine over to him. "It's my last one."

He reloaded his own pistol and then grabbed the shotgun from its back sheath, and slid his last four shells into it.

"Well?" she asked.

"Those are German tanks," he said.

"Those aren't Leopards."

"Tigers," he told her.

"Vadim?" she said, frowning.

He ignored her. The refugees were being loaded up into the backs of the trucks and the half-track, the soldiers and the tanks' machine guns providing inaccurate and undisciplined covering fire.

"Vadim!"

He looked up and saw the concern on her face. Zombies were still sprinting by. There was more shouting from the trucks. It sounded like a fight had broken out. Vadim heard a struggle, but couldn't make out the details. He stood up and started running again, heading straight for the tanks, sprinting into automatic fire. He felt something tug at his arm, making him half-turn. A bullet creased his leg, making him stagger, but still he ran. He wanted to scream at them, tell them not to get into the trucks. He recognised the silhouettes of the soldiers, their helmets, their weapons. He could hear the rumble of the tanks' engines switching gears as they started to turn, their turrets rotating so they could continue machine-gunning the charging zombies. The trucks and the half-track were leaving the beach.

"No!" Vadim wasn't sure why he was screaming.

Tank tracks churned sand and black snow as they climbed the sand dunes. Vadim was close enough to see the insignia on the tanks now. Not just *Wehrmacht* tanks; they bore the swastika, and the Nordic double-lightning bolt of the Waffen SS. Their insignia marked them as the 10th SS Panzer Division.

He came to a stop as the last tank disappeared over the dune. The remaining zombies continued chasing them.

"Vadim, what the fuck are you doing?" the Fräulein demanded as she caught up with him. Gulag wasn't far behind. Skull was still half-limping, half-running towards them, a grimace on his face.

"SS!" Vadim howled, pointing after the tanks. Gulag and the Fräulein stared at him as though he were mad.

"Vadim, they probably just took the vehicles from a museum," the Fräulein told him. Vadim spun round to face her. He'd seen the last soldier to climb into the back of the half-track.

"Their uniforms as well?" he demanded.

She had no answer for him. Gulag was staring past them both towards the sand dunes, a strange expression on his face.

"Will you look at that?" he said softly, with something approaching awe.

Vadim and the Fräulein turned to follow his gaze. Standing atop the closest dune, seemingly oblivious to the dead on the beach, backlit in the strange red light that suffused the fog, was a stag, its antlered head held high and proud.

CHAPTER EIGHTEEN

1405 GMT, 24th November 1987
Furness Peninsula, North-West England

IT FELT AS though Vadim had watched the stag for a long time, but it must have been only a few moments. It ignored the dead, now wandering aimlessly on the sand: they didn't seem to recognise the proud animal as a source of flesh. When Skull caught up with them, the stag bolted. Gulag turned to glare at the sniper.

The Fräulein stared at where the stag had been for another moment, then turned to Vadim.

"We're going after them." It wasn't a question. Vadim nodded. They both looked at Gulag.

"What?" he demanded. "Princess is with them."

"Can you track them?" Vadim asked Skull. The sniper looked momentarily affronted that the captain even had to ask if he could track a tank through snow.

THE TANK TRACKS followed the coastal road. The commandos found the odd car half buried in the black snow as they walked; broken glass and bloodstained vehicles told a story similar to what they had seen in New York. The tracks eventually turned north, following the road towards what looked like a reasonable-sized town, its skyline dominated by cranes and what looked like an indoor shipyard.

The tracks took them into the town, where they found evidence of tank damage to abandoned vehicles. They had seen little of the dead since leaving the beach, but as they entered the town they started to see more of them shuffling around. The zombies ignored them unless they made significant noise.

They passed neatly-ordered streets of red-bricked terraces with smashed windows and doors. They saw corpses frozen in the street. Some of the older buildings were made from red or brown stone; Vadim wasn't an expert, but he suspected much of the architecture dated back to the 19th century.

Led by Skull, they left the residential areas behind them and entered the docks. They crossed a bridge, the shipyard on their right, a large yellow crane hanging overhead. Somehow the presence of the wandering dead made it seem all the more abandoned.

The walk had given Vadim a lot of time to think, most of it spent trying to suppress his disappointment that the virus had already reached Britain.

They made their way through the docks, and then past more terraced houses. To the west they saw a narrow channel between the mainland and what Vadim assumed was an island, spanned by a bascule bridge, currently raised. At the east end of the bridge was a concrete barricade. A double-decker bus, with sheet metal wielded over the windows, acted as a gate between the barricades. Just behind the bus, Vadim made out what he suspected was another museum-piece armoured vehicle, this one with a mine roller attached to the front. Clever; the roller, designed to roll over mines and detonate them, would work equally well to clear the zombies milling around the gate so vehicles could cross the bridge. If any zombies did get through, they still couldn't cross the channel with the bridge raised.

The team were hunkered behind an abandoned van. They had seen movement behind the bus gate on this side of the channel; at the far end of the bridge, they made out sandbag-protected machine gun posts.

There were a number of small vessels moored in the channel, zombies dotted about them, stuck in the mud. Vadim was already considering using one of the vessels to cross the channel.

The whole situation seemed very strange. He couldn't understand why this shambles – they were too badly trained to be soldiers – were pretending to be an SS panzer division. All sorts of fantastical explanations were crossing his mind: the existence of zombies seemed to make anything possible.

"I don't fancy an assault with next to no ammunition," the Fräulein muttered.

"We need information before we make any decisions," Vadim said. Not for the first time since the refugees' apparent capture, he wondered what had become of Princess and New Boy. He would have expected some action from them by now. Not that he would necessarily be aware of it, if they did act.

"Reconnaissance?" she asked. Vadim just nodded. He noticed Skull staring at a pile of bodies. They were resolutely dead and unmoving; not a great deal of snow had settled on them, and they all had head wounds. Skull looked at him and nodded. Vadim signalled for the Fräulein and Gulag to keep a watch as he approached the pile of corpses with the sniper. They kept low, trying to avoid being seen by the guards at the double-decker gate.

"Try not to draw attention to me," the pile of corpses said. Vadim hadn't thought anything was capable of surprising him today.

"Princess?" he managed. He caught the barrel of her Dragunov sniper rifle sticking out of the pile; she was presumably using the scope to watch the bridge and the island. Skull and Vadim lay down next to the pile. Skull aimed his own .303 rifle at the bridge. He still had a few rounds left.

"Boss," Princess said.

"The bodies are a good idea," Skull commented.

"I think they mask my scent," she told them. She spoke softly, but even so, a couple of zombies stopped and stared in their direction. The three soldiers remained stock-still until the dead moved on. "I got the idea when Gulag saved those kids." Vadim glanced at Gulag. Had the criminal worked out that the dead ignored the dead before Vadim? Why hadn't he shared it? It was a conversation for another time.

"What happened?" he asked.

"We'd pretty much run out of ammunition by the time we'd made the beach. I was sure the refugees and crew were dead. I was going to try and make a break for it with New Boy, but we saw the tanks and the trucks. The refugees made for them, and New Boy followed, but I held back. Troops jumped out of the back and started ordering the refugees into the trucks. When the machine gun started firing, New Boy tried to intervene. He got clubbed down..." She went quiet again as another zombie walked slowly by. He was naked except for a sock.

"Who were they?" Vadim asked.

"They wore SS uniforms," Princess said. "But they had British accents."

"Soldiers?" Skull asked.

"I'm not sure, but they'd had training, some more than others."

"Equipment?" Vadim asked.

"The tank and half-track were from the Great Patriotic War, so was most of their weaponry. The trucks, however, looked like British Army: old, but not that old. And a few of them carried Belgian FNs."

"SLRs," Skull said. "It's the version of the FN that the British Army use."

The more Vadim knew about the situation, the stranger it became.

"The Territorial Army?" Princess asked.

"Then why are they dressed as the SS?" Vadim wondered out loud. "How'd you get away?"

"They started to beat Montgomery, New Boy stepped in. There was a fight. I made a run for it. A couple of them took shots at me, but they can't shoot for shit."

"Why'd they beat this Montgomery?" Skull asked.

"The policeman, Skull. Montgomery Harris. I'm not sure, it looked unprovoked. They called him names..."

"What names?" Vadim demanded, a little too sharply. Another zombie, an old man in a frayed tweed blazer and flat cap, jerked his head towards them, hissing. They went quiet again. After a little while, the zombie lost focus and shuffled off through the snow.

"I don't know. I didn't recognise the English. It sounded like gibberish, the kind of thing a child would spout; but I think they beat him because he was black."

It wasn't the snow that made Vadim feel cold. He wasn't quite sure what was going on here, but he was pretty sure the refugees, the crew of the *Dietrich*, and New Boy were all in trouble.

"What have you seen?" Skull asked.

"Foot and vehicle patrols along the opposite bank, work parties under the watch of the soldiers maintaining the defences. I'm not sure, but I think the bridge on the west side is mined, probably antipersonnel mines, claymores, something like that. If I can see it, it's not too subtle." That made sense to Vadim; zombies wouldn't know what they were looking at in any case.

"Work parties?" Vadim asked. "There are civilians over there?"

"Yes," Princess said, and Vadim found himself looking at the pile of bodies. The girl – woman, he corrected himself – on top of the pile looked to have been of an age with Princess. She'd probably had a very different life from the sniper's, at least until the war. The dead women's eyes were a mass of black, possibly the result of Princess caving in her head with a *saperka*. Just for a moment, Vadim wondered what her life had been like.

"Anything else?" Skull asked, breaking Vadim out of his thoughts.

"There are zombies stuck in the mud, but a bit further north of here I think the channel is shallow enough to walk across. But they've blown trenches in the mud and fortified the island side of the shallows. It's constantly guarded and the shore's been mined."

"Any idea where they took them?" Vadim asked.

"See the village just to the left of the bridge?" she asked. Vadim nodded. "In there somewhere. I heard the engines for maybe two or three more minutes, but some of that sounded like they were parking up rather than travelling."

"Okay, good work," Vadim said, and meant it. Vadim had known Princess was a very capable soldier, but even so, he was impressed. He started looking around for a place where they could keep their eyes on the bridge and the whole squad could plan with less worry of being interrupted.

THEY WAITED UNTIL there were no zombies nearby before Princess emerged from under the pile of corpses. The four dead Spetsnaz remained close to her as they made their way towards a tenement house. Vadim wasn't sure how the other three felt about it, but he was finding it difficult being this close to a living person.

Skull fell a little way behind. A couple of the zombies turned to look at them as they reached the open door of the house. Vadim had picked it because the open door was unbroken, as were the windows.

The black snow had drifted into the house's hallway. Princess was shaking, clearly freezing.

"Check for frostbite," Vadim told her. "We need to get your core temperature up." She nodded, but it was easier said than done. They couldn't risk a fire; the best she could do was wrap herself in blankets, assuming they could find any in the house.

Skull caught up and stayed with Princess while the rest of them checked the house, Stechkins in hand. Other than Vadim's shotgun and the two sniper rifles, the pistols were the only weapons anyone had ammunition for.

The house looked like it had belonged to an old person. They found signs of a struggle: smashed furniture in the lounge, blood on the carpet, the walls, the inside of the windows, but nothing else. Skull had closed and locked the door after them.

They made their way upstairs to the front bedroom overlooking the bridge. Gulag sat down on the bed. Princess had wrapped herself up and was moving around, trying to get warmer. Vadim didn't want to look at the black-and-white photos on top of the chest of drawers. He didn't want to recognise one of the zombies out in the street from the photos. Instead, he looked out the window. For a moment, Vadim could imagine the zombies outside were just pedestrians on a snowy day. Skull limped into the back bedroom, which looked out over the shipyard, but stayed close to the doorway so he could see down the stairs as well.

"Well?" the Fräulein asked, and Princess repeated the information she had told Vadim and Skull. "Any idea of numbers?" the East German sergeant asked after she'd heard Princess's story. It was the question Vadim should have asked.

"The two tank crews, and maybe another squad between the half-tracks and two trucks," Princess told them. "But I've seen more on the island."

"How many more?" Vadim asked. She shrugged.

"Even if it's just a platoon, which seems unlikely, we don't have any ammunition," the Fräulein pointed out.

"I'm aware of that," Vadim said, testily.

"Are we sure that they're hostile?" the Fräulein asked. Vadim stared at her. "All they've done, as far as we know, is rescue refugees from zombies. The shouting, the weapons, might have just been to get people moving. Shooting at Princess could have been their own panic."

"They were pretty hostile to Montgomery," Princess said.

"Who?" Gulag asked.

"Officer Harris," Vadim said. He didn't much like the look Gulag gave Princess.

"We need more information," the Fräulein said. Vadim and Princess nodded.

"Why?" Gulag asked.

The other three turned to look at him.

He pointed at the sniper. "We've got Princess."

"The refugees, the crew of the *Dietrich*," Princess surprised Vadim by saying.

"Very sad," Gulag said quietly, and then more loudly: "But we're at war with their fucking countries!"

"Will you *keep your voice down*?" Vadim hissed.

"New Boy," the Fräulein said.

"Oh, come on, the Ukrainian virgin? He's not one of us" – he looked between Vadim and the Fräulein – "and you both know it, don't you?"

"He's paid his dues," the Fräulein growled. Vadim could see her getting angry.

"He's not even been with us a month!" Gulag protested. "He was dumb enough to get caught. He could have fought." He pointed at Princess. "*She* got away."

"We had no ammunition. They all had guns and we were surrounded by civilians. And we didn't know if they were there to help or not, until the last minute," Princess said. Gulag opened his mouth to retort.

"Gulag, I'm sick of this," Vadim said, forestalling him.

"We all are," the Fräulein added. Princess nodded.

"New Boy's one of us. We're going to get him and make sure the refugees and crew are all right. Either come with us or don't, but I'm sick of arguing with you every time we try and get something done."

Gulag looked at Vadim, then at Princess and the Fräulein. "Women," he muttered. The Fräulein rolled her eyes.

"So what –" Princess started and then they heard the creaking. They looked out the window.

The bridge was lowering. The zombies had heard the noise as well and were shuffling towards the ad-hoc double-decker gate on this side of the bridge. They heard the rumble as the APC with the mine roller started up; then the bus began to vibrate as it was started up as well. The bridge came down and a six-wheeled armoured vehicle drove across it. Vadim was pretty sure it was a Saracen; he'd seen them used by the British Army in footage of Northern Ireland. The bridge was lifted again the moment it had crossed.

"Not taking any risks," the Fräulein said quietly. Multiple redundancies, it was clever. "The guards on the bus have to be in contact with the island."

The Saracen parked up behind the mine-rolling vehicle. The bus moved and the zombies surged forwards, but not at full sprint. It didn't look as though they had the scent yet. The mine-roller came forwards. It looked like a World War II tank, but not German; American, possibly. Pushing a big, heavy, gore-encrusted, zombie-flattening roller. The dead became red smears. The mine-roller came out just far enough for the Saracen to get past, and then it reversed and the bus rolled back into place.

"Did you see that?" the Fräulein asked.

"One of them ran in behind the tank-thing," Princess said.

"Give me your rifle," Vadim said. Princess looked conflicted for a moment and then handed her Dragunov to him.

"Don't mess up my scope," she warned him, and Gulag chuckled from the bed. Vadim looked through the scope. Even with the increased elevation, he couldn't see much – the bus and the concrete wall blocked his view – but he did see someone appear in the turret of the roller with an MP-40 submachine gun. He saw the muzzle flash, heard its chatter a moment later. "Wrong tool for the job," he said to himself. The guard wore a grey tunic and a German *stalhelm* helmet, with its distinctive coalscuttle shape. Through the scope, Vadim could see the swastika on the helmet and the two Nordic lightning bolts of the SS on the tunic's collar. He felt the old hatred bubbling up.

Suddenly the zombie – the one-socked naked man they'd seen earlier – bounded into view and started climbing up the tank. The guard was firing the MP-40 on full automatic, spraying it everywhere. Vadim saw an explosion of matter from the back of the zombie's head and it fell out of sight. It was sheer dumb luck that the man in the turret had hit anything at all. It was a shame; Vadim had found himself rooting for the naked zombie. He heard shouting coming from the bus. He couldn't make out what was being said, but whoever was shouting sounded angry.

He moved the scope off the bridge and followed the Saracen as it headed north and curved out of sight towards the town. He lowered the sniper rifle and handed it back to Princess.

"Are you coming with us?" Vadim asked Gulag.

"You're going after the vehicle?" the Fräulein asked.

Vadim nodded. "We're going to need to capture at least a couple of them alive," he said.

"To interrogate?" Gulag asked. He couldn't quite keep the eagerness out of his voice.

Vadim nodded again.

"I'm in."

CHAPTER NINETEEN

2014 GMT, 24th November 1987
Barrow-in-Furness Bus Depot, North-West England

GULAG APPEARED FROM behind the back door of the Saracen and wrapped his piano-wire garrotte around the neck of one of the SS soldiers. He dragged him backwards, clearing the Fräulein's field of fire to cover the driver. Vadim and Princess covered the last two soldiers. They'd left Skull to catch up.

"On your knees," Vadim ordered the men as Princess disarmed them and took their ammunition. Gulag's victim was drooling blood as the Muscovite started sawing through the neck. The SS soldiers ignored Vadim to stare at their friend's murder.

"Now!" Vadim snapped and they went down on their knees.

"Out!" the Fräulein snapped at the driver, dragging him out and pushing him onto his knees next to the other two.

"Watch," Gulag whispered in English to the three prisoners; the Fräulein had taught him the word at his request. He let the soldier slide to the ground, before putting his boot on the back of the soldier's head and sawing faster. The SS men watched in horror.

"Please," one of them whispered. He spoke with a British accent.

"It's the spinal cord that's the most trouble," Gulag muttered in Russian.

Vadim gritted his teeth. Even he didn't like the sound.

The Saracen hadn't been difficult to track through the black snow, even stopping at a hardware store en route for Gulag. By now they had worked out that they were in Barrow-in-Furness. Vadim was sure he'd heard the name before, from a list of sabotage targets; he was sure the shipyards built military vessels.

It had been a short journey further north through the town to a large depot housing the local bus fleet. The SS men had hurried in before attracting too much attention from the dead. It hadn't been difficult for Vadim, Gulag, Princess and the Fräulein to find their own way in, and Skull would have no problems following them.

Gulag's man's head fell off.

"No!" one of the soldiers cried out. Another soiled himself. The third man's hand shot to his mouth, tears in his eyes. Gulag let the dripping garrotte hang from his hand.

"Tell them it's harder than it looks," Gulag said in Russian.

"As members of the SS, I won't insult your integrity by assuming you'll talk after such a display. You are, after all, the Master Race," Vadim told them and nodded to Gulag. The Muscovite made a show of cleaning the garrotte, coiling it and putting it away. He took the hammer out of his webbing and one of the nine-inch nails from a pouch, then tipped the helmet off the crying SS man, the driver. He was a nondescript man, balding a little, with glasses. He looked soft, more like a bureaucrat than a soldier. He reminded Vadim a little of the photographs he'd seen of Himmler.

The man started begging.

"Shh, dignity," Gulag admonished in Russian. He tired to hold a nail to the man's head, but the man threw up, fortunately – for him – missing Gulag.

"What do you want? Please, just tell me what you want," he begged. Vadim held a hand up to forestall Gulag.

"Who are you people?" Vadim asked.

"My name's Bernie, Bernie Andrews. I own – I *owned* a garden centre," he whimpered. Vadim wasn't entirely sure what a garden centre was, but it wasn't the answer he was looking for.

"You're English, correct?" Vadim asked. The man nodded. "Why are you dressed like that?"

"We're re-enactors," he said, as though that explained everything. Vadim looked at him blankly. "We dress up as soldiers from the past and re-enact their battles."

"Why?" Vadim asked, mystified. Bernie stared at him.

"Y'know, history."

Vadim did not know.

"And they give you real weapons for this?" the Fräulein asked. "Live ammunition."

"Well, no, but some of the guys... we meet dealers and other enthusiasts, so we've amassed quite a collection."

"The tanks?" Vadim asked.

"Just the MGs, the main guns aren't functioning; that'd be insane."

"Yes. Yes, it would," Vadim muttered. "You bought the tanks?"

The man nodded again.

"For playacting?"

"To learn about history, by recreating parts of it."

"The worst parts of it," the Fräulein muttered.

"Why the SS?" Vadim asked, still not sure he understood what was happening. If members of a society could afford to equip themselves with military equipment for fun, then that society had to be pretty decadent.

Bernie shrugged. "They're interesting," he said.

"What's happening?" Gulag asked in Russian.

"They dress up like this for fun," Princess told him. Gulag looked confused.

"So you're not Nazis, then?" the Fräulein asked suspiciously.

"Of course not, that would be terrible."

"Where are the people you took prisoner on the beach?" Vadim demanded. There was a quiet tapping on the side door that they'd snuck in through. Gulag strolled over towards it.

"We didn't take them prisoner, we rescued them from the dead," the man said. One of the other prisoners, the one who hadn't soiled himself, shot a glance at the balding man. He looked younger, harder; he was bigger built and was frightened, but not frightened enough.

"Why'd you beat the police officer who was with us?" Princess asked. "And shoot at me?"

"I wasn't there," Bernie told her. Princess didn't look happy with the explanation. Gulag opened the side door and let Skull in. They walked back towards the prisoners with Gulag trying to explain the situation to the sniper.

"So you're just looking after them, then?" Vadim asked.

"Well, it's complicated, isn't it? I mean everything's changed. Somebody's got to be in charge."

"Shut up!" the younger one snapped.

"If you don't keep talking, *he*" – Vadim gestured towards Gulag – "will drive a nail through your skull, and get the answers we need from *him*." He pointed at the one who'd soiled himself.

"You want them as slaves, don't you?" the Fräulein said. Vadim hadn't quite got there himself yet, but the answer was written all over Bernie's face.

"It's not that simple –" he started.

"Don't say another word, you fucking traitor!" the young one shouted. Vadim nodded at Gulag, who knocked the younger one's helmet off. His head was shaved. It was a struggle for the Muscovite to hold him still, but eventually Vadim heard the all-too-familiar crack of nail through bone. The two remaining prisoners were screaming and crying.

"Shut *up*, or you get the same," Vadim hissed, wondering how many zombies would be attracted by their noise.

Gulag knelt and rolled up the sleeves of the dead man's camouflage tunic. "Boss," he said.

Vadim looked down. The shaven-headed boy had Nordic runes and a stylised swastika tattooed on his arm, along with the words *Meine Ehre heißt Treue*, written in gothic script. It wasn't often that Gulag looked disgusted.

"Not Nazis?" the Fräulein demanded. She sounded genuinely angry. Bernie held up his hands.

"Okay, look, there are a few nutters in the company; but most of are just ordinary guys with an interest in history!" he protested. Vadim wasn't sure what a 'nutter' was.

"And slavery," Princess added.

"Look, you're making that sound worse..."

"And your interest in history is still a priority during World War Three?" Vadim asked.

"It's practical in the circumstances. We were at a show nearby when the bombs started falling."

"If it was just a few 'nutters', then you stand up to them, ask them to leave," the Fräulein said.

"Have you invaded?" Bernie asked. He sounded eager to change the subject.

"Look, we can work with you..."

"Be quiet," Vadim snapped. He was struggling to control his distaste. It was the tattoos that bothered him the most. Perhaps most of them *were* just overzealous history buffs; but he couldn't understand why a citizen of a country that had stood up to the Nazis at the height of their powers had grown up to reject the lessons of history in such a way.

"Where are your families?" the Fräulein asked.

"Many of them were with us at the show," he told them.

"And the rest?" the Fräulein persisted, and Bernie stared at her. It was the first sign of defiance they'd seen out of him.

"We're from Essex," he said. "Y'know, near London." Vadim presumed London had been a target for nuclear weapons. "We were making our way back there when the dead attacked. One of the guys was in the TA; he said they had a centre, with an armoury and vehicles, on Walney Island. The bridge meant we could isolate it from the mainland."

"And the people on the island?" the Fräulein asked, disgusted.

"Are still there."

"As slaves?" Princess asked.

"We're just organising things."

That was enough for Vadim. He knelt next to Bernie. "Now, you need to answer these questions, and don't you dare fucking lie, understand me?" he said.

Bernie nodded, terrified.

"Where is your compound?"

"It's in Vickerstown, just off the A590 –" he started.

"Draw me a map from the bridge," Vadim demanded. The Fräulein found a piece of cardboard and a pencil. Bernie drew them a map, explaining as he went, obsequiously eager to please.

"Where are our people?" Vadim asked.

"They were in the yard when I saw them. Probably in one of the portacabins along the west wall, or in the assembly hall on the other side of the yard." Vadim wasn't happy with the answer, but he was also pretty sure that Bernie was telling the truth.

"How many of you are there?" Vadim asked.

"About a hundred of us," Bernie told him.

"Defences in the compound?"

"Towers at each corner with machine guns, then a lot of guns and the vehicles."

"Who's in charge?" Vadim asked finally. Bernie's expression changed: part fear, part awe. The other prisoner, the one who'd soiled himself, who was staring down at the concrete floor, started to snivel.

"Hauptsturmführer Kerrican, Steve Kerrican." Vadim had to strain to hear what the man was saying. "You don't want to mess with Stevie. He's a proper psycho."

"One of the 'nutters', then?" the Fräulein asked.

"He was the real deal, he served with 3 Para, Ulster, the Falklands –"

"You just watched my friend here saw one man's head off and drive a nail into the skull of another," Vadim pointed out. Bernie looked up at Gulag, who grinned back at him.

Bernie shook his head and looked down. "Look, I've told you everything, what are you going to do with us?" he managed. The other prisoner started to sob. Vadim regarded them both with distaste.

"What would your Hauptsturmführer do, I wonder?" he asked.

"Please..." Bernie said.

"We're going to let you go," Vadim said finally. Bernie looked up at him, hope in his eyes. Vadim nodded to Gulag and then climbed into the back of the Saracen with Skull, Princess and the Fräulein. Gulag made his way over to the main doors.

"Wait, what are you doing?" Bernie cried. Vadim closed the Saracen's rear hatch. In short order, the depot's metal doors ground open.

"You okay, Liesl?" Princess asked the Fräulein. Vadim turned to stare; even Skull looked momentarily surprised. Neither of them had ever heard Princess ask a question like that before. Vadim couldn't make out if the Fräulein was upset or just very angry. He wondered if it had anything to do with her being German. He himself had thought that the Nazis were the worst monsters that the world had ever seen, at least until he'd come to understand the extent of Stalin's purges. There were screams from outside, but they were screams of fear for the time being.

"Fools," the Fräulein muttered before looking over at Vadim. "We're going to get them, aren't we? All of them." He wasn't sure if she meant kill the fake Nazis or save the refuges. Vadim nodded anyway.

"You seem to be taking this very personally," Vadim said. Something hit the outside of the Saracen hard enough to make the vehicle rock on its suspension.

"Do you know what my first memory is?" she asked. Vadim, Princess and

Skull were all looking at her now. This wasn't the sort of thing Vadim expected from his second-in-command. The screams of fear outside had turned to howls of pain now. They ignored them.

"I was only three years old, and my insane mother took me to see my father executed. I'm not sure if I actually remember her saying this on the day, but she said it many times afterwards. She wanted me to know whom I had to hate: the bad people who had done this to my father for trying to stand up for his people. Just in case I might forget, she framed a picture of him hanging on the end of a rope. Black and white, artfully done. I saw it every day of my childhood."

"Your father?" Skull asked.

"He wasn't even a fighting man. A cowardly *Totenkopf* SS."

"Which camp?" Vadim asked.

"Ravensbrück, one of the women's camps." She shook her head. "She almost did it as well. Almost turned me. She spun all these lies that she'd convinced herself was the truth. An unrepentant SS widow. I found out, though; found out who my father was, what he'd done. Why he'd been hanged."

The screams had died down. There was a knock on the Saracen's armour.

"It's me," Gulag said. Vadim opened the rear hatch just long enough for him to climb in. The captain tried to ignore the sound of the dead feeding outside. Gulag sat down and looked around, picking up on the atmosphere.

"What'd I miss?" he asked. They ignored him. The Fräulein was still brooding. Gulag shrugged and inspected the weapons they had taken off the fake SS patrol. "This'll do." He picked up an MP-40 submachine gun. Vadim couldn't help but think it suited him.

VADIM AND PRINCESS had stolen a flat-bottomed dinghy, to present the smallest target. Vadim found himself having serious misgivings about its seaworthiness as they drifted across the channel towards the island. He and Princess were lying down in the dinghy, and there was a deepening puddle of water in the bottom of the small craft.

They had started just north of the heavily fortified area on the opposite bank, which Princess said could be crossed at high tide. They drifted north, occasionally leaning over the side of the boat to guide it with a paddle. The small village just north of the heavily-defended shore was dark, though there was smoke coming from some of the chimneys and candlelight shining through gaps in the curtains. They heard, but didn't see, a vehicle on the island. Vadim assumed it was one of the motorised patrols Princess had told them about.

There were hands waving in the water, zombies who had become stuck in the mud and left there for high tide. It lent their brief voyage an even more surreal feel.

Vadim and Princess were to make a reconnaissance before the squad made plans. Vadim would have preferred to do this with Skull, but the other sniper simply couldn't keep up on his leg.

They dragged the dinghy ashore into some nearby trees that bordered an airfield. There was little point in hiding; there were dozens of similar craft moored up and down the channel.

Vadim had left his AK-74 in the Saracen, which they were using as a mobile base; Princess had left her empty AKS-74, and the Dragunov, to preserve what little ammunition she had left, taking instead one of their stolen SLRs.

Vadim and Princess had crept back south, picking their way along the shoreline to the edge of the village.

"What now?" Princess whispered. "Go into a house?" Vadim was concentrating on the village, trying desperately to ignore Princess's proximity, the vibrancy of her life.

"How much were you taught about the British in your assassination squad?" he asked.

Princess gave the question some thought. "A bit," she said, "they were a potential target."

"Where's the best place to find British people," he asked, "even after World War Three?"

VADIM FELT THE atmosphere in the pub as soon as he walked through the door, even before the clientele had the chance to work out who and what he was. He could feel the anger in the room, and had seen the bodies hanging from the unlit lampposts outside. The people were frustrated, helpless.

Two men in SS uniforms stood at the bar laughing. Vadim was surprised by his own fury as he laid into the first man with his *saperka*. The man was screaming. Vadim felt the warm blood splash on his face, and it took every last ounce of self-control he had not to fall on the fake-Nazi and feed. He didn't even hear Princess shoot the other man in the head with her suppressed pistol.

"Boss," she said in Russian. His victim was a red mess on the bare wooden floorboards. Drool dripped from Vadim's mouth. He straightened up and looked around at the room as Princess closed the door behind her and leaned against it. With the burning log fire, he suspected it was the warmest she had been since they'd abandoned the *Dietrich*.

The pub was small, cramped, bowed and blackened; the modern furniture and fittings looked strangely incongruous. The clientele were mostly middle-aged men clearly used to life working outside. Rough hands ingrained with dirt told Vadim the kind of people he was looking at. They were all staring at him, horrified.

"Fools!" the woman behind the bar spat. "They'll kill us all." She was a plump lady, in her mid-sixties or so. Vadim turned to look at her and she took a few steps back. He reached down, removed the weapons and the ammunition from the dead SS men, and placed them on the bar. The room watched, silent.

"My name is Captain Scorlenski –"

"You 'ere 'a finish t' job?" a red-faced man in his forties demanded. Vadim had to play the sentence back in his head to work out what the man had actually said.

"Everyone thinks we dropped the bombs ourselves," Princess muttered in Russian. A few faces turned to her.

"I'm here to kill Nazis," Vadim finished.

"You can't!" the bar woman cried. There were tears in her eyes.

"We have to do *something*, Denise!" another man shouted.

"They'll kill them all!" the bar woman, presumably Denise, protested.

"Kill who?" Vadim asked with a sinking feeling.

"They took all the woman of a certain age, and all the children," said another man in the corner. He had the same build as many of the people in the pub: reasonably powerful, but running to fat. All of them looked like people who did hard, physical work but enjoyed their food and drink. Vadim guessed he was in his seventies. Something about him made Vadim think that he'd served in the military. He was old enough to have fought in the last war; if so, he couldn't have been pleased to see two men wearing SS uniform in his local pub. "They said the children were to be indoctrinated. That lunatic they have in charge is calling them the Stevie *Jugend*, but they're just hostages."

"The women?" Princess asked, her voice like ice.

"For their Joy Division," the old man said. Vadim went cold.

"They're not from here, are they?" he asked. "Why did you let them across the bridge?" It was out of Vadim's mouth before he could think. It was just frustration, it wouldn't help anything.

"'Tweren't us," the old man said. "They turned up a few days after the dead came, after we saw the flashes and the fires from Manchester and Liverpool. The way we heard it, they threatened to shell Vickerstown with the tanks, so they lowered the bridge."

They weren't to know that the main guns on the tanks weren't working.

"Why are you telling him anything, Bill?" a short, hatchet-faced man at a different table said. "He's one of them, look at him."

"The Russians fought *against* the Nazis, Sam," Bill said.

"I don't mean Russian. He's dead," Sam said. There was a collective intake of breath and some shuffling away from Vadim. Princess rolled her eyes.

"Can't be," someone else said. "He's talking, he's not trying to eat us."

"He's not breathing. Look at his colour," Sam persisted. Vadim caught a glimpse of himself in a mirror behind the bar. They were right. He didn't look human anymore.

"Yes, I'm dead," Vadim said. "But the Nazis have our people. We have a common enemy, that's all that matters."

"You people *did* this!" spat the red-faced man who'd first spoken. "You destroyed our cities, killed millions of people, brought this disease, turned our families – our friends – into cannibals!" He was on his feet, tears in his eyes. The men at his table were reaching up for him. Denise's hand was over her mouth. It looked as though they expected Vadim to kill him. Vadim took a step towards him, and he held his ground, shaking off his friends' hands. It was clear he'd had enough.

"My government did this. We had no part in the decision. My squad and I attacked New York, not Britain, but for what little it's worth, I'm sorry. I wish you and yours no ill will. We're deserters now, traitors. We just want to see our people safe. Yours too." The man had tears streaming down his face. Vadim wasn't sure why he did it but he took the man in his arms and hugged him. There was a moment of resistance and then the man was shaking in his arms, sobs wracking his frame.

Despite the heat of his life, despite the proximity of his flesh and the reek of blood from the corpses on the floor, Vadim felt none of his usual urges. He was just another sentient creature in pain. Pain inflicted on him by circumstances beyond his control, and compounded by petty, thuggish evil. Perhaps Gulag's vision of the world was right.

But if it were – if the new world belonged to warlords like this Steven Kerrican – then he may as well go down fighting.

"They took my daughter," the man sobbed. Vadim had nothing to say that would comfort him. They would try to get his daughter back – try to get everyone back – but they would be firing military weapons in a compound filled with civilians. It was a fight that had to be fought, but he wasn't going to make promises. He let the man go.

"What's your name?" he asked.

"Roddy," the red-face man told him. He sniffed and wiped away his tears, and then nodded almost apologetically to Vadim. There was nothing more to say, but somehow the two of them had come to an understanding.

"New York was you?" Bill asked from the corner.

Vadim suspected the question had been asked just to break the awkward silence. He nodded.

"We saw there had been terrorist attacks all over the US. Here as well. Greenham Common, Holy Loch, Faslane."

"That was people like us," Vadim told them. He wondered if it made any difference to explain that the virus wasn't supposed to have been used in Europe. He couldn't see how. If anything, it might make things worse.

"Any idea where the closest Soviet forces are?" Princess asked.

People shook their heads.

"We haven't seen any round here," Sam told her.

"A few of the zombies wear your uniforms," Bill added. "But that's all. We heard rumours that you'd invaded, but the telly went off shortly after the bombs fell."

For a moment, the futility of it all struck Vadim. Even if they managed to get the women and children out, it was only so they could die of radiation sickness or cancer from the fallout. This was assuming they didn't freeze or starve to death, or die of disease. *You have to keep fighting*, he thought. He wasn't sure why.

"We need you to tell us as much as you can about this Territorial Army compound, anything at all, but especially where the hostages are."

"No!" Denise cried from behind the bar. "You should be ashamed of yourselves! My Barbara is in the compound, so are her two little ones! You can't send people like that in there! They'll get them all killed!" She had tears running down her cheeks as well.

"They won't stop, Denise," Bill said, looking down at his pint. "They've had a taste of power. They'll fill the holes inside of them by hurting your Barbara, and Davie, and the tyke." He nodded down at the Nazis bleeding onto the bare floorboards. "I saw people like that in the camps in Burma. Doesn't matter if they're Japanese, German, their lot" – he nodded at Vadim – "or English; by the time they get to this point, all you can do is put them down like a dog gone wrong." He looked straight at the barmaid. "Now you won't like this, Denise, but there'll come a time that they've done so much damage Barbara and the children would be better off dead."

Denise tried to stifle a sob. "But you came back, Bill," she said through the tears.

He looked down, studying his pint again.

"It was a close-run thing, love. A lot of my friends died, too many by their own hand, and I very nearly became the worst kind of man. If it hadn't been for my Edna..." Another old man put a hand on Bill's shoulder, and he looked up and nodded in acknowledgement and thanks. "These dress-up Nazis, they just can't just let folk be folk." And then to Vadim: "Like your lot." Vadim wasn't sure he disagreed.

"We can't trust them," Sam said, glaring at Vadim and Princess.

"You hate them?" Bill said to Vadim, gesturing towards the two fake SS men.

"I grew up in Stalingrad," Vadim told him.

Bill crossed his arms and turned to Sam. "Good enough for me," he said.

"They're not just in the barracks," Denise said. "The ones with families took over the nicest houses in Vickerstown."

"Do you know which houses?" Princess asked.

"We can find out," Roddy said.

"Do you have any weapons?" Vadim asked.

"What little we had was mostly confiscated, but there are probably a few bits and pieces still lying around. Those'll help," Bill said, nodding towards the MP-40 and the two pistols on the bar that Vadim had taken from the bodies.

"Can you clear the ones out in the town and we'll do the compound?" Vadim asked. Bill thought for a moment, then nodded.

"Why were you drinking with them?" Princess suddenly asked. Almost everyone turned to look at her.

"They came here to look after me, love," Denise told her. Princess didn't seem entirely happy with the answer, but she didn't say anything else.

"You realise, if it gets out what we're trying to do, it's all over?" Vadim told them.

"We'll only get people we can trust involved. Nobody'll tell 'em owt," Bill assured him, to much mumbled agreement in the pub. Vadim wasn't sure what had just been said to him, but it seemed to mean they wouldn't share information with the enemy.

"Okay, tell me what you know, and be sure you get *where* the hostages are being held right," he told them. And then to Princess: "And then you're going back for the rest."

"Where are you going?" she asked.

"To meet with *der Führer*."

CHAPTER TWENTY

0001 GMT, 25th November 1987
Vickerstown, Walney Island, North-West England

VADIM MADE HIS way through the streets of Vickerstown past rows of mock-Tudor housing. The wind howled down the road, blowing the black snow around, creating drifts. There were very few candles burning in the houses, and the curtains were all closed tight against the horrors of the world. It was a joke; a place to hide and pretend that their world hadn't just ended. He had expected to see patrols, but found none. It seemed like the re-enactors just patrolled the shores of the island and manned the bridge and the shallow parts of the channel.

He was wondering why he was doing this. Walking into the wolf's den on his own. He remembered what the Fräulein had said to him on the *Dietrich* about their encounter with the national guardsmen in New York: *You look like you were trying to get yourself killed.* Was that it? It would be easier than carrying on, in this world, in his strange, terrible state. But he didn't think he was trying to kill himself.

He told himself he was going to negotiate, to see if he could arrange for the release of the hostages; but having sent Princess back to get the others, he knew he was on a clock. The Joy Division, the plan to indoctrinate the youth, were enough to want them dead. He suspected the real reason was to look into the eyes of this Hauptsturmführer Kerrican.

Vadim had done some very bad things over the years during various wars. He was already a monster before he died. He had *served* monsters, probably for most of his life. But he had limits, and when the likes of the KGB had tried to push him past those limits, he'd pushed back, as had the people he had commanded. Maybe it was the sickening maths of comparative atrocity. Maybe he was no better than Kerrican, but the Nazis' commitment to evil as an ideology, rather than a means to an end, had always staggered him. To find someone like Kerrican *aping* them, to the point that he would take advantage of the current horror to subjugate and brutalise his own people, disgusted Vadim. He had to look in Kerrican's eyes. He had to try and find himself in them; to see if he himself was anything more than a hypocrite unable to face what he really was.

Back in North Scale they'd agreed to move fast. Frightened people informed, especially when their loved ones were at risk, and they would be; the fewer people knew and the faster they moved, the less chance there was of someone tipping off the fake SS. Bill and his people would arm themselves as well as they could and contact people they trusted in other parts of the island. Then they would descend on the houses in Vickerstown that the re-enactors had taken over. They would leave the compound to Vadim's squad. It was a lot of ground to cover, a lot of personnel to deal with for just five people. Assuming Gulag came along with the others.

Vadim heard the compound before he saw it: loud music and raucous cheering. It sounded like some sort of sporting event.

The compound was a squat, ugly, high-walled square of red bricks. A heavy wooden gate opened onto the main road through Vickerstown. Vadim could make out scaffolding towers at three of the compound's corners, topped with sandbags. They were manned, and in the poor light Vadim could just about make out a machine gun in each tower. A larger building rose above the walls in the fourth corner, also made of red brick. No-thrills military architecture at its most utilitarian.

Vadim came down the middle of the deserted street under a dark sky. The moon and stars were still hidden from view by all the dust in the atmosphere. He managed to get quite close before the light of a powerful handheld torch stabbed through the night and blinded him. He raised his hands slowly and told them who he'd come to see.

* * *

THE FAKE SS men came rushing out of the gate to cover him. Before the war they may have been businessmen, or worked in shops, or driven lorries; but now they looked like Vadim's forty-year-old nightmares.

Their search was perfunctory; they didn't want to get too close to the dead, and they certainly didn't want to touch him. They took what weapons they could find before escorting him into the compound, into madness.

He had a look around as they marched him across the slush-covered yard. To his left the two Tiger tanks were parked between the gate and one of the towers. To his right was the half-track and another Saracen APC, with space for the one they had taken. Four prefabricated buildings ran down the right-hand wall, between two of the towers. If Bernie and Bill's information had been correct, and they seemed to agree, then the first hut was empty, unless the refugees and crew from the *Dietrich* were being held there. It looked dark. There was no way to be sure if there was anyone inside or not, though there were no guards posted outside it. The second hut was where the children were kept, the third hut was the so-called Joy Division, and the fourth was the barracks for the single men.

On the left in the back corner was the building he had seen, some kind of hall. A huge, blood-red banner with a swastika painted on it hung down from the roof. Vadim made out a number of military trucks parked against the rear wall.

In the middle of the grassy yard next to the hall, a pit had been dug out and then lined with multi-floored scaffold boxes, like crude bleachers around an arena. Nazis packed the stand, looking down into the pit and cheering.

Finally Vadim saw Captain Schiller, standing in the yard outside the bleachers. A chain ran from his neck to a substantial-looking iron ring that had been hammered into the tarmac. His ears had been cut off and he was very clearly dead. He was swaying from side to side like a caged predator, watching Vadim as he was escorted past the captain of the *Dietrich*. There was no recognition in his eyes at all. It took a great deal of effort for Vadim not to start killing there and then.

Then he got his first look at Hauptsturmführer Kerrican. Wooden steps ran up the side of the hall to a walkway overlooking the arena, ending in a door into the hall. Kerrican stood on the walkway looking down into the pit, like

Caesar on his balcony. The flickering light of a flaming torch illuminated his grinning face.

Vadim reckoned Kerrican would be thought of as handsome, though his high cheekbones and the cruel set of his mouth made him look arrogant. He looked at home in the grey SS smock and soft forage cap. Bernie hadn't been lying when he'd claimed that this man had served; it was plain to Vadim that he was looking at a soldier.

The guards marched Vadim up the wooden steps to the walkway where Kerrican stood. On the way up, he got a view into the pit. New Boy and a badly-beaten Harris were facing off against three zombies, armed with a broadsword and a cricket bat with nails driven through it. The body of a fourth zombie lay on the muddy ground of the pit. New Boy and Harris looked exhausted. Part of the pit had been fenced off to form a corral for more of the zombies.

Vadim was staggered by the waste of effort and resources. It had been only nine days since the world had ended, and yet somehow these people had decided this was the best use of their time. Nine days. Again Vadim had to force himself not to react. He just turned away as another of the zombies lunged.

The Hauptsturmführer tore his eyes away from the spectacle in the pit to face Vadim. Up close, the captain realised Kerrican was wearing a necklace of ears. He looked into his green eyes and didn't see himself. This man was irrevocably mad.

Kerrican looked him up and down.

"You look fucked, mate," he said, and then grinned. He had a charming smile. Vadim had seen smiles like that before on other psychopaths. "Let's talk in my office."

Vadim nodded. There was more cheering from the scaffolding, and Vadim risked a glance. Harris had embedded the nailed end of the cricket bat into the head of one of the zombies. It sank to its knees, spasming. Another charged the police officer but New Boy rammed the broadsword into the thing's mouth, the tip of the sword exploding out of the back of the dead man's head. "Looks like the nig-nog can fight after all," Kerrican muttered, before leading Vadim through the door and into an office. Vadim had no idea what a 'nig-nog' was.

THE OFFICE WAS warm and well-lit with electric bulbs, suggesting a generator somewhere in the compound. There was another door in the opposite wall.

Vadim figured it had once been the office for the commander of the TA unit stationed here. It was neat and ordered. It was obvious Kerrican had added the framed picture of Otto Skorzeny, a Waffen-SS officer who some credited with being the father of modern special forces operations. Vadim was not one of those people. Kerrican followed Vadim's gaze.

"Old Otto, he was a lad, wasn't he?" Kerrican asked, grinning. Three of his soldiers had escorted Vadim into the office. Kerrican nodded to one of them, who slung his SLR and went back onto the walkway to watch the end of the pit fight. The other two, both armed with double-barrelled shotguns, remained in the office, keeping an eye on Vadim. He assumed they knew how to kill him, or they wouldn't have lived this long, and the shotguns were good tools for the job in close quarters. Instead of answering Kerrican, Vadim turned his attention to a rifle hanging from a hook, along with two canvas pouches, each containing three spare magazines.

"Like that?" Kerrican asked. "That's an StG 44, one of the first assault rifles ever made."

"Came in towards the end of the last war," Vadim said. He couldn't shake the feeling that Kerrican was trying to impress him. He wasn't. "Still didn't save the Nazis. I thought Britain had very strict rules own gun ownership."

"Yeah, and they were just about to get tighter," he said with distaste. His accent was very different from the locals. Vadim was no expert but he was pretty sure he was from London, or its environs. "Some of us had licences, mostly for the bolt-actions. Some of the deactivated weapons weren't too difficult to reactivate if you knew what you were doing, but you'd be amazed at how much of this stuff was just left hanging around, if you knew where to look. Add to that a few shotguns off the farms" – he nodded towards one of Vadim's guards – "and what they had in the armoury here, and…"

"You've got all you need to equip your little army," Vadim said. A nerve over Kerrican's left eye twitched at the goad. Kerrican sat down behind the desk. Vadim's weapons had been laid out on top of it. The captain was losing count of the mistakes these guys were making.

"So what are you, then? Other than dead, I mean," he asked, looking up at Vadim. "KGB? GRU? VDV?" Vadim tried not to flinch at the mention of the hated KGB.

"Spetsnaz," Vadim told him. Kerrican wasn't looking at him; he'd picked up Vadim's NRS-2 knife.

"What's that when it's at home, then?" he asked, only half paying attention. It made sense that he hadn't heard of the Spetsnaz, very little was known about them in the West.

"Think of us as the Russian SAS," Vadim told him. That got Kerrican's attention. A shadow seemed to cross his face at mention of the SAS, as though he didn't want to hear their name. Vadim wondered if Kerrican had failed selection, perhaps on psychological grounds.

"Yeah, I don't think so, mate," he said. "But I'm guessing you're some kind of smart, Kremlin super-zombie sent over here to infect us with this plague, right?"

If I was, it would be foolish to let me get this close, he thought. Kerrican pointed at him.

"Ha! I knew it!" He turned to the guard to the left of his desk. "Ralphy, what'd I fucking tell you?"

"Aye, you were right enough, Stevie," the guard said.

Kerrican turned back to Vadim. "Before the Wartime Broadcasting Service stopped working, we heard that your lads had invaded down south."

Again Vadim said nothing.

Kerrican leaned back in his chair. "So I'm assuming you want something. What're you here for?"

"I want my people, the ones you took on the beach," Vadim said. "And get the two men in that pit out of it right now."

Kerrican appeared to be giving this some thought.

"So you came on the ship?" he asked. "Always wanted to go to New York; you see it in all the films, don't you? Well, maybe you don't. Problem is it's full of spicks, niggers and chinks, isn't it?" Vadim tried to keep his naked contempt off his face. "What do I get?" the Englishman continued. The guard behind him chuckled.

"What do you want?" Vadim managed.

"If you're just off the boat, then I don't think you'll have much sway with the occupying forces."

"I'm a colonel in the USSR's equivalent of the SS," Vadim lied. The KGB were much more like the SS – and the Gestapo – than the Spetsnaz were. "Let's assume that I'll have more pull than you. Will you make me repeat my question?"

"All right, mate, calm down," Kerrican said, leaning forward, raising a conciliatory hand. "I think the world would have been a much better place today if Hitler hadn't broken the Molotov-Ribbentrop Pact. He shouldn't have gone to war with the Soviet Union. You've seen what I'm capable of with next to nothing. I want control of this zone, ultimately under your command, but with autonomy to run it how I see fit. There's gas fields offshore, a refinery, there's people on the island who know how it all works. We could get it up and running for you. You give us the resources, we can take back Barrow-in-Furness, which means you get the dockyards." He sat back in the chair and looked up at Vadim, expectantly.

The little speech reminded him of Gulag's fantasy of carving out a kingdom. This is what it would look like: sad, pathetic and built out of other people's misery. Even for Kerrican to be talking to him about this was clutching at straws; Vadim could have been anyone with a Russian accent. Kerrican was accepting him at face value because he wanted it to be true.

"And for this, you'd turn on your own people?" Vadim asked, intrigued now. Kerrican shot to his feet. He dropped the knife he had been toying with and slammed his palms down on the table.

"*I* didn't fucking turn on *them!* They fucking turned on *me!* First the niggers in the 'fifties! Then the fucking Pakis! But oh, no! It's all right for young Stevie Kerrican to go and watch his mates get killed in Ulster, get fucking chewed up in the Falklands. I deserved a Victoria Cross for what I did down there, but you know what I got instead? Fucking binned, mate, that's what! And meanwhile the country's turning a funny colour!" Vadim wasn't following every word but he was getting the gist of it.

"Calm down, Hauptsturmführer," Vadim said. He didn't like using the man's assumed rank, but if he gave a little, he might be able to walk out of here with all the civilians. Then it would just be a case of exterminating these fools. "As you can imagine, our supply lines are somewhat stretched at the moment, so we would be grateful; and will reward any collaboration. I assume that you have worked out that we are in satellite communication with command? We can see what can be arranged."

Kerrican smiled and nodded. "See, what did I tell you, Ralphy?" he said.

"Sweet," Ralphy said.

"Of course, I'll need my people back," Vadim said.

Kerrican gave this some thought. "That's not a problem," he said. "But the nigger stays in the pit."

"Why?" Vadim demanded, trying to keep a grip on his temper.

"Because he offends me."

"How did he offend you?"

"No, *he* offends me," Kerrican said. Vadim silently apologised to Harris. He would get the policeman out as soon as he could. "Anything else?"

"Let the women and children go," Vadim said. Kerrican's eyes narrowed. It had been a long shot, and straightaway he knew he'd gone too far. Suspicion was written all over Kerrican's face. The guard standing to the right of the desk, Ralphy, shifted, bringing the shotgun up, but the so-called Hauptsturmführer raised his hand to stop him.

"Why would you want me to release the leverage I have over the people here?" he demanded. "Who've you been talking to?"

"It didn't take us long to work out what was going on in here. You give people nothing to lose and they fight back. You want to control them, subjugate them, they need something to live for." Vadim put both hands on the desk and leaned across it towards Kerrican. "And because this isn't the way that soldiers behave." He felt the twin barrels of Ralphy's shotgun pressed against his temple. He was quite surprised his head hadn't been sprayed all over the wall already, but it had been worth it. He'd managed to palm his knife off the desk and slip it up the arm of his jumper. He could feel it, pressed against the cold dead flesh of his forearm.

"No, mate," Kerrican said, shaking his head. "Wars are won by those who have the will to do what others will not. Look at what your lot did in Berlin in Nineteen-Forty-Five."

"Because having the will to do what others won't worked so well for your heroes in the last war," Vadim pointed out.

"Because they were fucking betrayed!" Kerrican was on his feet again. "One of the most shameful things this country has ever done. We should have been marching lockstep with the Germans. Instead the loony-left somehow took control and we fucking betrayed our whole race!" He pointed towards the prefab huts on the other side of the yard. "We're doing these children a favour. We're finally going to make Britain great again! All those women are doing is their fucking duty, for once! Breeding the next generation!" The madness was blazing in his face, now, panting and red. Vadim was struggling to control himself.

"What happened to Captain Schiller?" he asked through gritted teeth.

"He wouldn't kneel, would he?" Kerrican told him. His eyes seemed to glitter.

"He told me he'd made a mistake as a young man. He'd been conscripted, found himself in the engine room of a *Kriegsmarine* battleship. I told him that the only thing wrong with that was that he hadn't volunteered. He said that the biggest regret of his life was that he hadn't joined the resistance, fought the Nazis." Kerrican took a knife from a scabbard on his belt: a Hitler Youth knife. "See that? *Blut und Ehre*. Blood and honour, as in your fucking friend the captain had none. He was a race traitor!"

"So you cut his ears off?" Vadim asked, looking at the grisly necklace around Kerrican's neck. He could hear the sound of an engine now. Shouting from the gate. Kerrican glanced in that direction and then back, apparently unconcerned. He noticed Vadim looking at his necklace and held it up. Two of them, presumably Schiller's, looked very fresh, the rest were blackened and old.

"You like that?" Kerrican asked grinning. "Just like Vietnam, yeah? See I was 3 Para, proper green-eyed-boy me." Vadim had no idea what the colour of his eyes had to do with it. Kerrican was shaking the necklace of ears now. "Mostly Argies on here, but some of these belonged to American mercenaries. There's even a couple from Ulster."

"3 Para?" Vadim said, wracking his brain. Kerrican and Ralph were looking at his face, not his hand, and he slowly cocked the lever on the right hand side of his concealed knife's hilt. He'd heard the gates creak open. "Didn't they very bravely fight at Arnhem? Operation Market Garden?"

"Yeah, so what?" Kerrican said.

"And were nearly wiped out by the 10th SS Panzer division?" As Vadim clicked the knife's safety off he saw it in Kerrican's eyes, just for a moment: guilt. Then it was swept away by the excuses, the hate, the fantasies that had twisted the young man's mind.

"You are a disgrace," Vadim told him. "You deserve to wear that uniform." Outside the office, he heard the Saracen drive into the compound. There was no cry of warning. The fake SS soldiers were too stupid to make sure that it was their own patrol returning. "This is going to happen very quickly," Vadim told him.

CHAPTER TWENTY-ONE

0019 GMT, 25th November 1987
Vickerstown, Walney Island, North-West England

VADIM HEARD THE rockets in flight. The building shook, windows shattering, as the two Tiger tanks exploded, destroyed by the squad's remaining RPG-18s. The world turned orange. The fragmentation grenades were almost lost among the noise.

The explosion, not surprisingly, distracted Kerrican and Ralph. Vadim raised his left arm and pulled the trigger on the NRS-2 knife, firing the 7.62mm bullet out of the blade's hilt at Ralph. The recoil drove the blade into the dead flesh of his forearm, but a small hole appeared in Ralph's forehead and he started to fall back. Vadim grabbed his *saperka* from the desk with his right hand, swung round and threw it at the other guard. The sharpened edge of the entrenching tool caught him in the shoulder and he stumbled back, dropping his shotgun.

Vadim swung back to find Kerrican hooking the Hitler Youth knife in towards his head. More out of instinct than design, Vadim stabbed out with his own blade and caught Kerrican's knife arm with it, driving it back against the wall. Vadim tore the blade along the arm, opening it up, and the Hitler Youth knife dropped from nerveless fingers. Kerrican howled.

The door to the external walkway was kicked open and the guard with the SLR came through firing, almost hitting the screaming Kerrican. Vadim threw himself sideways as the rifle stitched a line of holes in the wall. He landed on Ralph's corpse, scrabbled for the shotgun and rolled over. The guard fired the SLR again, hitting Ralph's body; Vadim let him have both barrels, driving backwards out of the doorway and over the rail, into the pit.

"I'll fucking have you!" Kerrican screamed as he clawed awkwardly for his holstered Walther with his left hand. Vadim heard gunfire outside as he rolled to his feet. He hit Kerrican in the face with the butt of the shotgun, breaking his nose.

"Ow! You *cunt!*" he screamed, but it distracted him long enough for Vadim to grab the pistol and toss it away.

He retrieved his knife, stabbed it into Kerrican's leg and tore it downwards. The so-called Hauptsturmführer sat back down hard in his chair, trying to hold the wound in his leg together, shouting obscenities. Ignoring him, Vadim holstered and sheathed his weapons, before grabbing the StG 44 and the pouches of spare magazines. The guard with the *saperka* in his shoulder was trying to crawl through the doorway. Vadim crossed the room, kicked him screaming onto his back, tore the entrenching tool out of his shoulder and brought it down on his skull, almost bisecting it. He dropped the dripping *saperka* back into its loop on his webbing, then turned toward Kerrican.

"What are you gonna do?" Kerrican demanded. He was wary but not exactly frightened. Vadim strode back across the room, shoved the desk out of his way and picked Kerrican up. The Englishman thrashed ineffectually with his left arm as the captain carried him out onto the walkway.

Vadim took in the scene. Next to the gate he could make out the gutted remains of one of the Tiger tanks, torn open by the explosion. It looked like the 40mm fragmentation grenades he'd heard going off had hit the tops of two of the guard towers. Skull was limping as fast as he could towards the lorries parked against the rear wall, looking for higher ground to shoot from, and Gulag was running towards the prefab building that held the child-hostages. Once this would have worried Vadim, but not now, after what the Muscovite had done for Gloria and the Carlsson boy.

He caught a glimpse of Princess disappearing into the Joy Division prefab. The Fräulein was firing the MG 34 machine gun into the stands, using the Saracen for cover, belts of ammunition draped over her right arm. Nazis were tumbling into the pit, and Vadim saw tracers spark off the metal scaffold poles and fly into the night air. Such had been the ferocity of the attack that the re-enactors hadn't even started firing back yet.

Vadim dragged Kerrican to the edge of the walkway, over the zombie corral. The dead were already in a frenzy, feeding on the men falling to them under the Fräulein's onslaught. The so-called Hauptsturmführer could see what Vadim was about to do.

"I'm gonna come back!" he screamed. "I hate, like you do!" Vadim threw him down into the corral. Kerrican didn't even try to save himself; to hold onto him, or grab for the rails.

The zombies descended.

"You're nothing like me," Vadim muttered, even as bullets impacted all around him. He could see Harris and New Boy in the makeshift arena. They had harvested weapons from fallen Nazis; New Boy was dispatching the injured.

At last the fake SS started returning fire, if only sporadically. Bullets sparked off the Saracen's armour as the Fräulein took cover behind the APC. The shooters were on the ground floor of the hall beneath Vadim and in the prefab housing the barracks. The Fräulein turned the MG 34 on the prefab as Vadim shouldered the StG 44 and headed back into the office, in time to see the interior door opening.

Vadim dropped to one knee next to a filing cabinet, and watched the barrel of a rifle slowly push the door open. A stray bullet flew in through the window behind Vadim and put a hole in the interior wall. The door opened enough for Vadim to see another SS uniform; the man's eyes widened as he saw Vadim, and the captain squeezed the trigger on the StG 44. The rifle hammered into his shoulder, the recoil worse than an old AK-47, making the barrel climb as it stitched three neat holes in the enemy rifleman's chest and face. He fell back, and Vadim heard panic on the other side of the door. He could use panic.

He crossed the office in a few strides, and was through the door onto a mezzanine floor above a large hall stacked with looted supplies. He saw leather sofas, huge televisions and stereos, VCRs, crates of alcohol, fridges and freezers, all presumably powered by the as-yet-unseen generator.

There were about twenty of the re-enactors down in the hall, firing through the windows facing into the compound. They were probably all aiming for the Fräulein, but their inaccurate, undisciplined fire would be sending stray rounds into the prefab huts where the refugees and the local women and children were. There were three other SS men on the stairs up to the office, and they had been smart enough to have another two covering them from the floor of the hall.

Vadim started receiving fire the moment he stepped through the doorway. He felt one bullet open up his cheek, and another bury itself into his right arm just below the shoulder; more shots whistled by, powdering plaster all around him. Had he been alive, the impacts would have been more of a problem. As it was, he barely registered the pain. He fired one three-round burst, then another, and the two shooters on the floor hit the ground. The gunmen on the stairs were still struggling to react when Vadim turned his weapon on them.

The defenders shooting out the windows, realising there was danger in here with them, swung their weapons up towards Vadim. He emptied the rest of the StG 44's magazine and disappeared back through the door. Holes appeared in the walls off the mezzanine office and everything in the room seemed to explode as a rain of bullets tore through it. Vadim threw himself bodily towards the back of the room, feeling something tug at his leg in mid-air. He landed heavily and rolled over. A bullet had carved a furrow across his thigh. He curled up, trying to present the smallest target possible, and resisted the urge to scream. As a zombie, he knew he could take more punishment than a living human – short of a headshot, they'd have to more or less destroy his body to stop him – but he wasn't impervious to bullets, by a long shot. He assumed there was less liquid in his body than there had been when he had been alive, but ballistics was ballistics: one good hit from a machine gun bullet could easily blow a limb off through hydrostatic shock. Pistol and SMG rounds worried him less, but he couldn't just walk into a hail of bullets and expect to be fine.

The fusillade slacked off – presumably they'd emptied their weapons – and Vadim changed the magazine on his own gun.

The Fräulein returned fire for him. He heard her MG 34 as she poured fire into the hall below the office. Vadim made his way back to the door and peered out. He saw tracers flying through the hall, furniture and electronic devices exploding. He saw the slowest of the SS men dancing as bullets churned up their flesh. The rest were lying on the floor, hands over their heads, so Vadim started killing them.

Five people shouldn't be able to do this to a hundred armed men; had the re-enactors been soldiers, as opposed to well-armed but enthusiastic amateurs, they probably wouldn't have been able to. Even with trained soldiers, it took experience to function in the face of this sort of firepower, let alone when it was wielded by dead men and women with extensive special forces training.

The Fräulein's machine gun had stopped, but Vadim was still firing when they started to surrender. It was only when he ran out of rounds and had to reload that he actually heard their cries. The survivors downstairs had had enough, and were raising their hands in the air. Vadim moved down the steps, covering them. He had a choice: kill them now, which he suspected they deserved, but would probably descend into another fight; or accept their surrender and hope they were frightened enough not to try anything, since he had nobody to guard them. He chose the latter. The gunfire outside had died down some; he suspected that the Fräulein was changing the belt on the MG 34, and what he could still hear was from the barracks. The odd round ricocheted into the hall.

"Fräulein, do not fire into the hall!" Vadim shouted as loudly as he could in Russian as he made his way down the cracked, splintered steps. He half-expected the whole mezzanine to collapse. He thought he heard an answering call.

"Drop all your weapons and ammunition; that means grenades, knives, sidearms, anything! Then get into the middle of the room on your knees and lace your hands behind your backs!" Vadim told the re-enactors. "You move, we kill you; you try and run, we kill you; we find a weapon on you, we kill you; understand me?" There were nods from the six survivors. They looked dazed, in shock, as if their experience of war had not quite lived up to their fantasies. "Move, now!" They had enough sense of self-preservation left to scramble to obey him.

Vadim moved to the doorway of the hall.

"Fräulein!" he shouted in Russian. "I'm at the ground-floor door to the hall. I'm coming out, don't shoot!"

"Understood!" she called back, and Vadim risked glancing out of the door. The burning tanks illuminated the yard. Gunmen in the prefab hut against the rear wall, the barracks, were firing at the Saracen, rounds sparking off its armour. It looked like the fire was concentrated on the rear right corner of the vehicle, presumably where they had last seen the Fräulein take cover. He could also see muzzle flashes through the windows of the Joy Division hut and the hut where the local children were being held; and for the first time, he was aware of the sound of gunfire from outside the compound, in the town.

He glanced at the prefab closest to the gate. By process of elimination, that was where the refugees and the crew of the *Dietrich* had to be held. It was dark and still. That was either a good or a very bad thing. Vadim was preparing to sprint over when he saw four of the gunmen charge out of the barracks towards the Saracen. Presumably they had worked out that the Fräulein was reloading and had taken a chance. It was the bravest thing that any of the fake 10th SS Panzer soldiers had done.

Vadim raised his StG 44 and was about to shoot when they started dropping. The lead man was down, then the rear. The last two were looking around, trying to work out where the shots were coming from, and then there was one.

Peering through the bleachers around the pit, Vadim finally located Skull atop one of the lorries at the back of the compound. The last of the four men jerked back, his helmet spinning into the air.

Vadim lowered his weapon and again prepared to make a run for the prefab, but heard gunfire coming from the pit area and ran towards that instead. He saw the Fräulein emerge from the left-hand side of the Saracen, firing her machine gun from the hip, spraying the barracks, tracers zipping over the slush in the yard and punching through the hut as she walked towards it.

Vadim reached the scaffold stand and clambered onto the lowest level. Someone had thrown open the gates to the zombie corral, and Harris and New Boy were once again fighting for their life. New Boy was dropping them one after another with headshots from an SLR, while Harris was uselessly emptying an MP-40 SMG into the body of the zombie charging him. Vadim put a three-round burst into its face and it collapsed to the ground. He grabbed his KS-23 from the sheath on his back and dropped it down to Harris.

"Four rounds left, aim for their faces!" he shouted. Whether Harris heard him over the deafening roar of New Boy's SLR, or just felt more comfortable using a shotgun, Vadim didn't know, but the police officer dropped the SMG and grabbed the KS-23. Vadim raised the StG back to his shoulder, wondering who had freed the zombies, when a figure swung down from the level above. The newcomer caught the captain in the chest with both feet, hard enough that he heard a crack from his ribcage as something broke. He was knocked out of the scaffolding and sent sliding across the black slush in the yard. His attacker landed on his chest, their knees pinning his gun down, metal glinting in his fist.

"I fucking *told* you I was coming back, little man!" Kerrican yelled, flaps of skin hanging off his recently-feasted-upon face, the flesh pared down to the muscle. Kerrican drove the knife down towards Vadim's forehead. It was all the captain could do to catch the zombie's arms, stop the blade from being driven home. "I'm stronger than you!" he screamed, drool flecking Vadim's face as the blade inched closer and closer to his head. It seemed that the wounds Vadim had inflicted on Kerrican troubled him much less in his dead state.

There was no-one to help. The Fräulein was still marching inexorably towards the barracks. The makeshift bleachers stood between Vadim and Skull. Princess and Gulag were both still in the prefabs, and judging by the gunfire, New Boy was still fighting for his life in the pit. The flames from the burning tanks flickered in the blade of Kerrican's knife as the tip came closer and closer. Vadim felt the cold steel against his dead forehead, the sharp point parting it. He felt the tip meet his skull, felt the bone crack. It would be peace, at last; all he had to do was let it happen.

Vadim wasn't ready to stop existing yet. He screamed, and with all of his might tried to push the blade away, but Kerrican was right. He was stronger.

"*Lernen!*"

A rusted iron spike was suddenly rammed through Kerrican's head; he vomited blood all over Vadim and then collapsed to the ground. Vadim pushed the madman's body off him and scrambled backwards.

The earless corpse of Captain Schiller stood over him, staring down.

Vadim brought his weapon up.

"Captain?" he asked. A chain ran from Schiller's collar to the spike through Kerrican's head. "Are you in control?"

"Go." The word was torn from a dry throat. Vadim backed away from the other zombie, then turned and sprinted for the prefab by the gate. He heard a grenade explode behind him.

He glanced at the Fräulein, who'd made it into the barracks. Tracers zipped past the window; she was firing towards the rear wall, away from the other huts.

VADIM HIT THE door of the prefab hard and walked straight into a burst of fire from an MP-40. Three rounds stitched a diagonal line across his chest. *Overconfident*, he thought, as he squeezed the trigger of the StG 44 and returned the favour, killing the gunman.

The inside of the hut was spartan, with two rows of beds running down each side of the structure. The refugees and crew were standing at the far end of the hut, against the back wall. It took a moment to work out why. There were three guards still in with them, who had been organising them into a human shield.

"You just need to back out now," the one in the middle called to him.

"And then what? All your friends have surrendered," Vadim told him.

The refugees looked scared, but not terrified; there was very little snivelling or crying. After what they had been through over the last nine days, Vadim could understand why. "I want everyone to kneel down," he told them.

"Stay where you are!" the guard ordered.

"You know me," Vadim said to the refugees as he switched the selector on the StG 44 from automatic to semi-automatic. "Please do as I ask."

"If any of you kneel, I start killing," the SS man said.

"If he starts killing, just throw yourselves forward," Vadim told them.

"I'll get some of them!" the guard shouted, his voice breaking.

"I'm Russian. If you know anything about us, you must realise I'm prepared to accept losses to achieve victory. You know that as soon as you kill any of them, you lose your leverage. And my friends from the *Dietrich* know I will act whether they kneel or not." The refugees started to kneel. The SS guard screamed at them, but they ignored him.

With the refugees down on their knees, Vadim got a much better view of the situation. The SS man on his right, his knife to Colstein's throat, was young and frightened, tears running down his face. The man on the left, holding a pistol to the Carlsson boy's head, looked tense, but was handling it. The one in the middle, a big brutish man who looked like an Allied propaganda poster of a Nazi stormtrooper, had a pistol to Maria's head. As horrible as it sounded, Vadim was just relieved Maria wasn't in the Joy Division. He kept his weapon trained on him.

"Hello, Colstein," Vadim said.

"A fucking Jew, I knew it," the big guard snapped.

"Hello, Captain Scorlenski," Colstein said. Something strange seemed to be going on with Maria's eyes. She kept on looking down. Vadim glanced down and Maria opened her hand, showed him what she was holding.

"Do you trust me, Gerhardt?" Vadim asked Colstein.

"I'm going to have to say 'no'," the first mate told him. Vadim smiled.

"Do you hear how quiet it is out there?" Vadim asked the stormtrooper holding Maria. "All your friends are either dead or have surrendered. Pick one." The guard opened his mouth to answer, and Vadim swung his weapon to the right, squeezed the trigger, hitting the man holding the Carlsson boy dead centre in the head.

The switchblade in Maria's hand unfolded and she rammed it into the stormtrooper's arm. He howled in pain as she slithered out of his grip, then shrieked when she rammed the knife into his groin. Vadim cut off the screaming by shooting him in the head. Then he swung around to point his weapon at the young man with his knife to Colstein's throat. He was shaking and crying, and he appeared to have wet himself.

"Unlike you, I've cut a throat," Vadim told him. "It's a lot harder than it looks. You really have to saw it. You might cut my friend there a little bit, but you won't kill him. I, on the other hand, *will* kill you, assuming the lady with the switchblade doesn't emasculate you first." Maria was glaring at the frightened young Nazi, her right hand covered in blood well past the wrist. The boy dropped his knife and stepped away, and some of the longshoremen grabbed him. Vadim lowered his weapon and leaned against the wall. Dead or not, he was exhausted.

CHAPTER TWENTY-TWO

0030 GMT, 25th November 1987
Vickerstown, Walney Island, North-West England

CAREFULLY, VADIM PEERED into the yard. It had gone quiet. He could make out New Boy and Harris hunkered down in the scaffold stands. They were keeping an eye on Captain Schiller, who was standing over Kerrican's corpse, swaying slightly, as though drunk. Vadim looked back at the refugees and crew.

"Take their weapons, but stay in here," he told them, before turning back to the doorway and shouting to the others that he was coming out and not to shoot. He moved carefully out into the yard and slipped in the icy slush, landing hard on his arse in the cold and the wet.

VADIM MADE IT over to the scaffolding. Only now was he able to take in the full extent of the damage. The two Tigers had been gutted; one of them had hit a scaffolding guard tower. The force of the blast had blown the tanks into the wall, demolishing part of that as well. New Boy was cradling his SLR and had a finger in his ear.

"That is a really loud rifle," he muttered as Vadim joined him. Then he nodded upwards. Vadim glanced up. It took him a moment to make out Skull on the top deck of the stand. Harris had been ill-used and was clearly exhausted. He was covered in bruises and blood, though Vadim hoped that not too much of the blood was his own. New Boy didn't look much better.

"Were either of you bit?" he asked.

"No," New Boy told him.

"Which is a goddamned miracle," Harris said shaking his head.

"No," Vadim told him. "It's because you fought, because you wanted to live. I know you've been through hell, but I have six prisoners in the main hall; can you keep an eye on them until we ask you to bring them out? They give you the slightest trouble, just kill them."

Harris nodded wearily.

"Clear!" Gulag called from the second prefab. Princess repeated the call from the third prefab, and the Fräulein did the same from the fourth. Gulag, grim-faced, emerged from the hut and walked across the yard towards them. There were bullet holes in the grey SS smock he had worn to try and fool the re-enactors, and his head looked somehow more misshapen, as if a chunk were missing from it. Vadim noted that both his thumbs were red and blood was dripping off his face. He wondered just how traumatised the rescued children would be. The Muscovite didn't have any prisoners.

Princess emerged from the Joy Division, her left arm in a sling, and blood soaking through the upper arm of her jumper. Her SLR was slung across her back and she was carrying her Stechkin in her right hand. Her face was a mask of total disgust. She didn't have any prisoners with her either.

Two of the fake SS men emerged from the barracks prefab, looking utterly shocked. Smoke was rising from the hut. Vadim guessed a tracer had set something alight. The Fräulein followed them out. Even from this distance, it was clear she had been shot several times. Covering her two prisoners with her sidearm, she set the MG 34 down on the ground, resting on its bipod. Steam rose from the hot gun as it melted the slush.

Vadim looked questioningly at Gulag as he joined them.

"I lost one of the kids," Gulag said. He sounded miserable. "Stray round, it came straight through the wall."

Vadim didn't bother with platitudes. He just put his hand on the Muscovite's shoulder.

"Two of the women were killed," Princess told Vadim as she joined them.

"One was a stray round; the other because I didn't get to one of the bastards quickly enough." She sounded angry.

Vadim nodded. It could have been so much worse. Their attack had been more than reckless. Frankly, they had been very lucky.

The Fräulein ordered the hobby soldiers to kneel, hands laced behind their heads. Princess glared at them. Vadim was pretty sure the sniper would have happily killed them there and then. He wasn't sure he had the courage to enter the Joy Division prefab.

The barracks prefab collapsed in on itself as the flames spread; in a tired, but practical part of his mind, Vadim knew they would have to see to the fire before it spread.

The Fräulein joined them. Much to his irritation, Vadim could see the refugees and crew from the *Dietrich* starting to drift out of the hut they had been held in.

"What are we going to do with them?" Gulag asked, nodding towards the men the Fräulein had captured. Unusually, he seemed unenthusiastic about the prospect of prisoners.

"We take them back to the mainland, tie them to posts just high enough so their groins are at teeth height. Then we put signs around their necks with the word 'rapist' on them. It should act as a warning," Princess told them. The Fräulein nodded in agreement.

"There's something wrong with you," Gulag said. Princess ignored him.

"What do you want to do with him?" the Fräulein asked, nodding towards the earless Captain Schiller.

"He can understand you," Vadim said.

"I'm sorry, captain," the Fräulein told him. He turned and stared at her until she looked away. Then he turned the stare on Vadim.

"Kill me," Schiller said. Vadim opened his mouth to speak, but he kept going. "Kill me, you coward! It's the least you owe me."

Vadim could see it in his eyes, in the set of his jaw: the rage, the hate, the raw red hunger, warring with what was left of a justifiably proud man's dignity. Vadim did what he could for him. One more shot rang out across the yard, and one more body hit the ground.

"Boss!" Vadim looked up. Skull was aiming his stolen rifle at a figure standing on top of the pile of rubble from the collapsed front wall.

"Hold!" Vadim shouted as he recognised Bill from the pub. "He's one of ours." Skull lowered his weapon. The women and children were starting to move nervously out of their huts now. Vadim felt sick at the thought of what they had suffered. He looked up at the swastika banner fluttering from the hall.

"Let's cut that rag down."

1340 GMT, 27th November 1987
Jubilee Bridge, Walney Island, North-West England

AFTER SOME DISCUSSION, the locals had agreed to let the refugees stay. Vadim was pretty sure they all had some very rough years ahead of them. There was arable land on the long narrow island, but not nearly enough to feed everyone, even supposing the sun would rise anytime in the near future. This meant forays into the dead-infested mainland for supplies. Water would also be a problem. They would have to boil seawater to drink. This was of course assuming the fallout didn't get them, and they didn't freeze to death. On the other hand, they seemed like practical people. There was already talk of taking some of the smaller vessels up the coast to places called Whitehaven, Silloth and Maryport, to look for abandoned fishing vessels. There was enough expertise amongst the survivors on the island to crew them. There was also talk of finding some way to make use of the recently opened gas terminal. Vadim had no idea of the practicality of their plans, but at least they *had* plans. He was astonished that in this environment they were still looking forward, though it would take a long time for the wounds inflicted by this strange, wretched infection of Nazism to heal.

The locals decided that they approved of Princess's plans for the prisoners. Bill and his people had taken more in Vickerstown. Vadim and his dead squadmates had done the honours, although Princess insisted on accompanying them.

The surviving family members of the dead re-enactors were given one of the TA lorries from the compound, a full tank of gas, a few of their husbands' weapons, a very small amount of ammunition and no other supplies, and sent on their way with a warning not to come back. It was pretty much a death sentence. Vadim wasn't sure how he felt about that. They would have driven past the staked, half-eaten and by now reanimated remains of their husbands as they left.

The squad had given rudimentary instructions on the claymore mines the Nazis has set. The Fräulein had also taught some of the islanders and longshoremen how to drive the mine roller.

Then some negotiations had happened. Looking at a future of foraying into the zombie-infested mainland for supplies, the islanders had chosen to keep both the Saracens. Which made sense, though Vadim would have liked one to continue their journey. They were begrudgingly prepared to offer them one of the three remaining lorries, but the Fräulein had pointed out that the nearly-fifty-year-old half-track would be nearly impossible to maintain and more trouble than it was worth, so they might as well let them run it into the ground. The islanders had agreed. This was something of a relief; the half-track might be noisy but at least it was armoured.

Not surprisingly, the islanders wanted to keep the majority of the weapons, but the squad were more or less out of ammunition – barring Skull, who'd found two old crates of .303 rounds. Gulag had been for stealing the weapons and ammunition they needed, but Vadim couldn't bear to take anything more from these people. Besides, with their newfound knowledge about how to hide the living from the dead, they were hoping to avoid fighting as much as possible, although Vadim had no idea what was going to happen when they caught up with their own forces.

There was a doctor still alive on the island, and a paramedic who'd worked for the ambulance service. Between them they had seen to Princess's arm, and – once the living had been seen to – dug bullets out of the dead, sewing up the holes as best as they were able. They couldn't do anything for Skull's broken leg or Vadim's broken rib; the doctor suggested surgical screws or wire to hold the fractured bones in place, but such surgery was beyond her experience, and impossible with the facilities to hand.

TWO DAYS LATER, under what Vadim had come to think of as a nuclear sky, the remaining members of the squad were in the World War II German half-track, heading for the bridge.

The Fräulein recounted from the driver seat how Gulag had swum across the channel and killed the guards on the island side to lower the bridge. Princess and the Fräulein had stealthily taken out the guards on the mainland side. Princess had moved the bus and the East German had driven the mine-roller, allowing Skull to follow with the Saracen.

At the bridge, the Fräulein cut her story short and brought the half-track to a grumbling, bone-shaking halt. Bill, Harris, Maria and Colstein were waiting for them at the control booth. Dirty black snow was still falling from the sky, lying thick on the ground. The Fräulein switched off the engine to save fuel, which Vadim thought was brave given the problems they'd had starting the ancient vehicle, and all of the squad clambered out. Vadim found himself looking out over a muddy channel with bogged-down zombies stuck in it; at the industrial skyline of the dockyards, the roofs of the neat terraces, the steeples of churches and beyond that the black, snow covered hills.

Bill stuck his hand out first and Vadim took it.

"Thanks for this," Bill said, gesturing towards the island. "Not sure about that." He pointed at the mainland. Vadim just nodded. Despite his part in the attack on New York, he didn't feel like apologising again. "I'm not sure you'd exactly be welcome here, but we'd give some serious consideration into letting you on the island if you're ever back this way."

Vadim laughed.

"It has been beyond horrible meeting you," Colstein said as he shook Vadim's cold hand next. "And I hope I never see any of you again; but thank you. You didn't have to come back for us."

"I think I did," Vadim said. It wasn't just for Colstein and the others. In the end, he hadn't seen himself in Kerrican, but he wondered if he ever caught up with Varishnikov, would he see the same madness in the KGB hardliner's eyes? "I liked Schiller. He was a good man."

Colstein opened his mouth to say something, but thought better of it.

Maria didn't really want to look at him. It was clear she hadn't changed her views: she still felt that things would be better if he killed himself, and with the hunger always present, he wasn't sure she was wrong. Right now, surrounded by the living, the urge to feast was strong but not nearly as strong as his resolve. It came as a surprise when Maria grabbed him and hugged him, whispering 'thank you' in his ear.

"Keep that switchblade handy," was all he could think to tell her. She nodded. He looked down at Gloria, who'd accompanied her mother. The little girl was hugging Gulag. Vadim tried not to think too much about the future.

"Why *do* they call you 'Infant'?" Harris asked as he shook Vadim's hand.

"They don't, Gulag does to annoy me," he said, glancing irritably at the Muscovite, who was still talking to Gloria. The little girl appeared to be listening intently to him, despite not speaking any Russian, as far as Vadim knew.

Harris raised an eyebrow, and Vadim sighed. "We are given nicknames when we start training for the Spetsnaz. A... mentor of mine was already an officer, and he gave me that nickname." He wondered where Colonel Krychenko was now. Was he alive or dead? If he was dead, was he still moving? He'd be just as in control as Vadim was; he had never known a man with a stronger will.

"Why?" Harris asked.

"I was nine years when old I killed my first man," Vadim told him, and the smile disappeared from Harris's face. "A German soldier amongst the ruins of my city."

As he climbed back into the half-track, Vadim found himself thinking about Kerrican and his fake Nazis. The dead walked the earth looking for living flesh to feast upon, but humans had done this to other humans. He found that deeply depressing. After the bombs had fallen and their world had been destroyed, you would think people would come to the conclusion that perhaps more brutality wasn't the answer.

What about your mission? he asked himself.

I'm no longer human.

Skull poked him in the ribs, and Vadim turned, more surprised than anything else. The sniper nodded out the back of the half-track, smiling. Vadim looked to see Princess kissing Harris. They broke their clinch and she climbed into the back of the armoured vehicle. Everyone was staring at her.

"What?" she demanded. The Fräulein turned round and managed to coax the half-track back into life as the bridge started to lower. Unexpectedly, Vadim realised he was smiling.

ABOUT THE AUTHOR

Gavin G. Smith is the Dundee-born author of the hard edged, action-packed SF novels *Veteran*, *War in Heaven*, *Age of Scorpio*, *A Quantum Mythology*, *The Beauty of Destruction* and *The Hangman's Daughter*, as well as the short story collection *Crysis Escalation*. In collaboration with Stephen Deas, as the composite personality Gavin Deas, he has co-written *Elite: Wanted*, and the shared world series *Empires: Infiltration* and *Empires: Extraction*. *Special Purposes: First Strike Weapon* is his first World War Three/Horror novel and he enjoyed writing it a little too much.